A MEASURE OF DECORUM

"Miss East, as I have seen you in your night attire, you needn't talk to me as though I were entirely a stranger." Alaric lowered his voice to a murmur. The instant blush that appeared in her cheeks brightened her grey eyes before they were hidden beneath those dark lashes, so absurdly lovely for a girl with hair quite like spun gold.

"I never thanked you—"

"On the contrary, Miss East, you thanked me by allowing me to be of service. Forgive me for teasing you and for leaving you now as I must." Alaric stood up and turned away, his hand accidentally brushing against the silken coil of her hair. He sternly ignored the tingle that ran up his arm at the contact.

The temptation to tease her was overwhelming and dangerous. . . .

A Lady In Love

Cynthia Bailey-Pratt

JOVE BOOKS, NEW YORK

A LADY IN LOVE

A Jove Book / published by arrangement with
the author

PRINTING HISTORY
Jove edition / February 1993

All rights reserved.
Copyright © 1993 by Cynthia Bailey-Pratt.
This book may not be reproduced in whole or in part,
by mimeograph or any other means, without permission.
For information address: The Berkley Publishing Group,
200 Madison Avenue, New York, New York 10016.

ISBN: 0-515-11041-8

Jove Books are published by The Berkley Publishing Group,
200 Madison Avenue, New York, New York 10016.
The name "JOVE" and the "J" logo
are trademarks belonging to Jove Publications, Inc.

PRINTED IN THE UNITED STATES OF AMERICA

10 9 8 7 6 5 4 3 2 1

1

"Oh Lord," Sarah prayed. "Please don't let these two great boobies sit here all the afternoon. If only we could play a game of argue as we used."

She looked to her left. Harcourt Phelps nervously uncrossed his legs and sat up straighter, an uncertain smile coming and going across his long features.

She looked to her right. Harold Phelps's thin fingers touched his neckcloth and he too smiled, a pale copy of the boy she'd once romped with so merrily.

They were twins who, from the day of their birth, had done everything together. They were now twenty-one and, keeping strictly to the principle of their life to date, had unified in falling in love with the girl next door.

The girl in question was heartily sick of the entire business. Sarah got up and crossed to the french doors that looked out to the garden drowsing in the sunlight. "There are apples in the orchard. Let's go and pick some."

"Do you want apples?" That was Harcourt. She'd been the only one, outside their immediate family, who could tell them apart, though the similarity was less now that they no longer dressed alike. "I will be happy to go and find some for you."

"We could all go," she answered, turning. "I always could climb higher than any of us."

"The sweetest apples are always hardest to reach." Sarah sighed. Harold fancied himself as a poet and tried hard to turn everything into a compliment. "But it wouldn't be right for you to get your own apples. Let Harcourt go."

The older of the twins, by four minutes, thirty seconds, flashed an arrow glance of disgust at his brother. Not least distressing to Sarah was that their rivalry for her hand had disrupted a long camaraderie. "I am happy to be Sarah's champion in this as in all things," Harcourt said.

His brother smirked. "I said, you should go. I'm not dressed for bucolic pleasures. Go get apples, Harcourt. Sarah and I will wait for you to come back."

"Never mind," Sarah said. As she walked back and forth across the morning room carpet, she asked herself the question that so often occupied her of late. What had wrought the change in the brothers?

She couldn't ask them; she doubted they even knew. When she'd gone away to Aunt Whitsun, they had scarcely taken time from hunting and fishing to bid her good-bye. Three years her senior, their attitude had been one of relief for, though playmates in their childhood, when they had reached their teens they'd begun to think of her as being marginally more irritating than even their sister and her dearest friend, Harmonia. When she'd returned home early in August, however, their attitude had undergone yet another change.

She had not altered in the slightest, she had made certain of that. Aunt Whitsun had tried very hard to make her change, talking a lot of nonsense about being a woman now and not a hoyden any longer. And Sarah had been forced to put her hair up and lower her skirts, walk instead of run, and look archly across a room rather than bellowing when she wanted someone's attention. Her mother, who sent her away in despair, for she could get Sarah to do none of these things, had made it plain that the alterations must continue once she came home again.

But these things could not possibly have interested the Phelps brothers. Yet, she no sooner visited Harmonia than they began coming every day to sit in the morning room. And sit. And sit. No hints were sufficient to pierce their ardor. She could not, however, bring herself to hurt them by more direct methods.

She stopped pacing and tried again to gently dislodge them. "It certainly is a lovely day. I haven't seen so much water in the river since I was a child. Father says the fishing will be wonderful. And my, weren't there a lot of worms after last night's rain?"

Harold contrived to look as though he'd never touched a worm in his life. He probably would have swooned if reminded of all the ones he'd put down her back. "Oh, *country* pursuits will do for those with no higher aspirations. I wrote a sonnet to the moon last night. Would you like to hear it?"

"She just said there was rain last night. How could you write poetry to the moon when you couldn't even see it?"

"Need one see a thing to be vividly and intrinsically aware of it? I suppose you slept all through that cacophony of thunder and lightning. I never closed my eyes, enraptured by the majesty of it all."

Harcourt made a rude noise and folded his arms across his broad chest. "Is that why you were yawning like a barn door all the way over here?"

"I suppose all this rain is good for the crops?" Sarah interrupted. She always made an effort to address her conversation to neither brother in particular.

But they paid no attention to their lady love.

"I did not yawn, except at your chatter."

"Chatter? As if I would speak to a frilly thing like yourself."

"Frilly? And what are you but a cow-fisted chaw bacon with the manners of a highwayman?"

While Harcourt answered in the same vein, Mrs. East came in, bearing a basket full of cut flowers. "Good morning, dear."

"Good morning, Mother. May I take those?"

"Thank you."

"And who was it that fell off his new bang-up bit of blood the first time he'd had one bumper over the limit?"

"I've never seen so many roses so late in the season, Sarah. Poor old Marsh keeps going over his treatment of them, trying to remember what he's done differently from all the other years. I told him it's because he's been going to church regularly."

Sarah laughed. "If he's been more than once in the last six months, I will become a Dissenter."

"I know, but I like to think of him as a reformed pagan. I think it's his beard."

"But let us not forget who it was that couldn't even read the lesson without tripping over his tongue? 'Be not overcome of evil, but overcome evil with food.' Food, ha! The word is 'good,' you . . . puppy!"

"That was an accident! It had nothing to do with . . ."

Mrs. East smiled on the young men and said, "Good morning, Harold. Good morning, Harcourt." Shamefaced, they greeted her. "You should go home now. Sarah must help me with the flowers."

"Oh, yes," said Harcourt. "May I call again tomorrow, Sarah?"

She'd have loved to say no, to both of them. But how could she, when they'd been part of her world for so long? She merely smiled and shook her head noncommittally, as she did every day.

"One more bud among the roses," Harold said, bowing. "Farewell, Sarah. Until tomorrow."

As they left, she could hear them picking up their quarrel.

"What fine young men they've become," Mrs. East said, as she always said. Her daughter had been home six weeks and every morning found the Phelps boys in one room or another of her house. To Sarah's surprise, her mother never mentioned this manifestation, nor speculated upon its possible cause. If they were inconvenient, she asked them to go. If they were not in the way, they might stay as long as the fancy took them. Sarah wished they might be inconvenient more often.

"Do you need my help with the flowers, Mother?" She never had asked for help before.

"I beg your pardon? No, dear, I think I can manage."

"Then I shall go for a walk."

Mrs. East hummed assent. As Sarah left through the french windows, her mother's voice floated after her. "Take your parasol, dear. The sun is so strong today, I can't quite believe it is October."

For a moment, Sarah paused outside her father's study window. She could hear his voice, reading aloud his latest letter to the literary magazine of which he was a sometime correspondent. It was a peculiarly comforting sound, one she had known from childhood, a beloved voice roaring out condemnation of some distant blockhead. "In conclusion, let me say that the esteemed gentleman from the north has my sincere sympathies for his recent bereavement. To lose one's senses in the midst of penning a letter . . . perhaps I leave myself open to the same criticism? Fiddle! I shall let it stand. . . ."

Sarah went on. Though the sun's rays were almost hot on her

skin, the cool breeze made her think that a sun-shade would hardly be necessary. Certainly, it would be more of a hindrance than a help as she walked in the woods. She could smell the roses in the garden beyond the hedge, mixing with the recently cut grass and the fresh tang of rain. Her troubles faded. Sarah walked along the confines of her principality, completely happy, bestowing a smile on the elderly gardener as she passed.

There were apples in the orchard. But she knew where sweeter fruit yet grew on a wild tree that lived all alone in the woods. She carefully looked about. The Phelps twins were not above following her, singly or in unison. And lately, she'd had more than enough of their company. The woods, however, seemed empty of all human life.

Sarah had not thought to change her shoes before setting out. As she had no reason to walk on a hard road, she did not notice the oversight until she raised the hem of her skirt to step up into the low crook of the wild apple tree. The white kid slippers were marked by the plentiful leaf-mold of the old forest, and the ruffles around her hem were no less dirty. She sighed over it, but did not let it trouble her. Dresses were a botheration, as were hats, veils, gloves, and muffs, of both the summer and winter variety. Besides, her clothes were bound to look much worse by the time she was home again.

Reaching for the fruit above her head, she saw it was just ripened, deep green with a dusky red flush where the sun had touched most often. She reached high, her pale yellow dress gleaming among the rustling leaves.

The first shot flew by with a whine like that of a late bee rushing home to the hive. As such, Sarah did not regard it. Then she heard the crack of the discharge.

Twisting on her perch, Sarah tried to see who was shooting on Sir Arthur Phelps's property. If it were a poacher— Not in the daylight, she reflected. She knew all the local questionables, and they were almost never seen when the sun was high. The other possibility was that the "Smart London Visitors," guests of Harvey Phelps, the oldest son of Sir Arthur, had decided to practice their aim. It had most likely been a stray bullet, Sarah thought, and opened her mouth to shout so that they would know she was near.

The next bullet scattered leaves close to her hand. Sarah let go as she flung herself backward in surprise. Falling, she did not scream but protested in a wordless shout. Crashing down, she lay stunned, awake but unable for the moment to rise or even to think. She had not fallen from a tree in years, though she'd climbed many, and it seemed she'd forgotten the knack of bouncing up at once from such a calamity.

Not even a nearby voice roused Sarah from a bemused contemplation of the spreading branches above her head. "I made sure it fell somewhere near . . . oh, my God! Lord Reyne, Lord Reyne, come here! No, don't come here." His voice high with panic, the young man dropped to his knees beside Sarah's still form, throwing his gun down beside her.

"What are you playing at, Atwood? Come here, don't come here—do you fancy I am at your beck and call? What have you there?"

Atwood tried to hide the girl's body by flinging his arms out. "I thought it was a grouse. I saw it in a tree."

"Don't keep referring to her as it. You'll insult the chit. As if getting shot wasn't insult enough. Stand aside." The second of the men came within view of Sarah's dazed eyes. He was taller than the first by some inches, and yet was thinner. They were dressed alike, in leather coats and breeches, but whereas twigs broke beneath Atwood's stomping boots, the other man's feet were silent over the littered forest floor. The stock of his long gun was cupped in one hand, the barrel gleaming over his right shoulder.

He looked down on her with sleepy eyes. Yet, she saw a glint of blue beneath his lids, the same color as the sky visible between branches and clouds. Sarah felt this similarity to be somehow important and wanted to study it.

"Are you hurt?" he asked. His eyes roamed her body, yet she knew it was only in the interest of her health. Nevertheless, she felt a blush start in her cheek. She tried to push herself up using her elbows.

"Pray don't move. Are you hurt?" he repeated. His voice sounded so kind that she smiled dreamily up at him.

"No, I don't think so," she said, when he said nothing more. "Why did you shoot at me?" It was all right with her if he wanted to do it, though she'd rather he would look at her and go on speaking in his slow, dark voice that sent answering ripples through her body.

"I assure you I did not. My friend, however, thought you a

bird and so nearly made you an angel." Turning to that miserable man, he lay his fingers over Atwood's shoulder. "Run back to the house and get the doctor."

"But he might be miles . . ."

"His gig was before the door when we left. Seeing a sick child, I think. He'll still be there. If the brat's mother is anything like mine, he'll be staying for breakfast." The unhappy Atwood still hesitated. "I'll keep watch until you return," the other man said. "You know I cannot walk with any speed."

"Very well," Atwood said. He rose slowly to his feet. "I'm so sorry," he whispered before he turned around and ran, crashing through the undergrowth like a bull released from the pasture that separated him from the cows.

Sarah became aware that a rock or a stick was directly beneath her shoulder and had, moreover, been digging into her for some time. "Ouch," she said, wriggling.

"You should lie still," the man warned.

For a moment, she subsided, eager to do as he wished. "Oh, I can't," she burst out, and pushed herself upright. "It's exactly like trying to sleep on a lumpy mattress."

"You may have broken something," he insisted.

Sarah twisted experimentally, pushing her loosened hair back when it fell over her shoulder. "I don't believe I have." She bent her knees beneath her skirt, still pinned under her. "No, I am all in one piece, I think." Holding out her hand, she looked up at him, wanting to be pulled upright. She'd never wished so much for a man's touch before. Though Harcourt and Harold, as well as others, had often taken her arm to help her, she'd always shaken them off, not needing them.

"I can't help you," he said sternly. She seemed neither shocked nor surprised, so he unbent enough to say, "My shoulder was broken and I can't lift anything too heavy."

"How did you do that?" Sarah smiled, her laughter bubbling up. "Did someone shoot *you* from a tree?"

"No, from my regiment." For a moment, a shadow passed over his brow, but her only response was a low whistle and a murmured "too bad." He asked a question he'd wondered about for some moments. "Were you truly up a tree?"

"Of course, where else do you find apples?"

"I? On my dining table, or sometimes on a barrow. Or on the ground, surrounding you."

Sarah looked about her. "Oh, good," she said. Picking up a piece of fruit, shaken from the tree when she fell, she dusted it nonchalantly on her skirt, leaving a smear, and lifted it to her lips. "Do you want a bite?" she asked, hesitating.

Alaric Naughton, Earl of Reyne, had been offered many a proposition in the past. But few had tempted him less than this nonsensical Eve-child, offering the apple after her own fall. She might be a beauty when she grew up, he thought, but not now, not with dirty face and worse gown, not even with that splendid dark blond hair falling freely over the twigs and leaves that decorated her back. He noticed mildly that her hair was the exact color of the angels' in medieval stained glass windows.

"No, thank you, child. Eat it yourself. I prefer my fruit to come from my own forcing house." Cautiously, the earl lowered himself to sit upon a fallen log, resting his gun beside him. His thigh ached dully, the newly healed muscles protesting at the day's walk.

"I've eaten forced fruit at my aunt's. It doesn't taste like anything. Look, I'll climb up and get you another and you'll see how good it is." Taking a last bite of the core with her strong teeth, Sarah stood up, and the earl had to revise his estimate of her age.

"No, don't," he said in alarm.

"There's no danger," she called down. "Your friend left his gun behind."

What was climbing a tree, despite bruises, to fetch him an apple? She would have leapt over mountains, swum through pike-infested rivers, faced untold dangers to bring him anything he wanted. She knew proper young ladies never indulged in athletic behavior before gentlemen, except for walking or archery or such things unlikely to cast doubts upon personal femininity. But she couldn't let him think she was clumsy and weak, like the handless girls she'd met at her aunt's, good only for sleeping and gossip.

Sure-footed and easy, Sarah gathered apples, holding them in a fold in her dress. She glanced down to see if he were watching and felt a thrill of surprise to find that he was. Stepping lightly down, she went to sit by him on the log.

"Here," she said, holding out another apple. "This one is bound to be sweet. See how red it is?"

"It looks dirty."

"No! We had rain last night. Just rub off the spots on your sleeve." She showed him how on her skirt. "I love apples," she said indistinctly, for her mouth was full. "I'd eat them every day, if I could."

"I prefer pineapples," the earl said, though privately he admitted that a wild apple had a flavor no other fruit could match.

"That's not my favorite fruit," Sarah said, tossing her second core away. "They're not too bad candied, though," she added, reflecting that she would have to learn to like them now. She "cleaned" another apple.

"You'll need a doctor all right before you're through, if you keep eating those."

Sarah laughed, but did not lift the fruit to her mouth. "I'm Sarah East. Who *are* you?"

"My name . . . most people call me Reyne."

"Reyne?" She shook her head.

"You don't like it?"

"No. Is it your first name or your last?"

"Neither. It's my title."

"Oh, then I've no objection to it. You couldn't help it anyway." All the same, she could not help repeating it, tasting his name on her lips. "Reyne."

"My first name is Alaric. If you don't like that one, I've got five or six more." He shook his head in disbelief. It was impossible to continue sitting here conversing with a female, who, though her figure might suggest otherwise, was obviously no more than a child. He stood up. When he thought about all the women who would have been in high flight to have kept him chatting for one-tenth as long, what else could he do but shake his head?

"Five or six? I've only three myself."

"What are they?" Alaric asked, sitting down again, not noticing the absence of pain. A gentleman could not abandon her, though it was plain she needed no doctor. He wondered if she ever had, for she was obviously in the rudest health.

"Sarah Marissa Clivenden East."

"You weren't very lucky either."

"No." Sarah liked that he listened to her pleasantly, not avidly as if her every·utterance were of worth, as did Harcourt and Harold. Nor did he talk to her with the abstraction of a parent or other authority. Sarah tried to think of when she had last spoken to a man who was neither a relation nor in love with her. She had not wished to be agreeable to any of the presentable young men introduced to her at Aunt Whitsun's. None of them had been remotely like this.

Sarah looked at him openly. His face is thin, she thought, and the rest of his hair is darker at his temples. There were lines carved about his mouth and beside his eyes, yet he did not seem an old man. Not very old. Not forty. She decided she liked the lines just as they were. They made his eyes seem kind.

He turned his face to meet her gaze. Sarah smiled. She'd been right. They were the same color as the autumn sky.

"Atwood's taking a devil of a long time," he muttered.

"They'll be here soon," Sarah said. "I only hope they don't bring Harcourt and Harold."

"Who are . . . ? Oh, yes, the younger sons. How many children have Sir Arthur and Lady Phelps? There seemed a great crowd of young people at dinner last night." He thought he sounded just as old as he felt: ancient, desiccated like some Egyptian mummy slowly dropping to bits.

"There are five children. Harvey, Harriet, Harcourt, Harold, and Harmonia. Harriet married Mr. Randolph and they are visiting too, for a few weeks, with their two-year-old son, Harpocrates."

"Good God," Alaric said reverently. "Is it a mania?"

"They named Harvey after an uncle and the habit seemed to grow upon them," Sarah said in explanation.

"Let it be a lesson to me to know when to quit." Somewhat stiffly, he stood up again. "As it seems Atwood and the doctor have lost their way, let us go to meet them."

"I don't actually need a doctor," Sarah confessed. "I think I was only stunned by the suddenness of my fall. I'm not used to being shot at, you know."

"One never gets used to it, Miss East. No matter how hard one tries. If you please, will you pick up Atwood's gun for me?"

The grace she'd shown while ascending the tree was no less

when she bent for the unwieldy weapon. Alaric put the stocks
together and laid the barrels against his shoulder in a soldierly
way. "You know these woods well, I take it?"

"Yes, I've played here since . . . as long as I can remember."

"Then you may lead the way. Guide me to Sir Arthur's, if
you please."

"I'll take you to my house. You can ride back." Sarah
noticed that he had frowned with discomfort when shouldering
his arms and that he did not walk easily. "I'm certain my father
will lend you a horse, or even—"

"No, thank you," Alaric said not unkindly. "After the
Peninsula, I swore never to ride on a cart horse again."

Sarah pushed her hair back. For the first time, she realized
what she must look like to him. Her dress was torn and muddy,
her face grimy, and she could feel the twigs and broken leaves
in her hair. He must have mistaken her for a yeoman's
daughter, or even a gypsy. With a blush, she knew her behavior
had done nothing to disabuse him of that notion. Without
speaking, suddenly ashamed and self-conscious, Sarah showed
him the way.

Alaric felt tired. He'd walked farther than he'd wished, in
search of nonexistent game, on top of traveling which had
wearied him more than he'd ever known it to do before. And
the previous weeks had not been conducive to rest. He'd left
London for Brighton on a repairing lease, only to find it madly
giddy, with routs, races, and revelry every night and day. He'd
met a thousand old friends, some with the regiment there, and
had been swept into a social round he'd all but forgotten
existed.

Then a chance invitation to join a party traveling to visit
Harvey Phelps, whom Alaric had never met but heard described as an out-and-out cock of the game, though he'd not
seemed so last evening. Sir Arthur was undoubtedly plump in
the pocket, and his wife, an old tabby, seemed more than
pleased to entertain a houseful of eligible young men, though
she only had one unmarried daughter herself. The noise and
hustle at breakfast had tempted him to go out for a peaceful
morning's shooting with Atwood, though he'd soon lost
patience with the silly fellow. And then to be left with this

strange girl who he half-expected to see turn into a wood elf at any moment.

They topped a low rise at the rear of a sprawling two-story house, a grey slate roof blending harmoniously with the stone walls and shaven grass. From where he stood, still among the trees, Alaric smelled roses and smoke. Off to the left, he saw a neat stable, topped by an octagonal dovecote.

In answer to his look, Sarah said, with unconscious pride, "This is my house."

"Your house? You mean you work here?"

Though she'd hoped he had not assumed what he'd so obviously assumed, Sarah could not help laughing at the surprise on his face. "No, I live here. With my father and my mother. I have two brothers as well. They're both lieutenants in the navy. Mortimer, he's with His Majesty's ship *Restitution* and Sam is in *Ganymede*. We received a letter from Mortimer last week. He's just put in to Constantinople."

A female figure with a basket over one arm left the house and, walking on a few steps, bent down over a patch of green. "There's Mother," Sarah said. "She mustn't see me looking like this. She worries, you know. Listen, go down there and tell her who you are and that you'd like to borrow a horse to take you back to Hollytrees."

"I can't do that. She doesn't know me."

"That doesn't matter." Sarah gazed at him in wonder. Was it possible he did not realize that he could have anything he wanted just for the asking? "Tell her you're staying at Hollytrees, and she'll probably give you half a dozen commissions to Lady Phelps. Don't take any notice. She'll have forgotten most of them by the time they see each other tonight."

"Tonight? Oh, yes, there's some kind of entertainment. . . ." The long grey house, viewed through a haze compounded of autumn air and woodsmoke, was like an image from a half-remembered dream, or a picture glimpsed long ago. Alaric started down the hill and never heard Sarah say, "I'll save you a dance, shall I?"

2

"What in the name of mercy happened to you, Miss Sarah?" Molly asked, catching sight of the girl slipping up the stairs. "If one of them boys . . . what's that there on your skirt?"

Sarah put her back against the wall and looked down at the broad face of her mother's servant. "Mud, I think. Oh, Molly, Molly, what shall I wear tonight?"

"Tonight? I thought you weren't going to Hollytrees tonight."

"Not go?"

"That's what you said this morning. Talking on about how dull it all was likely to be."

"But that was this morning." Sarah dashed away to her room, leaving the heavier woman to climb up after her. By the time Molly came in, Sarah had shrugged off the yellow gown and was scrubbing her face in the basin with more enthusiasm than she'd ever shown before. Drying her face, she peered at herself. "I'm not absolutely ugly, am I?" she asked in sudden doubt.

"Handsome is as handsome does," Molly said, sniffing. "If you'd keep yourself neat and wear your stays, you'd be the better for it, though I don't hold with looking at yourself every moment."

Groaning, Molly leaned down to pick up the discarded gown. "Take me the good part of tomorrow to wash this, and look at what you've been an' done to your shoes!"

Sarah was not listening. Her quick ears had heard the sound of a horse's hooves, and she went to the window to look out. The shortest road to Hollytrees ran beside the house. Lord Reyne rode by, the sun striking red from his dark hair. He half-turned in the saddle to wave to someone out of her sight

13

and then went on. Sighing happily, she saw that he sat the horse better than any man she knew. Sarah watched until she could see him no longer but, remembering they would meet again tonight, let him go with no more than a single pang.

Harmonia Phelps had sent a note earlier in the day, requesting Sarah to come over before supper, so they might have the fun of gossiping together while they dressed. Sarah now replied to the invitation in person, with her mother's approval.

Unfortunately, as Sarah crossed the grounds of Hollytrees, Harmonia glimpsed her from an upstairs window. Throwing up the sash, she leaned out and hallooed. "Sarah, Sarah! View Halloo!"

Waving frantically for her friend to shush, Sarah hurried forward, clutching a brown-paper parcel under one arm. The sandy drive to the front door of Hollytrees seemed beyond human scale, like a never-ending path in a nightmare.

"Sarah!" her friend called again with a laughing face.

Increasing her pace, Sarah shot glances at the wood beyond the house, at the lake, at the stables just in view. She gained the safety of the pedimented portico and paused to catch her breath before entering the house.

Just then, Harold emerged from the small Grecian temple by the artificial lake. At the same moment, Harcourt sprang up from the bank, hurling aside his fishing rod. Like a thief seeking sanctuary in a church, Sarah turned the knob and burst, regardless of etiquette, into Sir Arthur's home.

"They're after me, Smithers," she panted as the butler came forward.

"Up the stairs, quickly, Miss East. Once you've reached Miss Harmonia, you'll be safe."

She raced for the stairs, hiking her skirts nearly to her knees so that she could leap them two at a time. Yet Harcourt's legs were longer even than her own. She'd lost too many races to the boys to hold any false hopes she could beat them without a longer start than she had.

Their voices, calling her name, echoed from the hall below. Sarah beat a fierce tattoo on Harmonia's door. When it was jerked open, she all but fell into the room.

"Harcourt first to the door, Harold next by seven seconds! Remind me I owe Smithers two pence. I can't help wagering on an outsider. I think the trouble with the odds is we have no third party. Do you think you could make Harvey fall in love with you too, Sarah? It would improve the turf enormously.''

Taking the glass of water Harmonia held out, Sarah sank gratefully into an armchair. "I wish you wouldn't do that," she said. "If not for my sake, for your brothers'. It can't be good for them."

"They don't seem to mind. I'd say they need more exercise, after all their mooning over you." Harmonia turned to look out of her window. "They've gone back to whatever they were doing. Are you going to dance with them tonight?"

"I suppose I'll have to, won't I?"

"Yes, I don't see how you're to get out of it, but I'd limit them to one set each. There's quite a few eligible gentlemen visiting Harvey. That's why Mama's giving this house party. She hopes one will want to marry me."

"Well, why not?"

Harmonia smiled at her friend. "Because one look at you, my dearest, and there lives not a man who'd look twice at me."

"Don't be so silly. Besides, do you want boys like Harcourt and Harold falling all over you? If they weren't your brothers I'd give them to you gladly."

"No, thank you. I don't care for hordes of young men, but it would be very pleasant to have one." Wistfully, Harmonia sighed. Her smooth brown hair and short, plump figure had never troubled her until this year, when Sarah had blossomed into such overwhelming beauty.

"Well," Sarah said lamely, "if you should like any of my admirers—though I don't see how you could—just name your choice and I'll give him to you."

Harmonia smiled again with mischief. "I'll remember that. There are second sons and lords aplenty. We've even a real earl staying here."

"An earl?"

"Yes, the Earl of Reyne. They say he was terribly wounded in Spain. Harcourt says he's going to try to get the earl to talk about it; you know how wild he is to join the army."

With a shake of her blond head, Sarah dismissed Harcourt's plans. She had not considered Reyne's rank, not caring whether he was a king or a woodcutter. She hid that she'd met him, for the hour in the woods was too precious to share with anyone, not with Harmonia, not even with her own mother. "This earl . . . what is he like?"

"Oh, I don't know. Handsome enough, I suppose. He was at dinner last night, but I didn't pay much attention. Harriet kept me busy, moaning about how sick little Harry is. The doctor told her it's just the chicken pox, but you'd think it the end of the world. He's been confined to the nursery, poor little fellow.

"Oh," she continued, as Sarah unwrapped the gown she'd brought and shook it to release the wrinkles, "I was hoping you'd wear that instead of your muslin with the blue sprigs. Remind me that Bumbleton owes me four pence; she said you'd wear the other, as it's only a family party."

After showing Sarah her own choice for the evening, Harmonia asked, "Are those the sandals you bought while you were away?" She came around to the other side of the bed to admire the cut steel buckles flashing in the late sunlight. The sandals were no more solid than a soft sole of wash-leather could make them.

"Yes, my aunt insisted they were the latest mode. They're rather too big for me, though. I almost have to shuffle, and if I wiggle my toes, the buckles come open."

"But they are beautiful."

"Yes," Sarah said, poking the silver satin with one finger. "I suppose they are."

As the hour for dinner drew closer, more young ladies of the county began to arrive, some already attired for the evening, others taking advantage of Harmonia's invitation. Soon her chamber was a riot of white muslin and giggling voices. In the window seat, Sarah nodded to the other girls, for she'd known them forever. She could not help but notice, however, that not even her most particular friends singled her out for a private coze. She shrank farther back into her corner, while the laughter went on without her.

Sarah came down the stairs as elegantly as a tall ship amidst a flotilla of lesser girls, all but a few dressed in pure white. The girls who had a Season already drifted last, languidly experienced if unwed. Sarah did not think for even a moment of her own Season, soon to come. She was looking for Lord Reyne.

As soon as she entered the salon, however, Harcourt and Harold came to her side.

"How are you, Sarah? You look . . ."

"I swear there's not another girl here to touch you. What's that, Posthwaite? Of course, too pleased. Sarah, this is . . . certainly, Sir Francis . . . this gentleman is . . ."

Though they frowned horribly at their brother's friends, crowding about, they introduced them each in turn. Sarah quickly lost any sense of which face went with what name. To them, she seemed a remote goddess, wreathed in sky-blue ribbons, dreaming of her lost home on some mountaintop.

In all, twenty-four pairs of seats were filled. Though comfortably casual in most regards, Lady Phelps was not as yet certain she approved of promiscuous seating, so a long row of women faced an equally long row of men. As was usual at an evening at Sir Arthur's, there had been no pairing off in order of rank, so it was not until they were all seated that two members of the party were found to be missing.

"Smithers," said her ladyship. "Kindly go tell Sir Arthur that we are all waiting. Politics," she said with an apologetic laugh, echoed by her guests.

The empty chairs were at the end of the table, far from Sarah. She hardly noticed the soup ladled into the bowl before her. Every nerve awaited Lord Reyne's entrance. He would walk in, sit down—or perhaps his eyes would wander over the assembled guests until he looked upon her. She could not imagine what would happen when he saw her, but as she picked up her spoon, her neighbor said, "Sarah, are you quite well? Your hand trembles."

Sarah looked at the quivering spoon in surprise. "Yes, thank you, Mrs. Flint. I'm . . . I'm a little cold."

"Cold? Yet it's such a warm evening. Quite unseasonable."

Putting the utensil down, Sarah folded her hands in her lap. Despite the noise all around her, she straightened the instant his voice sounded through the din. Perhaps it was wrong, unlady-like as her Aunt Whitsun would have said, but her eyes went at once to the door, ignoring her right-hand neighbor.

"You know," Mrs. Flint said. "My son, Nigel, suffers agonies from the cold. I'm always knitting him something warm. Why, last year . . ."

Sarah had to turn back and face Mrs. Flint while that lady spoke. She could not be rude and turn her back, though no one could expect reasonable answers under the circumstances.

When at last free to look again, she saw Lord Reyne, half-hidden behind a silver candelabra. He was listening to Sir Arthur. So far as she could see, he made monosyllabic answers. All she asked now was to be able to sit, chin in hand, and gaze upon him.

Evening clothes became him well, playing up his fair coloring against the black self-effacing fabric. His linen was white, bringing out his tanned skin. He was too thin but ate little. What was he thinking of, she wondered, to cloud his eyes so? She remembered well his brief smiles and longed to see one now.

All at once, as though he felt he were under observation, Lord Reyne ran his eyes down the table's opposite side. When his stern gaze passed over her, Sarah felt herself blush. Immediately, she began to talk to Miss Calpurnia Grissom on her left, although she had nothing to say to her.

"I . . . I . . . the hunting should be good this year?"

"Oh, without doubt. My father says . . . but I think . . ."

Fortunately, Miss Grissom was the sort of woman who possessed profound opinions on every conceivable subject. Safe from having to comment beyond a yes or no, Sarah dared to raise her eyes again to Lord Reyne. He jabbed without interest at the sliced beef that had replaced the soup. She wondered if he was thinking about pineapples. Would it be too forward of her to offer to go at once to Tahiti for one?

Embarrassed, Sarah recollected she could not spend the entire dinner staring at Lord Reyne, dearly though she would have liked to. When she at last turned her attention to the gentlemen across the table, it was to discover Harcourt Phelps staring back at her with a scowl. This cleared immediately upon her smile.

"I say, you will keep a dance clear for me?"

She was about to answer yes, when from beside him, Harold said, "And for me?"

"I get her first dance, because I'm oldest and asked first."

"Oh, have it your own way. I prefer to claim the final dance. Perhaps I can se you home, Sarah? Or did you come with your parents?" He half-waved at Mrs. East.

"I'm staying with your sister, tonight." The young male faces brightened. "Along with half a dozen other girls."

Harcourt surveyed the long line of ladies opposite with the

air of a sultan invoicing the latest bunch of harem beauties. "I shan't dance with anyone but you," he announced at the end of his appraisal.

"Neither shall I," his brother answered at once.

Lady Phelps had other plans. Between the older gentleman who did not dance and the younger gentleman who did not wish to dance, her duty was clear. Too many girls with their backs against the wall would ruin her party. Except for war, she found men preferred to shirk unpleasant duties. She glided about the ballroom, influencing her sons to do the pretty. Even Harvey, highly indolent as a rule, was persuaded by maternal authority to step out onto the floor with every female in the room.

In his adolescence, he had shot up two feet in one year, without growing the strength to match his length. He chose Sarah almost at once. "I have been many places," he said in his rather snuffling, drawling voice, aped, had she known it, from some of the finest bucks in the country.

"Yes, I know you have, Harvey."

"I mean to say, that I have *danced* in many places, and it is rare to find a girl who is . . . well, tall enough for me. It's a dreadful thing to talk down to a female. Quite . . . quite enervatin'." He smothered a yawn and smiled into Sarah's eyes.

"It isn't right," Harold muttered to his rival. "Harvey's the heir. He could sweep her away, and we'd never have a chance."

"True," Harcourt replied. "But he's dreadful weedy. Sarah likes the outdoor life." Inhaling, Harcourt imperiled the seams of his tight evening coat.

Unconsciously, Harold imitated him. Poet he might be, but there was nothing wrong with his thews or sinews. He'd kept up and sometimes surpassed his twin in many athletic feats, though he might despise mere brawn. Many young girls sighed.

Catching Lady Phelps' eye, the twins separated to perform duty dances, though they spent more of that set glaring at their eldest brother than flattering their female partners. During the rest of the sets, they glared at each other.

Though Sarah knew all the steps, her attention was neither on her dancing nor on her partners. The compliments passed around her like shreds of mist, because they did not come from

Lord Reyne. After dinner, he had disappeared. No, wait, there he was, talking to Lady Phelps. Looking over her shoulder at the earl, Sarah stumbled.

With a bow, her partner took responsibility for the mistake, then proceeded on, releasing her hand to turn away. Sarah began to follow. At her next step, however, the cold floor communicated itself to the sole of her foot. Sarah paused, as the dance went on without her, and looked down. Her delicately colored stocking peeked out from beneath the hem of her gown. She wiggled her toes, to be certain she saw what she saw.

One sandal had definitely come off. Looking about, she beheld it, only a foot away. Sarah began to bend for it, but the stays Molly had insisted she wear precluded any deviation from perfect uprightness. With a stricken look, she glanced up at her partner. Finding she had not followed him through the dance, he came over at once, kicking the sandal away, unaware he'd done so.

It slid across the slick floor, was checked by another girl executing a turn, and then was sent skidding backwards by another male dancing pump. Hastily, Sarah shoved out her shod foot to stop it, only to misjudge the distance. The sandal went shooting on. Revolving slowly, it came to rest against the foot of the Earl of Reyne.

Sarah saw Lord Reyne look down and then back to the face of his hostess. For a heartbeat, he continued to talk pleasantly before he glanced involuntarily downward again, a tiny frown drawing his brows together.

The brilliant blue eyes darted right and left, scanning the feet of the women present. The fashion was for skirts to be extra long this year and his investigation met with defeat.

He smiled once more upon Lady Phelps, even as he drew out his handkerchief to wipe his brow, though Sarah had not noticed any perspiration upon it. Dropping the linen square, he laughed at his clumsiness.

After a moment, he waved to one of the footmen, keeping his own foot upon the handkerchief. She saw him point down and smile apologetically. The servant, young Fred, hesitated when he stooped and touched the square of cloth. He looked up from his bent position and said, "My lord?"

"My handkerchief, if you please."

"Yes, yes, Fred, what is the difficulty?" Lady Phelps asked. "Kindly pick it up for his lordship."

Lord Reyne wore a bland smile. Picking up the handkerchief in both hands, the footman handed it to the earl, who, in return, handed over something that glinted in the candlelight.

Folding the handkerchief with some difficulty, Lord Reyne tucked it once more into his inner breast pocket. The sandal had vanished, but Sarah had not seen it kicked away.

Pleasantly, Sarah said to her partner, "I think we shall sit down now." The floor was cold, but she contrived to walk without favoring her right foot. She sat alone for a few moments after sending the young man off to fetch her a cooling sip of lemonade. Aunt Whitsun had said that this was the best method of distracting a man. Sarah felt a brief shock that Aunt Whitsun should be right about something.

Lord Reyne still stood beside Lady Phelps. Glancing at the card dangling from her wrist, Sarah realized she had only until the end of this second dance of the set, now beginning, to reclaim her sandal. Then some man, whose name she could not quite make out, would come to escort her through another.

Searching out Lady Phelps, very noticeable in a bright pink silk tunic over her evening dress, Sarah rose to approach the gentleman beside her hostess. Though she shrank from speaking to Lord Reyne about such an embarrassing subject, she could not pretend to have two sandals for the rest of the evening. The marble was very cold and quite slick beneath her silken stocking.

Hesitating behind the gentleman, she feared to break in on Lady Phelps' conversation. But that lady, best friend of Mrs. East and, she hoped, future mother-in-law to Sarah, smiled as soon as she saw her. "My dear, do you know Mr. Breed?"

The gentleman turned, and Sarah wondered how she could have made the mistake. He was dark, but utterly different in every other respect to Lord Reyne.

"Yes . . . I mean . . . no . . . how do you . . . that is, Lady Phelps, can you read the next name on my card for me?"

"Why, yes. Oh, dear, my handwriting grows worse and worse," said Lady Phelps. Craning her neck, she tried to spot the gentleman among her friends. "He was here speaking to me one moment ago. There he is, going out into the garden. He did say he wanted some air, but I thought he knew . . .''

"Thank you," Sarah said with a hasty bob. She saw the small door close, leaving no mark in the paneling to show where it had been. Having played nearly as often at Hollytrees on wet days as at her own home, Sarah knew the secret passage well. An earlier ancestor had not wanted to spoil the symmetry of the ballroom with any entrance other than the great main arch.

She scurried down a long stuffy hall, the music and laughter muffled behind the closed door. "Lord Reyne?" she called. The slowly moving earl paused.

"Miss East, isn't it?"

He remembered her!

"Yes, I . . . I believe you have my sandal?" What a bald way of putting it. Sarah could have kicked herself, shod or not. Why hadn't she listened when Aunt Whitsun had taught her how to comport herself around men? She'd seen other girls lower their lashes and half-turn their heads, but these tricks only made her dizzy.

"Is this it?" he asked, as if the floor had been littered knee-deep with misplaced footwear.

"Yes, it was too big. I couldn't keep it on." Taking it from him, she held it unsure of what to do. Without stays, she could have bent down at once or lifted her foot across her thigh to rebuckle it. She bit her lip in consternation.

Lord Reyne said apologetically, "Pray, forgive me for not replacing it on your foot, but as I told you . . .''

They regarded the inanimate object with frustration. "I can't go back without it," Sarah said.

"No, I quite see that. Permit me to give you my arm, Miss East. We'll step outside. It's too warm in this hall for thought." He pushed open the door under his hand. They both inhaled instinctively as the cool, scented breeze curled around them. "Lean on me, Miss East," he said.

"Oh, I don't want to hurt you."

"I think I can support this burden." The smile she'd waited for touched the corners of his lips and pulled powerfully on her heartstrings. Beneath her hand was pure muscle. She could feel it flex as he clenched his hand. Lord Reyne escorted her at once to a stone bench at the edge of the terrace.

"What are we to do about your . . . ?" He flicked his fingers at the sandal.

"I don't know. I'm . . ." She longed to seem competent in his eyes, as she had when climbing the tree, but it was impossible. With heat rising into her cheeks, she confessed, "I'd do it myself, but I'm wearing stays."

Had this interview taken place but one month earlier, it would have still been light enough at ten o'clock to see Lord Reyne's face. Now, however, there was only the darkening sky of twilight above them, the crescent moon hardly noticeable through a misty haze. Therefore, Sarah could not be certain of the meaning of the choked sounds coming from him. "You're all right? I didn't hurt you?" she asked in some anxiety.

His coughing fit ended, Lord Reyne said, "Why this concern, Miss East? I assure you I have offered support to far heftier ladies than yourself."

"You said you'd been wounded. Harmonia said horribly wounded, and I thought perhaps your arm . . . ?"

"So, I am the subject of girlish gossip?"

"Oh, no, I asked her about you."

"Well, permit me to put your mind at rest. My wounds are not horrible, but honorable. I was shot, I fell, and was . . ."

He'd received a ball in the thigh during the first charge. He could not recall now what it had felt like. That moment was too quickly overlaid by other memories, though he knew an obscure pride at having kept his seat and at turning about to lead the next attack.

The dust and the heat and the sharp smell of blood, cutting through everything else. The scream that he strove to keep behind his lips, only to fail as he tumbled from the saddle. The face of the dead Spaniard beside him on the field. And above all, the feel of a bayonet in his back, swelling up to override every other sensation, even of the pain of the ball in his chest.

But he had lived, and that was something. He could look down and see the gleam of bright hair beneath the rising moon and know the beautiful eyes of Miss Sarah East were looking back. He knew many men who would never see anything more, nor hear the gentle voice of a naive girl, nor, for that matter, breathe the scent of an English garden. Thinking of them, Alaric wanted to cough, to go back to that stuffy hall, for there at least he could inhale without remembering those others.

"Lord Reyne?"

He shook his head, and she saw a quick gleam of teeth. "I was decorated, Miss East, for my regiment took the hill we were after. And that is the total sum of my military career. The doctors assure me I should soon be as flexible as any acrobat. I do, however, regret that day has not yet come, for your foot's sake." He half-bowed, wryly.

"I think I know what we could do about that." How sweet to be able to combine herself with him, even if only for a moment. She stood up, the big toe of her right foot just brushing the ground. "You see how we are at the very edge of the terrace? There's a ha-ha down there. It's not very deep. If I sort of dangled my foot, could you . . . ?"

"Attach your sandal? I think I could. Where does one get down?" He took the sandal from her gloved hands.

"There are some stairs over there."

Looking up a few minutes later, Alaric saw a white oblong object hovering in mid-air. "Can you come down any further?" he whispered. Obliging, the object dropped a trifle.

Though he could feel the strain across his back when he lifted his hands, Alaric realized the girl was balanced precariously on one foot. If he made too many demands, she might tumble off the wall. Touching her foot, he felt her tremble and hoped to God the chit wasn't ticklesome.

"Good evening," she said from above his head. Alaric stayed his hands on the slim ankle. For the first time, he realized the strangeness of his position, deep in a ditch, looking up like a decadent Romeo at the girl above. "Oh, no," the girl said. "I'm just enjoying . . . enjoying the view. I mean, the night. Isn't . . . isn't the moon lovely?"

Sarah fought down a giggle. If only he wouldn't touch her so gently. She said to the elderly couple before her, "Mother? I know she's about some . . . somewhere. I saw her inside. No, no, she'll be glad to have you call at any time." She felt another laugh bubbling up. Containing it was painful.

Now her left knee began to shake with the strain of sole support. And the dear woman before her was telling her the entire recipe for eel soup that Mrs. East had requested. Then, the tormenting touch on her foot was gone, and in its place, a palm pressed under her right sole, pushing up to offer a steady platform on which to stand. Gratefully, Sarah rested against it, though by no means putting her full weight down.

When Sarah was once more alone, Alaric quickly fastened the last two buckles, forcing his fingers to hurry where they would have lingered, strictly of their own volition. Golden Sarah East, dressed in a white gown that hinted at the firm curves beneath, was as lovely as any woman he'd ever seen. But a blossom in her first youth was not the sort of girl a man of character engaged in a flirtation. Especially when he had but recently pledged himself to another.

3

Now that they stood together, Sarah realized it had been worthwhile to spend extra care over her appearance. Nothing less than perfection would do if she were to dance with Lord Reyne. With her sandal secured, she felt she could redeem herself in his eyes by stepping lightly over the floor. He had brought her in from the garden with considerable haste, and she hoped it meant he was eager to partner her. But here he was, bowing away.

"Lord Reyne," she said, crushed. "Lady Phelps wrote you down for this dance." Fumbling for the card, she showed it to him as though it were a writ from on high.

"Did she?"

"Yes, see?" When his face betrayed not even polite interest, Sarah felt like a fool, gauche and forward. Aunt Whitsun had often called these her faults.

"Very well, then," he said, touching his cravat. "If she wrote me down, I must fulfill my duty."

"If you are unable . . . if it will pain you . . ."

"Confound it, Miss East. I am not an invalid." Alaric held out his hand to her, commandingly. Yet, he'd danced little since returning home, not even at Brighton, gayest and giddiest of watering-places. He watched as the other couples took their places. "Do you know this one?"

"I learned it a few months ago, at Leamington Spa where I stayed with my great-aunt."

"Ah. Well," he said, swinging her hand a little as though unsure of what to do with it. He smiled at her. "I suppose I can stumble through somehow."

Sarah was astonished to see that Lord Reyne never put a foot wrong, though he acknowledged the steps of the *chassez bagatelle* were new to him. She'd had three weeks with a dancing instructor and still sometimes made a fiasco when embarked upon it.

No sensation had ever been so delightful as that of Lord Reyne's fingers upon her ankle. Yet, that had been nothing. In the course of the dance, he lightly clasped her waist with one arm to turn, and held her shoulders with both hands to step forward and back in time to the music. Looking up at his face from the vicinity of his shoulder, Sarah thought he was more wonderful than ever, though his eyes did not meet hers. They were too busy flicking little glances at the other men's feet.

Bowing, he sent her down the line. She wondered if he would miss her. Plodding past man after man, Sarah did not smile until she reached him again.

"You have always lived in Brandeton?" he asked.

"All of my life, Lord Reyne. Where do you live?"

"I have a house in Essex. And another in Middlesex. Did you enjoy Leamington Spa?" Briefly, he dropped his gaze to her heated face, only to look away once more to attend to the steps.

"No." Before she could explain her bluntness, it was time to proceed again down the line. For a moment, she had to concentrate on catching the correct next pair of hands. It shouldn't be hard for him to understand that city pursuits were unimportant to her. He rode like a man used to the country, and he certainly shot like one, which is to say he lifted his gun to nothing he did not see clearly.

Looking back, she stumbled when Lord Reyne put his hands on another lady's shoulders. Never mind that it was Calpurnia Grissom, never mind that his next partner was at the age of spots, Sarah watched each girl, waiting for a smile to light Lord Reyne's face. It was not the polite smile she minded, for she had one now affixed to her own lips. She feared to see that brief radiance of humor, like the swift flash of a shooting star, which had once been focused on herself.

As she returned to him the final time, he asked with a little bow, "Sandal all right?"

"Yes, it's fine, so long as I do not wiggle my toes."

"Please don't disturb them. We were lucky to get away with that antic once; I would not dare try it again. I know what I would think if I saw someone down there." His voice was low.

"I imagine," she said, "anybody who lived here would

think it was Harold or Harcourt. They'd often hide in the ha-ha so they could leap up and frighten whoever came to look at the view.'' She added sadly, ''They don't do it anymore.''

''Of course, I'd forgotten I was in the country.'' He bowed a last time, for the music reached its final bar. Sarah frowned at him as she rose from her curtsy. It had been a very strange thing to say.

Before she could speak, however, he waved at someone over her head. ''Miss East,'' he said, ''I wonder if you would forgive me our next dance.''

''If you like.'' Did he perhaps wish to return with her to the garden, misty though it was? Sarah would ask nothing more of life, if it offered her once again such bliss.

''I'm certain Mr. Atwood will be pleased to take my place.''

Sarah dipped into another curtsy, feeling she had not strength to rise. He had obviously found her so dull and clumsy that even the thought of standing up for the rest of the set was monumentally tedious. So he'd scraped her off onto this Atwood, a man without even the sense to be sure of his target before he fired. That memory seemed to be in the unhappy gentleman's mind.

''I . . . I hope you are well, Miss East,'' Atwood stammered. ''Reyne told me you were unhurt. I can't tell you how that relieved my mind. If I had thought . . . I don't know what I'd have done.''

''Pray don't concern yourself further.'' She saw Lord Reyne disappear in the direction of the card room Lady Phelps offered as a foil to the dancing.

Mr. Atwood was a new departure in partners. He had an infinite variety of apologies at the ready for any occasion. It was a good thing he did, for if he did not offer the wrong hand, he was stepping on the wrong foot, usually someone else's. Sarah was only too glad to retire to the edge of the room after this exercise and gratefully accepted Mr. Atwood's offer of punch.

Harmonia came to sit beside her. ''Will you introduce me to your partner?'' she asked without preamble.

''Mr. Atwood?''

''Of course. You did say I could have any of your swains that pleased me.''

''But Mr. Atwood!''

"Oh, I quite admire him. More than any of the other gentleman Harvey has up. I thought that first night at dinner that he was exactly the sort of man who would suit me." Seeing how her friend goggled, Harmonia continued, with a slight blush, "I think he looks like a lost lamb."

Just then, Mr. Atwood returned, his glove quite sodden from the punch that had spilled from the glass he held. "Oh, dear," Harmonia said, standing up. "Let me help you."

"I don't know how it came to happen." Looking at Sarah, his hand shook uncontrollably. The rest of the punch, bright red and sticky, shot out over Sarah. Leaping to her feet, she began to brush ineffectually at the clinging liquid. Mr. Atwood, all but weeping, repeated his apologies.

Accepting Harmonia's handkerchief, Sarah looked up to find the ballroom quite silent, as her neighbors twisted their necks to observe her. Even the seated musicians stood up for a better view. She knew she turned a brighter crimson than the stain, blooming now like fat roses against her shoulder and breast.

"Sarah, my dear?" said a gentle voice.

"Oh, Mother! Look what happened!" Sarah just knew that in one more moment, Lord Reyne would be bound to look out from the card room. It was that kind of an evening.

"If Harmonia will see to this gentleman, I will do my best by Sarah." The kind eyes turned upon Mr. Atwood, still incoherently expressing his regrets.

Harmonia said decidedly, "Yes, I will. Come along, Mr. Atwood. Smithers is certain to have another pair of gloves and then we can have our dance."

"I'm sorry, Miss Phelps. We were supposed to dance?"

"Oh, yes. I've lost my card, but I'm willing to wager your name was down for the next gavotte."

As Sarah left the ballroom, following her mother, she was prey to a strange suspicion. Hearing laughter, she wondered if it was at her expense. Though she feared to look about her, she felt as if a thousand fingers pointed at her back, while faces grew red with stifled mirth. Sarah increased her pace. There was a chance Lord Reyne might see her, and she could not have borne it if he'd laughed too.

In Harmonia's room, Mrs. East shook her head. "I can do nothing with this stain now. It's soaked right through. I'm

afraid you won't be able to go back down for the rest of the
dancing. Do you want to come home with Father and I?"

Sarah almost said yes. If she left, she'd not have to face any
laughter. But, on the other hand, she'd not see Lord Reyne at
breakfast. She might not see him for a week. "Oh, no, Mother.
I'd like to stay. I was growing tired, anyway. I shall get into my
nightclothes and wait for the other girls to come up. Harmonia
was telling me about this wonderful new novel she has. I'll
read that until they come."

Her mother helped her unfasten the white muslin gown.
Looking at the dress as Mrs. East folded it, Sarah asked, "You
don't think it's ruined, do you, Mother?"

"I shouldn't think so. Molly and I will get it out, or, if we
must, we shall dye it. I've long had a fancy to see you in red,
my love. With your hair and skin, I always thought you'd look
well in it."

"But Aunt says only white is suitable for young girls. I don't
think it flatters me, though. The brunette girls, like Harmonia,
look very well in it. I'm too pale already. Though I should love
a red gown. With gold slippers, I think."

Mrs. East did not widen her eyes at this sudden interest in
clothes, though she could not resist a gentle pry. "I thought
Harcourt looked very well tonight."

"No better than Harold, so far as I could see." Sarah curled
up in the window seat, her bare feet covered by the hem of her
nightdress.

"Oh, yes, Harold grows very handsome. My, when I think
what scamps they were as children."

"Sometimes they are still childish, I think. It's just as well
Harvey came first."

Mrs. East had achieved nothing. She was even less certain
which Phelps boy Sarah admired. It was even within the realm
of the possible that the eldest brother would now be her choice.
Reluctantly, she realized it might be none of them, which
meant her daughter would settle in a strange place, perhaps
miles away from her home. The house had been so empty
while Sarah was away in Leamington Spa and the boys at sea.
Mrs. East sighed.

"Anything wrong, Mother?"

"Oh, no, my dear. I'm a trifle weary. If I can lever your
father loose from his cards, I think we'll go home, too. With

you up here, the dancing will seem very dull. You've improved so much. I shall have to write Aunt Whitsun and tell her how you shone tonight. And, there's the matter of your Season. She wants to sponsor you then, too.''

''Must I have one, Mother? Leamington Spa was so slow.''

''I think you'll find London very different. The theaters, and concerts, and all the fine fashionable folk. I loved every moment of my time there.''

''Very well, if I must. But, you come too, Mother. I hated leaving you before. If you come, we can buy lots of new books for Father, and dresses for us, and you can go to parties and the theater every night. Or at least every other night. Each in turn. We shall have such good times. And you know Aunt would be so pleased. She says she never sees you. Oh, please do come.''

''I would, my love. But to leave your father for so long . . .''

''How long is a Season?''

''At least three months. April, May, and most of June.''

''Three months! But that's twice as long as . . . promise you'll try to come for a few weeks.''

''I should like to see your come-out. I will try. We have a long time to plan it. Six months at least. Now, I'd best go down. I'll tell Lady Phelps where you are, so she doesn't think you departed without thanking her. Sleep well tonight, my love.'' Mrs. East bent and kissed Sarah's cheek.

The novel was not so thrilling as Harmonia had promised. Sarah found her eyes turning more to the window beside her than to the page. Finally, tired of propping up the thick volume, she put it down beside her and blew out the candle.

Instantly, the silver-shadowed darkness of the misty evening filled the room. Sarah leaned her head against the cool pane and dreamed a tale of her own. This was a tower and she a princess. Somewhere beyond her enchanted window, dragons prowled. Never fear, the prince was bound to come along at any moment.

Behind her, the doorknob rattled. Though she could still hear the laughter of the guests, the small clock on the mantle had chimed twelve o'clock none too long ago. The knob rattled again, and a solid thud sounded against the panels. Assuming one of the girls who were also to stay the night had come up, Sarah unfolded her legs and went to the door.

"Enter," she said, as a princess should, sweeping it open. Then she gasped and fumbled for the open throat of her nightdress. The figure on the other side of the threshold was far too broad to be anything female.

His name escaped her, though she knew she'd been introduced by one of the twins. He was as surprised to see her as she was to see him. "Why are you in my room?" he asked thickly.

"This is Miss Phelps' room."

"No, it isn't." He shook his head and an admonishing finger. His small eyes were reddened.

Suddenly to Sarah's senses came a waft of alcohol. There'd been none in the punch; they must have been serving it to the card players. Both her brothers and the Phelps twins had dabbled with liquor in boyhood. Sarah had learned from them that it was useless to argue with someone who'd been drinking. "Good-night." Stepping back, she tried to close the door.

The man stiff-armed it open. "Prove it to you," he said, stumbling in.

"No, you can't . . ."

"Dark?" He looked about him, then at her. The light from the hall was sufficient to show her, gleaming in her white night attire. Sarah bit her lip in sudden fear.

"Pretty girl, pretty girl." He reached out and gave her cheek a pat. Then, as though that had been a last effort anyone could reasonably expect him to make, he fell down. The noise was thunderous, though not so hard to explain as the immediate snores that began to issue from his open mouth.

"Sir, sir?" she said, kneeling beside him. Shaking him did nothing but increase the loudness of the noises. Closing her eyes, Sarah wished him away with all her strength. But the rasping breaths went on. From the mantle, the little china clock sang the quarter-hour. Soon, the other girls must come up. What would they say, finding a man stretched out on the carpet? Sarah almost hoped they would come up at once. Together, they might be able to move him to his own room, as she never could alone.

If only she had not been here! Sarah understood about compromising situations. Aunt Whitsun had described several to her, with warnings about the unhappy fate of any girl caught in such a coil as this. "Fortune-hunters often entrap a girl of means in this way. To be alone with a man in a bedroom, especially at night, is a scandal that can only be hushed up by an immediate marriage.''

Sarah did not want to be married to the drunken fellow on the floor, no matter that she now recalled him as the second son of the Duke of Brae. She'd hoped to have more of a conversation with her affianced groom than a squabble about whose room she was in. At least he found her pretty, though he was not to her taste. He had not Lord Reyne's height for one thing, nor dark hair, nor eyes the color of a deep lost lake. Sarah dared not imagine what Lord Reyne would think if he saw her now.

Well, she thought, standing up, the first thing to do is to get some light. Then, perhaps I can awaken him. Surely, if I shake him extra hard . . .

He couldn't be harder to wake than her brother Sam. No one could be harder to wake than Sam.

Taking up the candle from beside the window seat, she maneuvered about the prone gentleman. With a glance left and right in the hall, Sarah stepped out to catch a flame from a near-by sconce. Footsteps approached from the staircase. She blew the candle out once more and faded back into the bedroom. Swallowing down a huge lump she assumed was her heart, Sarah watched until two gentlemen passed. Fortunately, her unwelcome visitor had flopped over onto his side, silencing himself.

''Damn fine lot of women they have in this backwater. Did you meet the blonde?''

''Indeed, I did. Lord Lumme, what a beauty! I hoped for a dance, but she seemed to have faded away.''

Wondering who they were talking of, Sarah waited until she heard their doors close. Then, once more, she snuck out into the hall to hold the taper to the flame.

''Miss East?''

Sarah jumped at the voice and the candle fell to the ground. A man's foot stepped on the wick before the long Axminster carpet caught. ''Lord Reyne?'' She shot a glance into the bedroom. ''I did not hear you.''

''Forgive me for startling you. My sisters complain I walk far too softly. They tell me I should whistle more.'' He eyed the candle. ''Once again, I am unable to come to your rescue.''

''Oh! Never mind.'' Sarah dipped and snatched it up. ''I

took off . . . that is . . . good-night.'' She wanted to stand there and look at him for an hour. He'd smiled the moment she'd turned. Perhaps that meant that he did not think her as foolish as her escapade tonight had made her feel.

At that moment, however, the Hallelujah Chorus broke out again with full crescendo. ''What in the name of—Miss East, what have you in your room?''

''I . . . that is . . . he just . . .''

Alaric's brows drew together as he listened. ''The only thing I've ever heard to compare with it is the growling of hungry bears. Miss East, have you a bear in your room?''

''Oh, I wish I did.''

If having one man in her room made for scandal, Sarah reflected, what on earth did two cause? She couldn't possibly marry them both; that would be illegal. Besides, she did not care for the idea of trapping any man into matrimony, but if she must, she would prefer her husband to be Lord Reyne. But the portly fellow on the floor had come first. She could only hope he was married already.

''What am I to do with him?'' Sarah asked.

Looking down at the prone Lord Dudley, a smile tugged at the earl's lips. Seeing it, Sarah relaxed. He said, ''I don't suppose there's a chance you could simply exchange rooms with him. I doubt, with so many guests, anyone will remember which room originally belonged to which person.''

''That is an excellent plan, except . . .''

''Yes, Miss East?''

''This is Harmonia's room, and I'm afraid she would know.''

Alaric chuckled. ''I suppose she would. Have you tried to rouse him?''

''I went to light the candle first.''

The amused expression with which he'd been regarding the snoring man now changed to disdain. It did not lessen when the sleeper snorted and began his song anew, though, blessedly, on a softer note. The earl asked, ''You had retired, then?''

''No, I was reading.''

''Without a candle?''

''I . . . I had put it out.''

Now he frowned at her, as well. HIs eyes traveled slowly over Sarah, taking in her loosened hair, pouring like melted gold over her shoulders, and her heightened color. He said with a twisted mouth, "Do you often read without light, Miss East? Or did your friend here suggest the two of you would agree better without a candle?"

"I don't understand. I had put out the candle because the book was . . . I couldn't see out the window with it burning. He knocked. I thought it was Jessica or Harmonia and opened the door. Lord Dudley fell in and started making that noise. Can't we do something before anyone else comes?"

"Well, at any rate, he is of no use to you in his condition. I quite sympathize with your wish to be shut of him. Now, the question is: how to remove him?" Alaric crossed his arms on his chest and prodded the sleeping gentleman with an inquisitive toe. There was no response. "Is there water in that jug?"

Sarah picked it up. "It's half full."

"Pitch it over him."

Swinging it backwards, she paused at the last moment. "I can't. How could I explain such a wet carpet?"

"Tell them you dropped the jug while washing your face. You won't throw the water over him? After all, he has caused you, if not disappointment, at least some anxiety of mind."

Sarah shook her head, saddened that she could not bring herself to perform the first action he'd asked of her. But how could she possibly soak Harmonia's carpet?

"No?" He took the blue-and-white jug from her hands. "Very well. Hop up into bed, Miss East, and pull the curtains close around."

Though she obeyed him, Sarah could not help peeking through a chink in the hangings. "Are you really going to do it?" she whispered. "How can you?"

"Oh, I've awakened many an over-due soldier this way, Miss East. One . . . two . . . three!"

Like a whale's spout, a wave broke upon the unhappy sleeper. The carpet, if not awash, was at least as damp as the rocks by the surf. Sputtering and coughing, portly Lord Dudley sat up paddling at his face. "I say . . . I say!" he said.

"Wrong room," Alaric said, in a surprisingly gentle tone, putting the jug down on the dressing table.

"Eh?"

"Wrong room."

"Oh, oh, quite, old man. Quite. Good-night." He had some

trouble steering for the door, but Alaric caught his arm and showed him out. As he himself left, Alaric paused and looked back.

"You'd better ring for a maid to clear this up.'"

"Lord Reyne!"

"I cannot stay, Miss East. I am not foxed. My presence here would be impossible to explain, with you looking like that."

"I only wanted to tell you . . ." No, she could not tell him what her heart truly felt for him. "Thank you."

"Good-night, Miss East." He bowed and left, closing the door to Harmonia's room with a soft snick.

The maid had the carpet dry, at least to the eye, by the time Harmonia came up. Nevertheless, Sarah apologized for the "accident." Her friend dismissed it. "Oh, it isn't important. Mother's been wanting to change this room around for a month. What do you suppose the odds are she'll pick blue again? She always declares against it and then chooses it anyway."

Sarah helped her friend with the laces at the back of her gown. "Is Jessica going to be sleeping with us?"

"Heavens, I don't know. She's still flirting with that fellow."

" "Which fellow?"

"He's an officer, I think, out of uniform. I wish they wouldn't come in civilian clothes. How are we to tell them from ordinary men?" Harmonia turned and caught her friend's hands. "What did you think of Harlow?"

"He seems a very pleasant man," Sarah said, without any clear idea of who she was approving. Had Sir Arthur and Lady Phelps found themselves another son?

"Then you forgive him for spilling that punch on you? I told him you never could stay angry very long. You should have seen how you looked when . . ." Harmonia laughed.

"You've already begun to call him 'Harlow'?"

With a dismissive gesture, Harmonia stood up. "I don't believe in standing on ceremony. Not when he is only to stay with us two weeks."

"Two weeks? Will the entire party leave?"

"I imagine they will. It's not very exciting here, as we both know. Once the hunting's over, they'll be off. Are you ready for sleep?"

The two girls got into the large soft bed, caps properly on their heads, and laid the blanket over them, tight up to the arms. Harmonia chattered drowsily for a bit about Mr. Atwood. Sarah tried to attend, though her thoughts wandered to Lord Reyne. Eventually, though, as the chimes sounded for two o'clock, Harmonia's voice hushed into sleep. Listening to the deep, low breathing, Sarah tried to let that sound carry her away.

It was no use. "Two weeks" sounded in her head. The very tick of the clock seemed to repeat the words. He would leave. She had only this time, a brief fortnight, to spend with Lord Reyne. Then, he'd be gone away for the winter. It was doubtful he'd ever come again. He was no great friend of Harvey's to come for frequent visits.

She might, of course, meet him again in London, but as her mother had reminded her, the Season was a long way off. Six months. Anything could happen in six months. He might even marry.

Turning her pillow, Sarah laid her cheek against the cool smoothness of the linen case. Her resolve was complete. In the next two weeks, she must spend every possible moment with Lord Reyne. Let the neighbors say what they would. Sarah was determined. He'd seen the sort of girl she truly was. The sort who made England great.

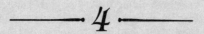

4

Sarah rose early for breakfast. For a moment, she hesitated on the threshold of the dining room. No one else sat there. Certainly not the one person she most wanted to see. Perhaps Lord Reyne hadn't come down yet. Or perhaps he didn't eat breakfast, though she could hardly imagine such a thing. "Good morning, Smithers. Am I the first?"

"Yes, Miss Sarah. May I tempt you with some eggs? Or Mrs. Smithers has done a very nice piece of gammon. And there's haddock, porridge, and toast."

"It all smells wonderful. I'll have some of everything."

Smithers respectfully served her, not forgetting the three kinds of jam and her tea. Sarah thanked him with a smile and sat down to wait. The hour grew later, and her food colder.

One by one, the rest of the family and guests trickled in. The butler and the footmen were kept busy exchanging plates, filling glasses, and ordering the table for the next influx. When Harold and Harcourt arrived at quarter to eleven, they immediately sat down next to Sarah.

"Did you enjoy your evening, Sarah? My heart burned with jealousy every time you danced with another!"

"Oh, yes, I enjoyed it very well. Thank you, Harold."

"I can't believe that ass Atwood spilled a drink all down your . . . um . . . gown." Harcourt laughed at the memory.

"Please, let's not talk about that." She winced just thinking of it. Her discomfort increased when Lord Dudley rolled in with a pale face. He shuddered delicately when Smithers offered kippers. Accepting a glass of water, he sat down across from Sarah and hung his head between his hands. His only participation in the morning table-talk was an occasional groan.

Harmonia bounded into the room twenty minutes later,

38

closely followed by Mr. Atwood. "You were right not to go," she said to him. "I'm certain the morning mist would have done your throat no good at all."

He gave a slight cough in answer, like a sheep about to give his first public speech. "Just a trifle of milk-toast, if you please," he said to the butler.

Catching his brother's eye, Harold nodded significantly. Not troubling to lower his voice, Harcourt replied, "I said he is an ass."

Harmonia shot them both a glance of disdain, and her tone when she spoke again held unaccustomed mildness. "Come and sit out of the draft, Mr. Atwood." With the gentleman settled into the chair at the head of the table, Harmonia consented once more to notice the others present. "My goodness, Sarah, I was surprised to see you up so early. Did you sleep at all?"

"Why, yes."

"You couldn't have told it by me. You were so restless all night long."

Knowing the boys were casting worried glances at her, Sarah said, "I'm sure you're mistaken, Harmonia. I slept excellently. Truly, I did."

"I'll wager you shouldn't have eaten the ham in the refreshments. It was much too greasy and never should have been served," Harmonia said. Across the table, Lord Dudley groaned. "I shall speak to Mrs. Smithers about it."

Beside her, Harold fervently grasped Sarah's hand. "You must take care of yourself. So delicate a blossom . . ."

"Oh, Harold," she said, wiggling her hand free. "I never even touched the ham."

"Besides, it couldn't have been better. I ate half a dozen slices and slept like a top." Harcourt drew his brows down as Lord Dudley muttered something. "I say, what's the matter with you? Lifted two or three too many? You should have gone out with my brother and Lord Reyne. Nothing like a good gallop to rid a fellow of the collywobbles!"

Lord Dudley rose unsteadily to his feet and weaved his way out of the room. Harcourt laughed. "Thought that'd get rid of him. Can't have a death's-head at breakfast—it's un-English!"

"Where did Harvey go?" Sarah asked. She'd sat here for nothing. Lord Reyne was already gone out. She pushed her plate away, suddenly not the least hungry, even if her food had not lost all its appetizing quality long ago.

"Oh, there's a pair of horses he's wild to buy, and he took some of the more sporting fellows over to examine 'em." Harcourt became aware that Harold scowled at him. He frowned back, purely on general principles, until a thought occurred. Hastily, he added, "That's Harvey all over. Spending money he don't have on horses he don't need."

It hurt him to say such things about his revered brother, but he'd heard once that the end justifies the means. Sarah couldn't fall in love with anyone but himself. It was unthinkable.

Harmonia, however, couldn't let this insult go unchallenged. "What nonsense!" she said. "You know Harvey's last pair were touched in the wind."

"That's just what I mean. Who told him to buy those old nags anyway? Even I knew what to expect. I mean to say, they were deuced narrow in the chest."

"Well," Harold said offensively, "if you found it obvious, anybody should have seen it."

Sarah broke into this infant argument. "Where did they go to see these new horses?"

"Brocklebury. And another thing . . ."

"Oh, I see." Lord Reyne would be gone most of the day. Sarah excused herself, unheard amidst the Phelps children's brangle, and went upstairs to gather her belongings. Halfway through her packing, Lady Phelps came in to help her.

"Are you going so soon, my dear?" Lady Phelps asked, gathering Sarah's brush and comb. "Why not stay to luncheon? We've hardly had a moment to talk. And I know Harriet is longing for a good coze with you."

Smiling, Sarah refused Lady Phelps' invitation. Talking to Harriet, who had never been a particular friend, could not be considered a substitute for the sight of Lord Reyne. Besides, Harriet's conversation revolved solely around the myriad perfections of Mr. Randolph and Harpocrates. Sarah now had her own standard of perfection, and she knew she'd be unable to keep from mentioning Lord Reyne's name. At home, she could wander in the woods, thinking of him without interruption.

As Lady Phelps escorted Sarah to the front door, she invited her to a picnic she'd arranged to entertain her guests next week.

Sarah agreed immediately. "Excellent!" Lady Phelps replied. "Shall I send Harvey over to fetch you on Thursday?"

"No, thank you. Not unless it's wet."

"If it's wet, we shan't have a picnic, silly girl."

"Then you won't need to send Harvey," Sarah said, smiling at Lady Phelps' joke. She'd been walking over to Hollytrees in all weather for years, and Lady Phelps knew it well. Thanking her for her kindness, Sarah's words were drowned by a raucous huzzah from out-of-doors.

"What in the world . . . ?" Lady Phelps asked, hastening forward. All the younger and spryer male guests, with Harcourt and Harold frowning in the forefront, waited on the steps of Hollytrees. Addressing her sons, she asked, "Are you going to play a game?"

"No, Mother. We are walking Sarah home."

"What? All of you?"

"Not ideally," Harold replied. "But it seems to have turned out that way."

"Really," Sarah said, addressing the assembled gentlemen in a tiny voice. "It's very kind of you, but I . . ."

A man stepped up and offered her his arm, to a chorus of cheers. "Permit me, Miss East."

"Gallant Sir Francis," some wit called in a falsetto voice.

"Thank you," Sarah said, awkwardly shifting her brown-paper parcel to her other side. Sir Francis had an abundance of dark, curling hair and a definite dimple in his well-tanned cheek. Sarah turned a look of dismay on Lady Phelps.

Meeting Sarah's gaze, she coughed and said, "Then, I needn't worry anything will happen to you. Good morning, my dear. Tell your mother I shall come to see her tomorrow afternoon."

Sir Francis proudly led Sarah through the cluster of her admirers and proceeded to be charming. He had to speak rather loudly to be heard above the rattle of twenty Hessian boots all striking the road at the same time. Sarah nodded and tried to smile, but the effort lost all pretense of reality when she chanced to lift her head. At the end of the road, by the double gates, sat a man on horseback.

Her escort stopped, more or less as one. "I say, Reyne," Sir Francis drawled, "back so soon? The bits of blood not worth the trouble, I suppose."

"I decided not to accompany Mr. Phelps." Alaric cast a look over the younger men assembled before him. "I've seen less elegant turnouts in the Guards, gentlemen. If you ever decide to join the militia, do let me know. Though I misdoubt me you'll ever again find such a charming commander." He touched two fingers to the brim of his hat and bent slightly forward in the saddle, his glance falling on Sarah.

She felt the embarrassment she'd undergone at the first sight of the young men had been worthwhile if that same sight made Lord Reyne laugh. A smile of rare radiance lit her face. It remained there all the time she walked home, leading Sir Francis to think himself a devil of a buck.

Fortunately for Sarah's peace of mind, her mother and Lady Phelps had always maintained a steady traffic between their households. Rarely in the history of their friendship had a day passed without some child trudging back and forth with a note or jar of jam or skein of silk. The only change in this routine was that Sarah could now be found immediately whenever her mother had a small commission for Hollytrees, instead of having to be searched for. This eagerness to be of service continued, despite the dangers Sarah found in the journey.

The difficulties were lessened by Harmonia's loss of interest in the conduct of her friend's beaus, having found one of her own. Without Harmonia to give the alarm, Sarah found it easier to evade the younger men. All the same, Sarah did not abandon her caution, still looking both ways before emerging from the trees and listening carefully for the sound of male footsteps before advancing down a seemingly deserted hall.

Despite her care, it was a near run thing on one or two occasions. Lord Dudley had the knack of appearing around a corner just as Sarah came out of range of cover. Fortunately, he seemed to have no memory of their encounter in Harmonia's bedchamber. Furthermore, though he'd smile when he saw her, he did not appear intent on overwhelming her with his charm. The same could not be said of the others when they found her.

Though the nearly universal demand for her company continued, every day she was disappointed in her own dearest wish. Sometimes, no matter how indiscreetly she inquired, she couldn't even manage to find out from Lady Phelps and

Harmonia where Lord Reyne was, or what he had done that day.

On Tuesday, she came up to return a shawl her mother had borrowed. Mrs. East had been unable to locate it until almost four o'clock, so when Sarah arrived, Harmonia asked her to stay to tea. Entering the green drawing room, she crossed to take her teacup and then searched for a place to sit.

Lord Reyne sat in an armchair, pulled around near to the fireplace. Though until that moment she had found the touch of autumn in the air invigorating, she now went closer to warm her hands. She felt almost afraid to look at him, yet she did not miss his self-absorption. Sad lines sculpted his narrow face. She wondered if he were in pain.

He glanced up, his frown still in place. Recognizing her, his features seemed to relax. "Ah, Miss East. Have you climbed any more trees? Or led any more parades?"

Sarah could only shake her head, too happy to speak. He actually remembered her after nearly an entire week without seeing her! She seated herself on a hassock near his feet. Sipping her tea, Sarah did not dare raise her eyes above Lord Reyne's knees. Finally, an idea of something to say crossed her mind. "Are you enjoying your stay at Hollytrees?"

He nodded. "So much so that I have agreed to remain for several more days. I had thought of leaving tomorrow."

Sarah's heart leapt painfully and she nearly spilt her tea. He was not going soon, though not staying long. "But you are to be here for the picnic?"

"I have been persuaded. I think young Harvey wishes to question me about my experiences during the last campaign. Somehow, I find it difficult to talk about that now. I suppose my memory is failing. The price of old age, you know." His mouth twisted, and Sarah made haste to change the subject.

"You said, I think, that you've a house in Essex. What is it like?" She hoped to picture him in his home, if he would tell her enough. It would give her something to dream of, after he left.

"Miss East, as I have seen you in your night attire, you needn't talk to me as though I were entirely a stranger." Alaric lowered his voice to a murmur. The instant blush that appeared in her cheeks brightened her grey eyes before they were hidden beneath those dark lashes, so absurdly lovely for a girl with hair quite like spun gold.

"I never thanked you—"

"On the contrary, Miss East, you thanked me by allowing me to be of service. Forgive me for teasing you, and for leaving you now as I must. I am engaged to discuss the Corn Laws with Sir Arthur." Alaric stood up and turned away, his hand accidentally brushing against the silken coil of her hair. He sternly ignored the tingle that ran up his arm at the contact.

Dealing with the hero-worship of the sons of the Phelps family wore on his nerves, but he enjoyed the freedom of the house. He'd found some old friends in their library. The gently rolling countryside admirably suited a man who needed to hone his skill in the saddle without overtiring himself. And yet, Alaric had not felt quite at ease until he saw the East girl hesitating beside him. The temptation to tease her was overwhelming and dangerous. He'd write to Lillian tonight.

Sarah had not another opportunity to speak to Lord Reyne that afternoon. But she could watch him, even when ostensibly speaking to one of the others. She could only hope the cold breeze would fade by Thursday, for it would be too bad if the picnic must be canceled. Prayers for fair weather would be within the bounds of sanctity, she supposed, if she prayed for the success of Lady Phelps' plans, rather than selfishly.

Thursday dawned clear and sunny, more or less, a summer day let down in the middle of October. The sky above emulated the exact color of Lord Reyne's eyes, though stern mountains of white and grey cloud were building up on the horizon. In the lane that led to Hollytrees, Sarah danced as she walked, bowing to a he-rabbit waiting beside a mushroom and kissing her hand to a tree that burned with crimson leaves.

Emerging on the hillside where the house sat, she could see all the lawn. The servants had already brought out tables and chairs, setting them up beside a rivulet that lead to the Phelpses' artificial lake. This was a new addition, having been dug out of the native soil but three years before. Picturesque though it might be, regrettably the lake had rendered the nearby soil quite marshy. Lady Phelps decided the picnic would be more seemly some little distance from the lake. It shone enticingly through the framing trees.

Though he stepped no less quietly than before, Sarah felt

that Lord Reyne stood beside her and turned sharply to see if it were true. No witty greeting came to her. She could only look at him, happy to see him well. Whatever had troubled him at tea the day before seemed to have left him.

After waiting for her to speak, Alaric said gently, "Good afternoon, Miss East. I had hoped I might see you today. Are you ready to go down, or do you wish to wait for Miss Phelps and her brothers? They're not far behind me; I left them gathering a multitude of rugs."

At the sound of his voice, she lost all the fear that had kept her tongue-tied. "I don't care to wait, and I know Smithers won't mind if we go down in advance." As they went, she said, "This is the best hill in the county to roll down, and it makes wonderful sledding in the winter. You only have to be careful not to run into that fence. Or the water."

"Do you often roll down this hill now that you are grown?"

"No, not anymore. Not since last summer." Sarah's feelings glowed in her cheeks. Not only had he said he hoped that he would see her today, but he thought her grown up. Molly had been wrong about her best nainsook muslin gown not being suitable for a day on the grass. She could not regret disregarding the country-woman's stern predictions of rain. The weather could not be so cruel as to change!

They reached the table. She greeted Smithers and the rest of the staff. They were putting the final touches to the tall pyramid sculpture of vegetables in the center of the main table, silver and china dishes radiating out from this artistic center like a mosaic.

"It must have taken hours, Mr. Smithers."

Alaric agreed with Sarah. "The Duchess of Richmond's alfresco occasions are nothing to it, Mr. Smithers."

The portly butler bowed from the waist. "A fancy of my own, my lord."

"How hard you have worked," Sarah said. "You know, it's a pity it won't survive. Once the boys come down, I mean."

Walking around the other side to get another perspective, Alaric said, "An artist must take every opportunity to practice, eh, Mr. Smithers? If it were not a poor recompense for Lady Phelps' hospitality, I would try to steal you away for my own household. You're rather wasted down in the country."

"Thank you, my lord. I could not leave Sir Arthur's service."

"Of course not," Sarah said. "They'd never get on without you. I know I couldn't. All the times you've rescued me! Do you remember . . . ?" Just in time, Sarah recalled that the tales of her hoydenish escapades might not please Lord Reyne. Glancing at him, she saw him attending with polite interest. "I forgot what I was going to say."

Smithers, equipped with the god-like perception of a truly gifted butler, merely bowed again and murmured, "Always happy to be of service to Miss Sarah."

Harmonia called her name from the top of the hill. Sarah waved and Harmonia ran down, going faster and faster as the slope increased. It seemed as though Smithers' work was destined for a premature destruction, when Lord Reyne stepped out and caught the flying girl against his chest. He steadied her, tilted his hat, and walked away. Sarah sighed. If only it could have been she who fell into his arms, even for a moment.

"Are you all right?" she asked Harmonia, as the girl panted for breath.

"Goodness, yes! I wanted to talk to you before Mother came." Taking her friend by the hand, she set off briskly, out of earshot of the servants and the guests. "You'll never guess what horrid thing has happened."

"What?"

"Miss Dealford, a dreadful friend of Harriet's, is visiting us. With her mother. They're frightfully correct and the worst bores. You've got to help me get rid of them or they'll stay for days."

Sarah's attention still turned toward Lord Reyne, now in a group with Sir Francis and several other young men. But when her friend enlisted her aid, she asked, "Why do you want to be rid of them?"

"Because she has her hooks into Harlow, that's why. They arrived last night, and what do you know? They know him from London. I've hardly had the chance to speak to him since. He's so pleasant to everyone; he doesn't have the heart to give her the kind of set-down she deserves. Look there, and you'll see what I mean."

The weedy figure came down the hill, feeling with his small feet for firm footholds, quite as if he were descending an Alp.

He seemed to be escorting an opened parasol. As they came closer, Sarah saw a frail-seeming young woman gripping his arm, wrinkling the blue superfine. She seemed especially frightened of the cows, who walked up to the fence as stately as dowagers to see the visitors. Mr. Atwood brandished his stick at them and steered a path somewhat farther away from the enclosure.

"You would think," said Harmonia, "that with all the unmarried men who are staying with us, she'd find someone else to attach herself to rather than my Harlow."

"Your Harlow?"

Harmonia blushed. "Oh, Sarah! If you only knew!"

"I'm sure he's being polite. I'll wager . . ." Sarah waited for Harmonia's eager questions, but her friend did not take her up. Perhaps the matter was serious.

Miss Dealford smiled; Harmonia grumbled. "That creature . . ."

"What do you want me to do?" Sarah would throw her heart into this project, if it meant Harmonia would be happy.

"I don't know, exactly. If we could but get her away from Harlow! Mother's seen us; we have to go back."

Miss Dealford already felt put out because Harriet had been too busy at her son's cradle to talk last night. Now she and her mother sniffed at Miss East and sneered at the ill-taste of the men who went at once to her side. Harlow remained beside them, but he shifted awkwardly from one foot to the other and had to be spoken to twice before he replied. Only Alaric kept his manners and his sense, bringing each woman a cup of punch.

"Who is that young person?" Mrs. Dealford inquired of him, peering at the tall blonde through her lorgnette.

"Miss Sarah East, the daughter of a neighbor of Sir Arthur's."

"And who is her father?" she asked, repeating herself like an owl.

"A scholar of some note." He had listened for quite an hour, his first night at Hollytrees, to Sir Arthur's stories about the incomprehensible behavior of Mr. East, which seemed to consist chiefly of corresponding with papers other than *The Morning Chronicle*.

"Oh," said Miss Emma Dealford, exchanging a glance with

her mother. As though it had been spoken, the phrase "Undistinguished Antecedents" hovered in the air. "She's tolerably pretty."

"Is she?" Alaric asked, stifling a yawn. He rose. "May I refill your glasses, ladies?"

Sarah had no opportunity to sit even an instant with an empty glass or empty plate. If she had not kept on her feet, she would have been too stuffed to move, like a force-fed goose. The young men seemed intent on having her taste at least a little of everything Smithers thought necessary for a special luncheon.

Sarah saw Lord Reyne bow and speak a moment to his hostess. Lord Dudley Tarle was taking a glass of wine with Lady Phelps, and the two men talked, seemingly at ease.

Beside her, Harcourt asked, "Do you want Mother? I'm sure she'll be glad to get away from that old stick, Lord Dudley. Reyne's not a bad sort, however. You know, he's interested in butterflies?" The boy's disgust was palpable.

"That's not so terrible," Sarah said, determined to cultivate a passionate interest in winged insects.

"No, but he wants to talk about them. All the time. And you know, I leave that sort of stuff to Harold."

"What do you leave to me? Are you making out a will, old man? I trust this treasure is among . . ." He bent and kissed Sarah's hand. Harcourt made an expressive face. "But I forget. Sarah is not yours to give away." Harold retained her hand, and Sarah had to tug forcefully to get it back. She wiped it surreptitiously on a napkin.

"We were talking of Lord Reyne," she said.

"No, we weren't, either," Harcourt said sharply, then, recalling to whom he spoke, he softened his tone. "Don't you remember? We were talking about that fool, Tarle."

"Oh, him," Harold said. "How dull. I can entertain you better than that, Sarah. Wouldn't you like to walk with me by the water? I'll read you my latest poem. It's . . . I'm dedicating it to you. It's called 'To S. E.' 'Oh, eyes that mirror heaven's hue . . .'"

"But my eyes aren't blue," Sarah said, thinking of a pair that were.

"They aren't?" Harold stooped and tried to see past the brim of her hat.

Sarah thought Harcourt was going to be sick. " 'Course they ain't blue, you fool; they're grey. And she don't want to hear any poem you wrote. It's bound to be rotten. Come down to the lake, Sarah. Do come. Some of us are going to fish.''

"No, thank you," she said, touching his arm for a brief moment, smiling at him. "But you go. And you, too, Harold. Maybe you can alter your poem." Because she'd known him forever, she added, "Then I'd be so pleased to hear it."

"Of course. I'll just arrange the rhyme so it's a stormy sky. That should be simple enough." He squinted in concentration and began to count meter on his fingers.

As Harcourt led his brother off, Sarah found herself alone. The rest of her admirers, with the goddess monopolized by the twins, had gone off to do their duty by the other girls Lady Phelps had invited for the afternoon. They were the same who had come to the evening party last week, and Sarah felt their attitude toward her had not warmed. It troubled her, but she didn't know what to do about it. On trying to approach Jessica, the girl blatantly turned away and pretended not to see her.

Lord Reyne still remained by the Dealford ladies. So did Mr. Atwood. She didn't know what to do about that, either. Harmonia did not seem to be about. Smithers said, when asked, "Miss Harmonia has gone down to the lake for the fishing."

Perhaps Harmonia did not really mind Mr. Atwood's attendance on the enemy. Because Lord Reyne stood there, Sarah crossed the grass, closer to the chairs set a little way off from the rest of the party.

In a piercing tone, Mrs. Dealford said, "Lord Reyne, you promised me an introduction to Miss East." He obediently performed this office. "Now, be off, sir! We want no tiresome gentlemen. We want to talk. Sit down, Miss East. Emma, let Mr. Atwood show you those cattle. No. It is foolish to be afraid. You must persevere."

Mrs. Dealford proceeded to turn Sarah's mind inside out in an apparent effort to learn her every thought since babyhood. She had just wrested free the facts regarding last year's irksome meeting with a traveling portrait painter when the inquisition was broken into by a scream. The sound went on and on as though emerging from some machine.

"My dearest!" Mrs. Dealford said, starting up. Horror-stricken, she pointed toward the paddock. "She'll be gored!"

Mr. Atwood, Miss Dealford and several other intrepid gentlemen had entered the paddock to come closer to the cows. Unfortunately, the cows were not alone. Without so much as a preliminary paw at the ground to indicate his displeasure, the bull thundered forward. His chest was deep, his horns sharp and glinting in the sun, and his hide as black as an evil wish.

The others turned to flee, supporting Miss Dealford. But upon departure, she tripped on her trailing skirt, landing directly in the evidence that this had long been a cow enclosure. Instead of rising, she remained sprawled on the ground, screaming incessantly. With word and gesture, the gentlemen encouraged her to hurry and be gone.

Among the horrified onlookers, paralysis seemed to have taken hold. Then, Sir Francis called, "I'll get a gun!" and began to run up the hill to the house as fast as his long legs would carry him.

Sarah said, "Carrots!" Mrs. Dealford gave the girl a pained glance before once more gazing at her soon-to-be destroyed daughter in an agony of fear.

Already dashing toward Smithers' tower of greenery, Sarah passed Lord Reyne. He went the other direction, carrying an unfolded tablecloth. It was dyed a mild pink. Grabbing the carrots from the base of the pyramid, Sarah followed him.

Nimbly as any boy, she climbed the white fence. Lord Reyne approached the line of gentlemen, who stood between the fallen girl and the fearful beast, as they prepared to defend her life at peril of their own. "Pick her up, you fools!" Sarah heard Lord Reyne growl as he passed them.

Stopping a few yards from the bull, who had paused as though deciding which body he'd juggle first on his horns, Alaric extended the tablecloth as a breeze billowed the material. The bull snorted and shook his head. He dashed forward a yard, then turned away as if uninterested. However, Alaric saw the animal look back at him as if judging the distance.

"Miss East!" he said, as Sarah came to his side. "Leave at once." The bull came around to face them. Shaking the cloth at the bull, Alaric asked mildly, "Are you daft?"

"Not at all. What are you doing?"

"A technique practiced in Spain." He walked slowly forward, the tablecloth at the ready. "Will you please leave?"

Sarah watched him, admiring the set of his shoulders and the cut of his coat over his narrow hips. Realizing she should not even be thinking of his person let alone permitting her gaze to dwell upon him, she stepped out from behind the shelter of his body. Holding out the carrots, she said, "Here, Petey."

The bull trotted past Lord Reyne and stopped before Sarah. He lowered his massive head, as large as a man's chest, and took the carrots, stalks and all, from the girl's hand.

"Petey?" Alaric asked, as he folded the tablecloth. "A family pet, I take it?"

Though he approached with caution, in a very few moments he was scratching the bull's woolly head. He murmured, "Did that woman's screaming bother you, boy? Sounded like a night at the opera—something I'd advise you to avoid."

The bull's fringed ears twitched as though taking heed of this advice. He almost seemed to nod in agreement before placidly chewing the prized vegetables. Alaric took Sarah's arm as he escorted her back to the fence. "You're a very brave young lady."

"Oh, I've known him since he was a calf. I wasn't frightened at all."

"You're rather remarkable, aren't you, Sarah East?"

For the length of a single heartbeat, they looked into one another's eyes before Mrs. Dealford came forward. Lord Reyne moved away from Sarah, leaving her both breathless and confused. To be called remarkable seemed very fine, but somehow the meaning and his expression had not agreed. It was almost as if she'd displeased him somehow. Yet there had been some other feeling present in the depths of his eyes— something she could not recall ever having seen there before.

5

Having heard the commotion, Harcourt, Harmonia, and Harold ran up from the lake, closely followed by the other fishers. Eagerly, they listened as several people described what had happened to Miss Dealford.

"Oh, is that all?" Harmonia asked. "She frightened the fish because of Petey? Poor fellow, he must have been terrified. I'm going to eat some cake. Mr. Atwood, pray join me."

The thin gentleman, lurking at the rear of the crowd for fear Mrs. Dealford would forget that showing Emma the cows had been her own idea, brightened up at hearing his name spoken by a friendly voice. "Miss Phelps, I should like it above all things."

Harvey, delayed all this time at the house getting the proper shine on his boots, put his arm around the weeping Miss Dealford, not noticing that she was reeking rather from the mingled mud she'd fallen into. "There, there, old girl. Come up to the house, and we'll soon have you put to rights."

Miss Dealford ceased calling brokenly for her mother and raised her glistening eyes to young Phelps. "Yes . . . yes, please. Oh, he can't get out, can he?"

"Certainly not. Old Petey—that is, we keep him stoutly penned. Yes, quite stout, those pens. Helped put 'em up myself."

"Did you really?" Reluctantly, she turned her attention once more to her mother, approaching with Lord Reyne. "I beg your pardon, Mama?"

"Of course, Emma also wishes to express her appreciation for your bravery just now. Don't you, dear? That bull would have charged you, Emma, if not for Lord Reyne."

"Actually, Mrs. Dealford," Alaric said, "it was all Miss East's doing. Any thanks going about belong to her."

52

Mrs. Dealford affected not to hear. "Emma . . . Emma, thank Lord Reyne. Poor child, she's so distraught."

"I'm going to the house, Mother," Emma Dealford said. "Mr. Phelps is going to help me."

Mrs. Dealford might be convinced that Lord Reyne's bravery alone saved her daughter, yet the young gentlemen were of the opinion that it was all due to Sarah. Then and there she was voted the Order of the Carrot, with Parsley Clusters. That made her laugh, causing Mr. Posthwaite, who'd thought of the jest, to preen himself for quite half an hour.

When handsome Sir Francis arrived just too late for glory, the jokesters did their best, but his *amour propre* was too great to allow him to reply in kind. Valiantly, he pretended the pistol he'd hastily shoved into his waistband was not there, until relieved of it by Smithers. Freed from this encumbrance, Sir Francis bowed low over Sarah's hand and said, "I'm most happy violence was avoided. Especially as the bull is an old friend of the family. Your lovely hands could gentle any wild beast, even a man."

Sarah shook her head as the other gentlemen echoed the young baronet. "I know he was only curious to see what all the noise was about, same as anyone. Of course, I wasn't frightened. Why would I be?" They paid no attention. Lord Dudley Tarle proposed a toast in her honor and Smithers went for glasses and wine. They drank and laughed, while Sarah replied only absently to their pleasantries. Her attention was fixed on the other group of excited young people.

Her friends gathered close to Lord Reyne and pressed him to show them exactly what he would have done with the tablecloth if Petey had proven hostile. In a few moments, they gave a collective sigh. Looking over at the cluster, between the heads of the gentlemen that surrounded her, Sarah saw that Lord Reyne had gone from their midst. The disappointed girls looked toward the lake. Had he walked down to the water?

Try as she would, to follow him at once was impossible. But then Smithers, bringing more wine, accidentally dropped Lady Phelps' largest silver tray. It fell to the ground, ringing like an alarm bell. The thick green bottles which had been upon it dropped with thuds onto the grass, shaking beyond aid the fine wine inside. As her admirers spun to see this latest disaster, and the butler scrambled to collect the bottles, Sarah stole away to the lakeside.

Parting overhanging branches, Sarah stepped as carefully as a deer coming down to drink. The ground was not too boggy except by the very edge of the water. Sarah went as near as she could without getting her feet wet. The ornamental lake kept company with the sky, adding touches of silver-blue to the thickening clouds. The sun's glow had dimmed and little waves had begun to rise from the still water. Sarah suddenly felt lonely. Lord Reyne was not to be seen.

"There you are. Watcher doin' down here all by yourself? Come back to the picnic." Lord Dudley stumbled over the slight lip between the grass and the lakeside, yet contrived not to spill any of the pale red liquid in his glass.

He'd been so pleasant this last week that Sarah spoke politely. "I was just about to go back, Lord Dudley. Please excuse me." His small eyes seemed very red. And surely his smile had never been so broad before, except for the night of the party.

With an apologetic smile, Sarah attempted to go around him. He grinned as if her movement were a joke and spread out his arms as though to trap her. His smile widened still further, until it seemed to Sarah that she could see nothing else. "Please, excuse me, Lord Dudley," she repeated, raising her voice a modicum. Aunt Whitsun had told her a lady never shouts, but perhaps in exceptional circumstances she could.

Advancing, Lord Dudley nearly tripped again and the wine in his glass slopped back and forth. He seemed to regard this with considerable apprehension. Hastily, he drained the glass, doubtless for safety in case of accident. While he was thus distracted, Sarah tried once more to edge around the nobleman.

"Don't go so soon. Have a little kiss first." He dropped his emptied glass onto the hummocky ground. "Pretty girl, pretty girl." He reached out as though to pat her cheek. Remembering that he'd fallen down and gone to sleep after performing this action before, Sarah stood still. But instead of patting, Lord Dudley grabbed for her arm. His hand was hot. "Little kiss first," he repeated.

Lord Dudley had an uncommonly strong grip. Before she quite knew what to do, his arm had snaked about her waist and he pulled her against him. Sarah attempted to twist free. No one had ever tried to force a kiss from her before. Disgusted, for his breath stank, she fought to keep her face turned away, pushing at his chest with her free hand. Feeling his lips against her neck, she shoved harder. All at once, her striving fingers found another set on Lord Dudley's shoulder.

For a moment, Sarah ceased to struggle as she prayed. Oh, Lord, let it be Harcourt or Harold. Let it even be vain Sir Francis. But please . . . please don't let it be Lord Reyne.

In this case, her prayers were not answered. Alaric jerked hard on the tipsy fellow's shoulders, peeling him away from Sarah by main force. He stepped between them, a laughing glint in his eye as he looked at Lord Dudley and then at Sarah. "What a way to behave at a picnic."

The second son made another grab for the girl. Sarah stumbled back towards the water's edge and watched as Lord Reyne restrained Lord Dudley's flailing arms. "Just a moment, old man," Alaric began in a tone of amused reason. "You're a trifle elevated, you know."

"I demand satisfaction for that insult!" Jerking free, Lord Dudley struck the other man across the face with his open hand.

Red marks came up in vivid relief on Alaric's cheek. His spine stiffened as he drew back, glancing briefly at Sarah. The laughter had died in eyes that now seemed all pupil, save for a flicker of fire in their depths. Sternly, he said, "You're drunk, man. And you've embarrassed a lady."

"I'm not!" Lord Dudley attacked again, his eyes closed. As he was not paying the slightest attention to where his blows fell, one smacked Sarah quite hard in the shoulder.

She stepped backwards to maintain her balance, stepping squarely into the mud at the very edge of the lake. "Oh, dear," she exclaimed.

While Alaric tried to stop the other man without hurting him, Sarah pried one foot out of the mud, wondering how storks managed. Therefore, she was in no position to recover when Lord Dudley reeled into her. She fell back at full length into the water, sending a splashing wave high into the air.

As she sank, the bubbles singing in her ears and the wash swirling over her mouth, Sarah wished she might never emerge. But the lake wasn't deep, at most reaching her knees. Sadly, she found her footing and stood up, water streaming from her falling hair as she coughed and spluttered. Pawing the seaweed-like strands from her face, she dared to look around.

"I'll save you!" Lord Dudley shouted. Breaking free from Lord Reyne's hold, he plunged in toward her, swimming wildly as though the lake were a storm-tossed ocean. Cold water on top of the wine-induced exertion proved too much. The shock laid him out.

As the breeze struck her skin, making the mild autumn afternoon feel like a frigid winter's night, Sarah's first thought was that Molly had been right as usual. White nainsook muslin was not perhaps the best choice for a garden party.

Her second thought was that she ought to remove Lord Dudley from the lake before he swallowed it. She floundered over to the now semi-conscious second son to prop him up. "Pretty girl," he muttered as his eyelids fluttered. "Mermaid . . . ?"

"I'm coming in, Miss East," Alaric called.

"No, don't. There's no reason for you to get all wet. I can probably manage him. He's not very heavy, and the water is not deep, as you can see."

But when she looked in his direction, Lord Reyne already had removed his blue coat and cream-colored waistcoat. She repeated her reasons for his staying dry as he waded toward her, though she was glad he disregarded them. Shivering, she waited for him to help. True, Lord Dudley wasn't heavy, but neither was he exactly seaworthy. Though she'd managed to keep his head above water by putting her arm under his neck, she daren't tow him to shore. He was too drunk to keep himself afloat.

For some reason, when he reached her, Lord Reyne looked only at Lord Dudley. "What a priceless ass," he said.

"That's what Harcourt said. No, that was about Mr. Atwood."

"It seems I have a great deal in common with young Harcourt." He almost glanced at her then, but hastily averted his gaze. As he reached for Lord Dudley's collar, a stone must have shifted under his boot, for suddenly he was no longer standing. "Damnation," he said, rising. Then he begged her pardon, as he wiped the water out of his eyes.

Sarah was not attending. His shirt, as fine a muslin as her

own gown, had suddenly become quite transparent. Wet, it molded itself against every sinew of his masculine form. She felt like Eve looking for the first time at Adam, after the incident with the Tree of Knowledge.

Until this moment, she'd thought all men were like statues. That he had dark golden hair on his body, growing in circles across his firmly built torso and leading down, surprised her. However, her gaze soon fell on the red, star-shaped scar above the brown areola.

"Oh," she said, putting out her hand as if to cover the mark. She did not make contact with his body, though a longing to do so surged through her. It was foolish to believe that her touch might heal him, yet the certainty that it would pounded in her mind and heart.

Alaric clasped the hand she held out to him. "You're cold," he said. "This wind—"

"Yes," she said, knowing it was not the sharp breeze causing her trembling. Lord Dudley stirred, and she was forced to look at him. He was not a pleasant sight. "I don't suppose throwing water over him will do much good this time," she said wistfully.

"We'll see what good dry land will do. Why in the name of heaven anyone wants a lake on their property . . . Remind me to have mine filled in. I never knew water could be so very wet. I've been drier in my bath."

Alaric brought the dead wood ashore. Sarah followed, her eyes fixed on Lord Reyne's back. Another scar, puckered and long, ran down from his triangular shoulder blade to almost the last rib. She no longer wondered at the occasional stiffness of his movements, but felt ashamed that she'd ever asked him to do anything for her. "Is he too heavy?"

"Of course not," Alaric replied, heaving the fellow out of the lake. The sloppy embrace of the mud seemed to rouse Lord Dudley as nothing else had been able to. All the fight had gone out of him, as though it had never existed at all. He pulled himself upright and fluttered small, sheepish eyes at Lord Reyne while he murmured an apology. Tarle began to offer one to Sarah when his jaw dropped.

Hastily, Alaric picked up his coat and draped it over Sarah's shoulders. She thanked him, adding, "I am rather cold." The wind blew harder now, and the sun could no longer be seen even as a bright glow through the clouds.

Alaric was astounded that Sarah had not, even as yet, realized the appearance she presented. The memory of Miss East in her nightclothes was enough to keep a man smiling well into old age. The vision she made with soaking transparent muslin adhering to every curve was enough to send him mad. Alaric grabbed at the fast-disappearing reins of his sanity.

"You'd better hurry to the house, Miss East," he said, catching and holding Lord Dudley's eyes. "Before anyone who heard our splashes comes to investigate."

"Quite, quite," said Lord Dudley, his rubicund face abnormally pale. "Hurry along, Miss East. And pray forgive me. I don't know what came over me." Any temptation he felt to steal a last glance at her exquisitely revealed figure was dampened by the suppressed rage in Reyne's expression.

"Yes, I suppose I had better. But neither of you should stay here in those wet things. You'll catch your deaths." She turned away, and began squelching across the shore.

Alaric muttered, "Any word of this gets out, and I'll see to it you're unable ever to drink again. Is that entirely clear?" Perhaps the way Alaric twisted his waistcoat between his hands contributed to the enthusiasm of Dudley's nod.

Sarah said, "Did you hear that? It sounded like thunder."

Alaric wasn't sure it hadn't been the grinding of his teeth. "I don't think . . ." Then there was a second, nearer rumble. Moving away from Lord Dudley to Sarah's side, he saw that the sky had darkened appreciably in the last few moments. "We'd better hurry or we'll—" He chuckled. "I was about to say we'll be drenched, but it's a trifle late for that kind of caution."

He glanced over his shoulder, but the sobered nobleman had bolted. Sarah presented a finer picture, anyway. Her hair, darkened by the water, puddled on his coat in soaking tendrils. Her lashes starred into spikes about her large grey eyes, nearly black in the swiftly failing light. Impulsively, he touched her livid cheek. "You're chilled to the bone, child!"

"If we run . . . I mean . . ."

"Yes, if we run . . . ?"

"That might warm us up. But I forgot about your—"

"Miss East, I give odds of seven to one that I best you in reaching the house. We begin at the next lightning flash."

With a smile that would have dazzled Zeus, Sarah swiftly bent and removed her shoes. What would Molly say about two ruined pairs in a week? Wet stockings clung irritatingly to her legs, but she knew better than to take them off before him. She tensed as she waited for the lightning. She knew it would be a deadly insult if he won by any but his own best efforts.

All at once, the skies delivered a downpour. Sarah and Alaric stood close enough to the trees to miss the full power of the water, yet the rain stung as it struck. Sarah turned instinctively toward the only shelter provided.

Alaric found his arms wrapped tightly about a shivering girl. A girl whose body was as lush and full as a Roman emperor's favorite statue. When she lifted a perfect face to his, Alaric discovered the limits of temptation. It would be easy to kiss away the water droplets, to press his lips to hers, to feel the marble grow warm and real beneath his breath.

He thanked every immortal that he'd been so cold a moment ago. That accident of temperature was all that enabled him to stand so close to her and merely pat her shoulder comfortingly, sternly ignoring the beauty of the limb beneath his hand.

"Now then, my dear. Were you frightened? Let's hurry along to the house. We'll be warm and dry in the shake of a lamb's tail." He sounded, he thought, like a maiden aunt, which was just as well under the circumstances.

Sarah did not want to let go. Had it been but two hours ago that she had wished she were lucky enough to be in his arms? Now her hands were flat against his back and her head rested on his collarbone. His hard ribs expanded and fell beneath her elbows, while the warmth of his hands spread throughout her body. For all this, however, Sarah suddenly felt something was wrong. Perhaps it was the voice of Aunt Whitsun, like a distant whine, or that Lord Reyne's hand on her shoulder never ceased patting.

Sarah pushed away from him. "Yes, of course. We must hurry." She could not bring herself to meet his eyes.

They found the main hall crowded with dripping, complaining men and women. No one had noticed the storm until it was upon them, and even if they'd sensed it, who could have guessed it would drop so much water so quickly? At least four others, who had wandered beyond the lawn, were as wet as Sarah and Alaric.

Sarah went at once to Harmonia's room. Though her friend was not there, a maid had a huge fire aglow. As soon as Sarah saw the flames, her teeth began to chatter. She'd not realized how thoroughly chilled she was until she felt an overwhelming hunger to stand nearer the blaze.

"What you want," said the maid, after a searching glance, "is a mustard bath for your feet. Oh, never you mind. There's more than one being stirred in the kitchen at this minute. Strip off them wet things, and I'll see if I can dry 'em for you."

"Th-thank you."

"My Aunt Molly'd skin me if I didn't do my best by you, Miss Sarah."

In a few minutes, Sarah was not the only girl with her hands held out to the licking flames. Harmonia hadn't enough dressing gowns to go around, so they wrapped themselves in rugs, blankets or whatever else they could find, and shared mustard baths. After a whispered apology for her earlier rudeness, Jessica plunged her feet in with Sarah's. Smithers had created a hot punch. Sarah sipped the golden liquid from a silver cup and soon felt not only warm but dizzy.

Trading her blanket for Jessica's *robe de chambre,* Sarah went into the hall. Now that she was reasonably dry, she wanted to find Lady Phelps to offer aid. A door slammed at the end of the corridor and Harmonia came striding past. Sarah had actually to put out a hand to stop her. The sleeve she touched was clammy with damp. "Harmonia, you should put on dry clothes."

"That's what Mother said, but I haven't time now. Harlow's unwell. I'm going to send for Doctor Reeves."

"Is he that sick?" Sarah matched her friend's swift steps.

"He's complained of a headache all week, and I think the wetting he took has brought on a fever. But he wouldn't hear of sending for the doctor. He's so unselfish!"

At the head of the stairs, they met Miss Dealford. "Miss Phelps," she said, "I wonder if you might send for your local physician. I'm afraid Mama has caught a cold." From the door behind her came a mighty sneeze, followed by a cough that sounded like Petey with corn in his throat.

"I was about to send for Doctor Reeves," Harmonia said. "I'm sorry your mother is ill. She's not the only one."

From the bottom of the steps came another sneeze. "I beg

your pardon, Miss Harmonia,'' the butler said, looking up at them. ''Sir Francis Coulterwood asks if you were thinking of sending for the doctor. He seems to have discovered—I beg your pardon, ladies—he seems to have discovered dots.''

''Dots?'' Harmonia asked.

''Oh, dear,'' Sarah added.

''I must tell Mama.'' Emma Dealford went again into her mother's room. Just before closing the door, however, she turned upon the other two girls a speaking glance of friendlessness.

From within, her mother snapped, ''Don't stand with the door open. There's a draft!''

''Is there anything I can do to help?'' Sarah asked. Emma only shook her head and closed the door.

''Smithers,'' Harmonia said, ''send Robert Groom for the doctor at once. And you'd better ask at every door who wishes to see him. Sarah, I'll find you something to wear and you can help Mother and me.'' As they returned to her room, Harmonia said, ''You know, I almost feel sorry for that girl.''

The doctor came in due time. Sarah greeted him as he entered, shaking water off his hat onto the clean hall floor. He seemed irritated to be called out in the middle of the storm. However, by the time he went away, he beamed. ''Lady Phelps,'' he said, ''you have four guests and three servants with head colds. For this group, I have prescribed bed rest, hot baths, and a mixture which receipt I shall give you.''

''I'm sure we can manage to care for them so that they will think they are at home.''

''Also, Harcourt and Harold are ill with the same trouble.''

The lady's face lost a measure of its confidence and Sarah sympathized. From boyhood, the twins had been trying sufferers, losing all their spirit in distressing demands for coddling. ''And . . . and my other children?'' Lady Phelps asked, after a moment to deal with this first burden.

''Young Harvey, Harmonia, Harriet and Mr. Randolph all seem quite healthy. I've told his mother that Harpocrates should be allowed up for a few hours tomorrow. Which leads me to my next group of patients.'' The doctor glanced at the list he held. ''The Earl of Reyne, Sir Francis Coulterwood, Mr. Posthwaite, and Mr. Atwood are all showing signs of chicken pox, undoubtedly contracted from your grandson.''

"Chicken pox?" Lady Phelps and Sarah exclaimed together.

"Without a doubt. I believe these gentlemen paid a visit to the nursery last week. Most unwise. I warned Mrs. Randolph that her son should be kept from the company of those who had never been exposed to this disease. We of science now know that the merest contact leads to contagion." The doctor shook his head, safe in his superiority.

"What can be done?"

"Nothing, except to let the business run its course. Of course, they'll require nursing. A low diet will suffice in case of fever. They must be kept from scratching the blisters, for fear of scarring, and I shall send you up some bottles of carbolized oil, to aid in removal of the crusts, when they appear. And they must be kept from undue exertion. The same treatment I recommended to Mrs. Randolph in every respect."

"And my other guests?"

"I've seen every person in the house. Those who show no signs—pustules, fever, and so forth—should stay for three more days, to assure themselves they are free from contagion. Lord Dudley Tarle seems especially anxious to be gone, but I've warned him of the consequences if he leaves too soon. After all, we don't want the entire county to break out with it, do we?"

After ringing for Smithers to show the doctor out, Lady Phelps all but collapsed into her chair. "I never expected to turn the house into a hospital," she murmured. One by one she said the names of the stricken guests. "And then, three of the servants are ill as well, which makes for thirteen people in need of care. An unfortunate number."

As Sarah chewed her thumbnail, commiserating, but unable to offer a helpful suggestion, the butler entered. "I beg your pardon, my lady, but I fear . . . I fear . . ." Smithers sneezed violently, flourishing a handkerchief. "I regret to inform your ladyship," he continued in an oddly thickened voice, "that I am about to become inconvenient."

"Fourteen!" Lady Phelps exclaimed, becoming a trifle more cheerful. "At least that is not a number of ill-fate."

"Glad to be of service, my lady."

Sarah said, "You should put your feet in a mustard bath, Smithers, and drink a glass of that punch you sent up to us. And have Mrs. Smithers put a hot brick beside you when you retire. Mother always says that's the way to drive off a cold.''

Inexpressible yearning came into the butler's face. "Hot punch,'' he echoed.

"Yes, do go along to bed, Smithers. We shall manage without you—somehow.''

After he'd gone, Lady Phelps said, "Poor man. Yet I don't feel as sorry for him as I do for myself. However shall I care for all these people without a complete staff? And the twins sick, too. This is the last time I permit Harvey to hold open house. I shall speak to Sir Arthur about it directly. I do hope *he* isn't going to be ill. You've no notion how horridly difficult—'' Lady Phelps recollected to whom she was speaking. "Whatever shall I do?'' she repeated.

Sarah tried to imagine herself in Lady Phelps' position. What would *she* do if faced with this predicament? "You could send for Mother,'' she said. "Shall I take the message for you?''

"Of course.'' Quickly, Lady Phelps crossed her pink boudoir carpet to seat herself at her desk. Taking up a pen, she removed paper from a burl-wood box. "Marissa's never flustered by anything. I shall write her immediately. And, Sarah, I don't want to sound unwelcoming, but you'd best stay away from the house until the course of this chicken pox is done. I shouldn't like you to fall a victim to it. You heard the doctor say it can leave scars.'' She touched her own cheek, looking at the smooth cream of Sarah's skin.

Marissa East read the incoherent note her friend had sent. "Oh, dear, what a dreadful thing to have happened. And after all her trouble over that picnic.'' She glanced at her daughter, especially at her mud-splashed legs. The dress she'd borrowed from Harmonia was far too short, allowing full sight of Sarah's ankles and much of her calves. "Do you feel quite well, dearest?''

"Oh, yes, Mother. Not even a sniffle.''

"Good. For I shall need your help at Hollytrees. All those poor people are going to require nursing. Dorothea cannot do it all alone. Run up and ask Molly to pack us some clothing, then you change into your warmest dress. I shall order your father's suppers for the next several days.''

"But Lady Phelps doesn't want me, Mother. She said so."

"Ah, no doubt she is concerned for your safety. She mayn't recall your having the chicken pox when you were three. I do, though. You gave it to everyone in the house, even to Molly."

"I don't remember, either." Yet, she smiled. It was one more link between Lord Reyne and herself.

— 6 —

When Molly took the bundle that had been the nainsook dress and her shoes, the maid said all that Sarah thought she might. "Haven't you even sense enough to come in out of the rain, child?"

"Yes, Molly." Sarah was thinking of the rain, and the surprising warmth she had felt when enveloped in Lord Reyne's arms. She sat on her bed, leaning her cheek on one knee drawn up close to her chest.

"You may smile, miss. It's not you that's got to clean 'em. If you ruin your shoes this way, you'll go to London barefoot. And all the fine ladies and gentlemen will laugh at you."

Sarah's smile faded. Once more she found herself at Lady Phelps' dancing party with wine punch all over her bodice. Had the guests been laughing at her? More painful a thought even than that—was Lord Reyne laughing at her now? He had not embraced her there under the trees; she had thrown herself into his arms. Sarah remembered the rigidity of his body and the impersonal pats he gave her shoulder. Pressing her hands to her burning face, Sarah slid off the bed into a heap on the floor.

Molly, turning from the clothes press with gowns in her arms, froze. For a moment, only her eyes moved. "Isn't that just like the girl? To run out and leave me with all the—" A terrible groan seemed to float up from the floorboards. "Mercy! I never knew the house was haunted." More loudly, she said, "Come out from there and let me see you!"

A disembodied head floated over the edge of the bed, looking at her with mournful eyes. "Oh, Molly, I've been such a fool!"

Tossing Sarah's gowns onto the bed, the maid came around to seat herself on the other side. Blond hair, loose and rather wet, rested against her black satin knee. Molly smoothed the

65

heated temples, as she often had when Sarah was a child. "What is it you've done that's so horrid?"

Sarah wanted to confide in someone. Molly listened to so many of her fancies and dreams; she would surely understand the feelings Sarah had toward Lord Reyne. Yet, even as she opened her mouth to speak, something held her back. With the echo of laughter still hurting her ears, she would not risk even the slightest upward curve of the maid's lips. Sarah straightened, and carelessly picked a leaf from her skirt. "Nothing, Molly. I've done nothing. Oh, your niece who works at Hollytrees—"

"'Lizabeth."

"She was very kind to me when I was all wet."

"Why were you all wet?" Molly asked.

Sarah guessed Molly was still trying to find out why she had called herself a fool. "The rain caught me, unexpectedly. That's how my shoes got wet. Everyone at Hollytrees was caught. 'Lizabeth took good care of us."

"I reckon she'll have her hands full now. Do her good; all young girls are lazy."

"Yes, Molly." Sarah stood up, pretending to be strong. "What shall I help you with?"

Molly frowned. She was all the more suspicious because of Sarah's exaggerated aspect of innocence. Slowly, the maid said, "They'll be needing extra linens at Hollytrees, what with all them fine folks bedridden, as you say. They'll need to make up beds for you and the missus as well. Go count out a dozen sheets to take Lady Phelps. Not the ones with the lace edges, mind."

In the fragrant depths of the linen-press, Sarah laid her cheek against the cool ecru sheets. A tear was absorbed and lost. Loving Lord Reyne from the moment she'd seen him, it had never until now occurred to Sarah that he did not love her in return. Everything he'd said and done, reinterpreted, meant only casual kindness to a girl, same as he would have shown to any stranger. After all, Lord Reyne was an earl, trained from infancy always to be a gentleman.

Sarah saw now what an utter, utter fool she had been and reproved herself for it. There'd be no more hurling herself into his arms and seeking out his company. Though she loved him no less, an infant self-esteem demanded she behave as a well brought up young lady should. Aunt Whitsun would be proud of her, though she hoped that lady would never find out how her niece had behaved.

Resolutely, Sarah began placing the folded sheets in a basket. A sob shook her. "One, two, three . . ." Tears spotted the second-best sheets. "Ten, eleven, twelve." Sarah sighed and wiped the dampness from her cheeks with shaking fingers.

Half-closing the door, she glimpsed the best, the finest sheets waving their lace-trimmed edges at her. Quick as a thief, Sarah grabbed a set and buried them under the others, so Molly would not see them. She slammed the press door.

"No!" Lord Reyne said, pushing the tray the young footman attempted to place on his lordship's blanketed lap. "Blast it, man, I don't care what the doctor said. Eating in bed is for old women and invalids. Take it away and bring me my breeches."

Fred left open the door to Lord Reyne's room. Sarah, in the hall after taking Mrs. Dealford her tray, paused to eavesdrop. Mrs. Dealford had made no objection to dining in bed, contenting herself with asking Sarah to send up Emma as soon as she returned downstairs. Sarah would not hurry to do the lady's bidding.

From Harmonia she'd heard that Emma had not left her mother's bedside even once during the afternoon, which Harmonia thought monstrous. From hostility, Harmonia had swung over to Emma Dealford's side. "No doubt her mother forced her into it. I'm sure Emma didn't want to talk to Harlow at all."

Sarah felt a certain hesitation in meeting Lord Reyne after that impulsive embrace, but she overcame it, feeling he needed her help. Stepping into the room, Sarah coughed gently, her lashes downcast. With a muffled exclamation, Alaric swung his naked legs under the covers. When he was decent, he said, "Miss East, perhaps you can explain that dining cannot be considered undue exertion. I've been trying for five minutes and all I hear is 'Doctor's orders, my lord.'"

Stung by his mockery, the footman said, "So it is, my lord."

"I think it will be all right if Lord Reyne sits over there." She pointed to a rather old-fashioned style of table, banished from the library, that possessed a matching chair. "There isn't going to be a formal dinner this evening, just trays for everybody. It makes more work, of course, but Lady Phelps thought it would be best.''

"Oh," Alaric said. "I didn't know that."

Sarah smiled, laughing a little. "You're not the only one who's sick, you know. There are thirteen of you."

"Thirteen!"

"Fourteen. Smithers has a dreadful cold."

"That's true enough," said Fred, from the corner where he laid out Lord Reyne's supper. "We can hear him sneezing like a grampus all through the downstairs." He stood back and surveyed his handiwork. "Will that be all, my lord? Miss Sarah?"

"No, you can stay to valet me," Alaric said.

"I ain't been trained for that work, my lord. I'll make a hash of it, sure to." Fred backed toward the door.

"At least find me a bowl of hot water so I may shave. Once these spots turn to blisters, I shan't be able to use a razor. Please forgive me for speaking so frankly, Miss East."

"I don't mind." Sarah wandered over to look at what Lord Reyne was to eat for his supper. She had not thought the thin gruel and dry toast looked very appetizing when she'd carried it to Mrs. Dealford, though that lady said it was the very thing she wanted. Mrs. Smithers' attention was less on her cooking than on her husband's wants, as was natural, and the under-kitchen maid had prepared the meal.

Sarah glanced up inquiringly, feeling Lord Reyne's gaze upon her. When he did not speak, she prompted him with a "Yes, sir?"

Alaric could not help smiling at the girl, despite a headache like a lowering cloud. "Will you ever get over this habit of being alone in men's bedrooms?"

"But it wasn't Lord Dudley's room! I told . . ." Sarah blushed. "Excuse me. I'll just see about finding you some beefsteak—if you want it, that is."

"Beefsteak? Miss East, I am in your debt unto half my worldly goods. I may be ill, but I'd rather not starve to death. Call it an invalid's whim."

Sarah cast one more look at him as she hesitated in the doorway. In the light thrown by the shaded candles beside his bed, she could not see any dots on his face, only the disorder of his fair hair and the strong neck revealed by the open throat of his nightshirt. "I can find you something. It may be cold."

"As long as it is food for a man, not for a Bath widow. Sarah?" he said, calling her back.

"Sir?"

"Why are you doing this work?"

"I beg . . . oh, my mother and I came to help Lady Phelps. There isn't anyone else, what with so many of you."

"You've had this revolting disease, then, I take it?"

"When I was a baby."

"Gad, the things one leaves undone through absence of mind. I kept meaning to have it, you know. Well, if you are immune, will you sit with me while I eat? I promise not to alarm you by dining in my shirt. I shall at least wear breeches, if that fellow can be prevailed upon to hand them to me."

She laughed happily. It had just come to her that he'd called her by her name. She all but sang as she went down the stairs. When she reached the kitchen, the tune came bubbling up.

"You're cheerful," Harvey said.

"Yes, I am. Where's Annie?"

"Gone to bed with the same thing Smithers got."

"Oh, no! Not another one. Who's to cook?"

"Your mother said she'll do breakfast. Mother will make dinner tomorrow night. I'm to create some sort of luncheon."

"You, Harvey? Perhaps I should."

The young heir quirked his lips in his attractive, lopsided smile. "No, no. I shall enjoy it, I think. Father's livid about it, of course. But I always rather fancied my chances in the kitchen. Some very notable gentlemen have special dishes they prepare themselves. I mean to say, punches and such. Why not meals? With Mother's help, naturally."

Sarah could only shake her head in surprised admiration. "Do you think you could find a beefsteak for Lord Reyne? He's frightfully hungry."

"I . . . I suppose I might be able to. There may be some of sliced roast beef from the picnic. I know there must be, as we hardly had the chance to sink a tooth in it. I wonder where they would keep it?"

Through the swinging door came Emma Dealford. "Mr. Phelps, I think—" Seeing Sarah, Emma said, "Ah, Miss East. Is Mother looking for me?"

"No, I don't think she is." Sarah saw Harvey's face when Miss Dealford spoke. The expression passed in less than a finger snap, yet it was enough to clear Sarah's conscience of her lie. Sarah knew Mrs. Dealford thought her stupid, from the way she'd very slowly repeated her instructions two or three times. Let her go on thinking so, if it would please Harvey.

"I'll be back in a moment," Sarah said. "There's something I want to ask Mother. Do try and find that roast beef, Harvey. Perhaps Miss Dealford can help you."

"So this is your kitchen," Emma said. "Isn't it beautiful!"

When Sarah returned, the sliced beef stood on the scrubbed wooden table, with some rolls, butter and a small dish of cold mashed turnips. Harvey and Miss Dealford were not in sight. Muffled noises came from within the pantry. Harvey exclaimed, "Look at that! Have you ever seen anything so enormous?"

"I've never seen anything like it before. Though I'm not certain it's right to hang it from the ceiling. And what do you suppose caused it to be that odd color?"

"Miss Dealford, I believe, yes, I do believe it's a ham. Smoked, I think."

"Amazing."

After a moment of silence, Harvey exclaimed, "Bottled peaches! So that's how we manage to eat them in winter."

"Remarkable! I never knew. Do you think I could learn how to do that?"

That was all Sarah heard. Carrying up Lord Reyne's supplementary meal, she passed Harmonia in the hall, going the opposite direction with a covered tray. "You're late with that; it's after eight o'clock," Harmonia said. She paused and frowned over the food. "Who's that for?"

"Lord Reyne."

"A lot of indigestible food isn't going to do him any good. Why, Harlow said he could hardly eat what I brought him, for fear it would lie too heavily on his stomach."

"It's what Lord Reyne asked for."

"Oh, men never know what is good for them."

"How is Mr. Atwood?" Sarah asked, though her tray was growing heavy.

"Very low. Sitting up tires him so much. And he has a

perfectly horrendous headache. I'm going back to sit with him as he sleeps. In case of nightmares.''

"Won't you be tired?" Sarah asked. In answer, a mistiness came into Harmonia's eyes. She set off at a great rate down the hall, no doubt so that she might not be too long away from her ailing idol's bedside.

Perhaps, Sarah thought, she oughtn't let Lord Reyne eat the roast beef. And the half-bottle of claret she'd added at the last moment might push him into an apoplexy. Sarah hesitated. On the one hand, she hated to disappoint him, but on the other, what if the meal made him worse than he was? Fortunately for Lord Reyne, at that moment, Fred Footman looked out and said, "Please, Miss East, hurry along with that! He'll have my head off in a minute."

Alaric sat up in an armchair, tucked about with pillows and blankets. He wore a fine quilted dressing gown over his nightshirt, the open collar filled in with a silken handkerchief. The silver-blue gleam of the banyan had been chosen by a sister to play up his dark good looks, but he knew that it also brought out the color of his spots. However, it was all he had with him.

Sarah thought he looked impossibly handsome. She quivered where she stood, setting the crystal glass to ring against the bottle. "Claret?" Alaric exclaimed. "Miss East, my dear Sarah, more than half my worldly goods are yours. Bring it here."

Though she yearned to do his bidding, Sarah still hesitated. "I don't know if you should . . . Mr. Atwood says . . ."

"Atwood? Why should he concern himself with my habits? Besides, Fred tells me he's yet more ill than I. If he thinks that good food can harm me, he must be delirious. Please, Sarah, I'm dying of hunger."

She enjoyed watching him eat. He praised the wine, but when she offered to find him some more, he refused with a laugh. "You drown me and would now drown my wits? No, Sarah, this is an admirable sufficiency. I shall have enough to do to keep my eyelids propped up. Don't go."

"You're tired."

"Yes, devilishly, but I don't want to sleep yet. Do you play cards?"

"No, sir, but my father taught me cribbage."

"Cribbage is cards. Fred?"

"Yes, my lord?" All this time the footman had been busying himself with straightening Lord Reyne's chamber. He seemed already to imagine himself a valet to some notable, having weathered the perils of shaving an exacting gentleman.

"Find me a cribbage board; there's a good chap."

Alaric found himself bested two games of three. He knew shame for assuming Sarah would be an incompetent player. He lost the first game through underestimating his opponent and the third through utter demoralization. Her card sense was impeccable, never leaving him an opportunity to cry "Muggins" and take the points she'd passed by.

Furthermore, she had the most confounded luck. "Are you certain you haven't another jack or so up your sleeve?" he'd asked once, delighted when she merely laughed and shook out the lace that encircled her wrists. The beauty of the inlaid board was a pleasure to play on, and the beauty of his opponent made it almost a pleasure to lose. He said as much at the conclusion of the third round and looked up to see Mrs. East in the doorway.

He suddenly felt uncomfortable. His attire was not at all what a gentleman entertaining a lady in his room should wear, and Fred had been dozing by the fire for quite an hour. Alaric would have stood up the moment he saw Mrs. East, but the tucked-in blankets held him fast.

"I won again, Mother," Sarah said with an irrepressible smile.

"How clever of you, dearest. But it's quarter to eleven and Lord Reyne is unwell."

The man and the girl turned surprised faces to the clock. "So it is, ma'am. I apologize for keeping Sarah so late. I plead, however, that her company did me more good than any medicine by keeping me from dwelling on my complaint."

Mrs. East entered and gave a gentle shove to Fred who woke up, nearly falling into the fire irons. "Help Lord Reyne to bed," she said. "Come, Sarah. You can play again in the morning."

"Please come back," Alaric added. "After all, I must get my revenge. I think I shall lie awake and plot it."

Before Mrs. East could say the words that so obviously hovered on her tongue, Sarah said firmly. "No, you shall not.

You must rest. Your mother would say the same, were she here.''

"No doubt she would. It is as well she has been spared the experience. She worried to excess whenever I fell ill.''

"That is a mother's right. Isn't it, Mother?''

"Yes, my dear. Are you ready?''

Sarah put the pegs safely into a secret slot under the board. "Until tomorrow, Lord Reyne.''

The next morning, a yawning Lady Phelps told Sarah that the twins were asking for her. She promised to stop in their room after carrying up breakfast to Lord Reyne. Fred, serving in Mr. Smithers' absence, told her, "He already et, Miss Sarah. Well, that is, he drunk a cup of tea. The rest didn't please him. He damned my eyes, saving yer pardon, and asked me when . . .''

"When what, Fred?''

"When you was coming up to see him. But you didn't hear it from me, miss. He'll have my ears if he finds out I told you.''

"All he took was tea? No wonder he's in a bad temper. I'll run up.'' But when the bell Lady Phelps had given her sons shrilled, Sarah looked to where the older lady sat, drowsing over her plate. "Never mind, I'll go,'' Sarah volunteered when Lady Phelps shied at the sound.

The twins lay in two beds. Harcourt was just raising the bell again in one languid hand when Sarah said, "Good morning.'' The larger boy's eyes brightened before a bout of sneezing struck him. Seeing he was unable for the moment to speak, Sarah turned toward Harold. "How are you this morning?''

Sadly, Harold shook his head, touching his throat. As he swallowed, a look of pain, equal to any worn by the most profound martyr, closed his eyes and contorted his mouth. "Can't you talk?'' Sarah asked. Harold shook his head again.

"No, he can't,'' Harcourt said, opening his hand and letting the white cloth drift to the floor. It lay atop a mound of others between the boys' beds, silent testimony to the severity of their colds and the devotion of their mother. "And it's ever so dull up here with a funeral mute for company. Can you stay?''

"No, I'm sorry. I daren't even come in. I have to take care of . . . some of the others, and I can't find time to become ill. But I'll come by sometimes to see how you are. Do you want a book?'' Harcourt rolled his eyes but Harold nodded eagerly. ''Which one?''

Harold wrote something on the slate his mother had given him to make his wants known. From her place of safety in the clear breezes of the hall, Sarah couldn't make out what he'd written. *''Tristram Shandy,''* Harcourt translated.

''I'll see if I can find it. Are you certain you don't care for anything, Harcourt?''

Gruffly he said, ''I'd rather have my horse, or dog. But you might as well bring me the estate books. I promised Father I'd look them over, and I haven't anything better to do.''

''All right.'' Lord Reyne's room was in another wing so Sarah was not tempted, at least not much, to stop in before performing the boys' commissions. Sir Arthur gave her the account books, but the ledgers were so large and awkward that he agreed to take them up for her. Harold's novel she sent by Lady Phelps.

Free of her obligations, Sarah flitted up the steps to Lord Reyne's door. She stopped to smooth her hair and straighten her dress. Her mother, coming out of Mr. Posthwaite's room, saw her daughter perform these significant actions. She also saw the enraptured smile that lit Sarah's face when a patrician male voice called out, ''Come in.'' Last night, Mrs. East had lain awake a long time, prey to obscure worries. Now her fear had a name. Alaric Naughton, Earl of Reyne.

He sat by the window, his elbow on his knee and his chin in his hand, staring out at the mist that hung from the trees like veils on ugly women. ''A glass of water, if you please,'' he said.

''Certainly.'' Sarah poured it out from a pitcher on the table and carried it across to him. Standing near him, as he stretched out his hand for the glass, she saw that the spots, faint last night, had now come up like a fresh crop of freckles. ''I hope you're feeling more the thing this morning. You seem much better to me.''

''Please don't lie. I can't bear it. Where were you?'' When he asked this question, he did not turn his head to look up at her, but went on gazing out the window at nothing. He drank the water as though he were very thirsty.

''I felt I must visit Harcourt and Harold.''

''And no doubt tomorrow I shall be sneezing.''

"I stayed by the door and never even breathed their air."

"Yes, yes. Well, what do you want?" He turned the empty glass restlessly between his fingers. She took it. His fingers continued to move until he seemed to realize what he was doing. Then he laid both hands in his lap, lacing the fingers as though to prevent them getting away.

"More water?"

"Yes. I mean, thank you." Then, as though he could no longer control his feelings, he cried out, "Damn, but I itch! Worse than lying on an ant's nest. I itch in places no gentleman—" Alaric clamped his lips shut.

"Can I help?"

"Absolutely not!"

"Mother says you should cut your fingernails. If it becomes very bad, we have some oil to rub on."

"It's only that . . . I can't even expect compassion! Chicken pox is more likely to cause my friends to laugh than to sympathize. I have a headache. And it's warm in here."

"Drink this. Then, I think you should return to bed, sir. If I close the curtains, you'll be able to sleep."

"What will you do?"

"I shall visit Mrs. Dealford—"

"I pity you."

"And Sir Francis. I've not been to him, yet."

"You must tell me how he gets on. Handsome Sir Francis. At least, I am not so violently fond of my reflection that I cannot bear a spot or two. Or even a hundred, as you in your kindness were about to tell me I wear."

"I wouldn't have said that. I told you how well you look."

"Then you lie, Miss East, as I said. Take this." He pushed the glass once more into her hand. Sarah was shocked by the heat radiating from his hand.

"You're running with fever," she said. "Into bed at once, and I shall send my mother to you. She knows many remedies for bringing your temperature down."

"Better she than that doctor fellow. He laughed when he told me I was going to be laid up here for another week." Alaric stood up, only to find that the room swayed. He flung out a hand and clutched Sarah's arm. "Pray excuse me, Miss East, but I find I must make some use of you."

"I don't mind," she said, though he leaned almost all his

weight against her. Sarah felt a hard lump in her throat at the realization of his need for her, even in so small a matter as guiding him to bed. She knew already the difficulty he found in admitting that, due to his imperfectly healed wounds, he couldn't easily and with grace do what other men did. To fall ill now must leave Lord Reyne feeling as though all destiny were against him.

He sat with a sigh on the bed. Quickly, Sarah knelt and removed his slippers. "Here now," he said, rousing. "You shouldn't do that!"

"It's done. Now, off with your banyan. I had 'Lizabeth change your sheets. Feel how cool and smooth they are."

"Yes, I remember her coming in with Fred. Neat little figure."

Sarah stood by, with her eyes turned modestly away, as Lord Reyne lifted the covers to climb beneath them. He still wore his breeches, though he seemed to have forgotten about them. His eyes were already closing. Sarah leaned down and untied the silk from about his neck. Alaric's eyes flicked open. "You're a good sort, Sarah East. Damn this itch!" His hand darted upwards as though he would scratch.

Seizing his hand in her own, she stroked it. "Just be patient, Lord Reyne. A few days and it will all be over."

"Why, Sarah! Your hands are cold."

"It's just that you're so warm. Sleep now."

When his fingers were lax and limp in her own, Sarah laid them on the counterpane. They seemed to seek after her own until curling under one another. His hands were narrow and long-fingered with a faint golden gleam on their backs where the light burnished the hair.

She was about to leave the room, to find her mother, when gazing a last time at the figure on the bed, she saw that he was trying to scratch in his sleep. She put down the pitcher and crossed to once more hold his hands still. They turned beneath her own and grasped tightly. His eyes, very bright and shining, opened. After wandering a moment, they fixed on her face.

She whispered, "I didn't mean to wake you, but you mustn't scratch."

She attempted to pull her hands free, but his grip was firmly gentle. Thinking he was playing a game, she laughed and said, "Really, you must let me go. I'll come back."

"I'll never let you go." With surprising strength, he pulled her off balance to lie against his chest. Then he turned, and she found herself lying beside the heat of Alaric's body, his face only inches from her own. He posed above her so all she could see was the depths of his eyes. They were not sky-blue now, but dark as the midnight swell of the sea.

"Lord Reyne . . ." she began, but he began to speak to her in an underbreath, words that made her cheeks burn as hot as his own.

"There's never been another woman as beautiful as you. When you appear, all the others faded into insignificance. I can't recall even their faces. You're like a dream—that's not original, but it's true for all of that. The arch of your brow would make a Roman architect weep, your lips would shame a rose for never achieving such a perfect color. And as for shape . . . The way you walk with your breasts held so high . . . the curves of your waist and hips . . . the curve . . ."

Sarah gave up twisting her wrists to get free and lay, passive and trembling, beside him. Her eyes closed as one thought filled her mind. He's going to kiss me. She held her breath and waited.

After a long time, she dared to open one eye and cast a swift glance at Lord Reyne. His cheek had fallen onto the pillow, and his chest rose and fell in the tidal rhythm of sleep. Around her wrists, his hands were relaxed. She found it disappointingly easy to slide free.

Her knees felt weak, Sarah only had strength enough to walk to the armchair and to sink down upon it. Whatever love she had felt for Lord Reyne before was but a child's for a painted image compared to what feelings kindled now in her heart. Taking his fever into account, she could not rejoice that he loved her too, though his words might lead her on to hope. He admired her and more. It was not impossible to dream that one day Lord Reyne might feel the full power of love for her.

Sarah sat in the armchair and dreamed so long that Mrs. East and Lady Phelps both came in search of her. First, they saw the man asleep and changed to a tiptoe pace. "Sarah? Wake up, dear," her mother whispered, taking her daughter by the shoulder.

"Oh, I wasn't asleep." Perhaps she had been, though, and all that went before was no more than a dream.

Lady Phelps said, "You mustn't tire yourself, or you'll be indisposed as well. And you missed luncheon."

"Did Harvey do it?"

"Everything was delicious. I was rather surprised."

From behind them, a hoarse voice said, "Your whispers, ladies, would rouse a sleeping stone." The two women turned, showing Sarah between them. "Ah, there you are," Lord Reyne said, propping himself up on his elbows.

Sarah saw, by his glittering eyes and reddened face, that his fever had not yet passed. Swiftly, she glanced up at her mother and Lady Phelps. They smiled still, the formal smiles of a sickroom call. Rising and pressing past them, she poured out more water into his glass to carry to him.

"Mind you don't spill it," he said. "You've dampened my ardor often enough already. How can it be that every time I see you, you're more wonderful than before? But you shouldn't wear your hair up; let it be loose and free as it was the first time we met. Every time I run my fingers through it, I hear music."

He struggled upright to be in a better position to drink. Before he lifted the glass to his lips, however, he flourished it in a toast to his gape-mouthed audience. "I must compliment you on your daughter, Mrs. East. A most radiant and loving woman, or so I have always found her. Did you say something about luncheon? I have quite an appetite today. I don't know why."

The two older ladies exchanged a single glance which seemed but compressed thought. Lady Phelps stepped forward, while Mrs. East escorted a red-faced Sarah out. "Certainly, Lord Reyne," Lady Phelps said. "Wouldn't you enjoy an iced pudding?"

"You're too kind."

But by the time she returned with it, he was once more asleep. The sweet was too good to waste, however, so she took it along to the chamber Mrs. East and Sarah were sharing during the emergency. Sarah was too happy to eat it and her mother shook her head at this sign of love, before indicating silently that she'd like to speak to Lady Phelps out in the corridor. "I think it best if Fred continues to take Lord Reyne his meals. And if the man requires entertainment, let him be content with a book.''

In a low voice, Lady Phelps said, ''Do you think . . . has he trifled with Sarah's feelings?''

''I doubt it.'' Yet Mrs. East's plump cheeks, so admirably suited to her cheerful outlook, were drawn down by her worried lips. ''She is so desperately in love with him! It is better if they do not meet while he is . . . disturbed.''

''I needn't tell *you*, Marissa, that you must warn her. Men's affections, especially when ill, are so easily caught and once caught, easily changed.''

''I've warned her, yes, but I fear it will do no good. She says nothing, though she sighs frequently. I have never known Sarah to sigh for anything before now.''

''This is positively the last time Harvey holds open house!''

United in kindness, they made Sarah promise that she would not visit Lord Reyne's room again, even if other persons were present. She protested, knowing that her mother relied on her word, and once it was given, she could do nothing further, except think of him every moment.

From Fred, she heard of the drying and fading of the blisters, and the triumph of the first shave. From 'Lizabeth, coming in to do Sir Francis' room, she heard all the details of Lord Reyne's return to good humor. But Sarah did not see him again until the day he arose from his bed to reenter the world.

Though she knew it most likely contravened the spirit of her promise, Sarah lurked in the hall to see him descend. He came down quickly enough, his fingers still smoothing the wings of his cravat. Harvey was close behind, and Lord Reyne addressed a few words to him. ''All the other guests are flown, Phelps? Believe me, it was never my intention to overstay my welcome.''

''On the contrary, I fear we have overdone our hospitality.''

Reaching the hall, Lord Reyne said, ''You must call on me when you are next in London.''

Harvey was visibly gratified. ''I shall, sir. Gladly.''

''Just leave your nephew at home, eh, Phelps?'' Laughing, Lord Reyne pushed his fist against Harvey's shoulder. Then his smile went directly to the pillar which Sarah clutched in front of herself like a shield. ''Is that my playmate? Come out.'' He took her wrist and pulled.

Sarah could only stare dumbly at him, certain the gesture would bring everything back to his mind. However, he only said, ''What of all those promises to let me win at cribbage? You've not been near me since. Afraid your victory was a fluke?''

''No, sir.''

''Ah, then you're confident you'll best me tonight! The good doctor forbids travel for two more days, so I must impose further on the good offices of the Phelpses. And yours.'' He stood before her, looking into her eyes. Then a frown came between his brows, and Sarah thought a memory stirred. Though she knew it wrong, she longed to hear those breathless phrases in her honor repeated, again and again. But all he said was, ''Do you hear something?''

''Something?''

''Like the blowing of horns.'' The front door was beside them. He opened it and dimly, yet growing nearer, came the sound of horns lustily blown. ''Someone's coming,'' he said, stepping out onto the half-round steps.

Sarah stood by his shoulder as a team of outriders came up the drive, gravel spraying from beneath their horse's hooves. The men wore grey-and-blue livery, silver braid contrasting with the brass of their instruments. They put them to their lips for one more blast that brought servants, guests, and family members to every window.

Then a darkly varnished carriage, its exquisite lines showing beneath the dust, drew around the sweep of the drive, the four horses seeming fresh from the stable. The footman swung from the back as lightly as a whirligig on a stick and bent like a sawdust doll when he bowed on opening the door. Sarah expected at least a wattled duchess for all this ceremony, yet the first person to come from the carriage was obviously a maid. The next personage, though much finer and grander than the first, also turned and waited for the last one out.

A small foot, a ruffle of gleaming petticoat beneath a soft strawberry-colored pelisse, a gloved hand, and at last the face of a lovely girl beneath a large yet tasteful hat. She cast one glance up at the house, and a ripple of laughter broke from the rosy lips. ''Alaric! My foot's asleep. Help me out.''

Lord Reyne said, ''Lillian?''

Sarah stood wondering on the step as Lord Reyne went

down to her. He'd mentioned sisters. Perhaps this was one. Now they were returning, she leaning on him and saying, "Isn't it just like me to come to you a little too late? How dare you recover before I could nurse you devotedly."

"Well, I shan't fall prey to it again just to please you. Besides, I had excellent nursing as it was. Miss Canfield, may I present Miss Sarah East?"

Sarah was ready to curtsy, but the other woman put out her hand. "I'm surprised you aren't malingering, Alaric, with such a fair one as this to look after you. How do you do, Miss East. Thank you so very much for looking after my fiancé."

——— • 7 ·———

"May I join you, Miss East?" Miss Canfield parted from Lady Phelps and crossed the drawing room to sit beside Sarah on the silver-striped settee. A scarf floated from one shoulder and reflected the candles' light in its rosy threads of shot silk.

"Certainly," Sarah said, prompted only by politeness.

"What a charming home Hollytrees is. Lady Phelps says that it is historically nothing, however, compared with your own. I hope I may come to see it while I am here?"

"Lady Phelps is very kind."

It was after dinner. Mrs. Smithers, joyful because her husband felt more the thing, had created a splendid feast for the mere eighteen persons who now sat at the family table. The gentlemen, replete, lingered over their wine while the ladies departed to take tea in the drawing room.

With Miss Canfield's arrival at Hollytrees, a new spirit seemed to have taken hold. When his wife gave him an embroidered waistcoat on his last birthday, Sir Arthur had declared no power on earth would make him wear such a dandified garment. He wore it tonight. Lady Phelps selected a dashing turban to complement her husband's choice. The twins, heavy-eyed and sniffling still, rebelled at staying in bed any longer and had come down with marvelously inventive cravats. The rest of the guests were fine enough for a ball. Even Mr. East had taken trouble enough to brush his hair over the balding spot at the back.

Sarah's choice, if left to herself, would have been mourning. Today she had discovered the truth of the proverb that declares "Eavesdroppers never hear any good of themselves."

"Sarah East?" Lord Reyne had said in answer to a question put by his fiancée. "She's a beauty, I quite agree. But I'm afraid babes in arms have few attractions for me." Miss

82

Canfield had laughed and then said something in an undertone. "Well, yes, you are rather long in the tooth, aren't you, Lillian? What are you now, twenty-one? Ah, twenty-two! Our marriage is off."

She had not meant to listen. Lady Phelps had sent her to ask Miss Canfield if she needed anything in her room. Sarah couldn't say that she'd rather walk barefoot through alligator-infested waters than speak to Miss Canfield. Approaching the open door, she'd heard Miss Canfield say, "What an amazingly lovely creature you introduced as your nurse. Is her character as charming as her face?"

Upon hearing Lord Reyne's cool reply, Sarah kept only enough wits to glide, rather than clatter, away. In a vacant room, she caught her breath with a sob. The odor of flowers, placed here to drive off the bad air that came with sickness, filled her lungs. Raising her eyes, Sarah saw that this was his room. Here, on that bed, he'd poured out his admiration for her. That, she now realized, was only the ravings of a fevered man. If dreams went by contraries, so might delirious praises of her beauty mean something entirely different.

Once, she'd found a wounded rabbit under a bush, pressed into the moist ground as though praying to be absorbed by the sheltering earth. Picking it up, she'd felt it shudder, yet it was too wretched even to kick out against her. Her father had delicately removed the wire that had lacerated its leg. Though it recovered, it always lay flat in the bottom of the hutch, until Sarah could bear its sadness no longer and let it go.

She felt like that now, dumbly miserable, yet there was no hand to free her. Sarah felt the impossibility of sharing her newest sorrow with anyone. She had no more words to express it than did the rabbit.

Mrs. East, approaching the settee, was in time to hear her daughter's ungracious reply to Miss Canfield. "Of course, you must visit," Mrs. East said. "We are returning home this evening."

Sarah looked up. "We are?"

"I hope you shall find time to visit us, Miss Canfield."

"Thank you, I certainly shall. Having made Miss East's acquaintance, I am reluctant to sever our friendship so soon. I have such cause for gratitude towards you."

At the warmth of Miss Canfield's tone, Sarah straightened her sloping shoulders and said, "I haven't done anything."

Miss Canfield's dark eyes smiled. "You cared for Alaric when I could not. What greater cause could there be? I wonder . . . would you accept some token of my gratitude?" She wore, as was the fashion, five or six beaded bracelets on her left wrist. Now she unfastened one, and with a glance upwards to receive Mrs. East's approval, Miss Canfield pressed it into Sarah's limp hand.

It was a pretty thing, of lozenge-shaped blue stones flecked with gold, separated by golden spheres. Sarah looked at it, cool and solid in her hand, and dully said, "Thank you."

As Sarah fumbled with the tiny hook, Miss Canfield said, "The stones are lapis lazuli from Afghanistan. I spent several years in India with my father, where we collected many beautiful things." Fleetingly, she touched the fine sapphires that dazzled with blue fire about her slim throat.

"Is he a scholar?" Mrs. East asked.

"No, a merchant. He retired, more or less, last year, but I'm afraid he is still susceptible to the lure of business." Sarah noticed that Miss Canfield's easy posture became the tiniest bit rigid when she explained, though her smile was as gracious as before.

When Mrs. East said, "I understand that soldiers often have the same difficulty adjusting to civilian life," Sarah saw Miss Canfield relax. Sarah herself was too unhappy to attach any meaning to the other's behavior. Her interest only awakened when Miss Canfield used Mrs. East's comment to discuss Lord Reyne.

"He actually resisted his doctor's suggestion to visit the seaside because he'd be unable to keep regular hours away from his home. He has the most completely correct manservant, who quite terrifies me. Barton used to be his orderly and raises military precision to an art."

"I was surprised to learn Lord Reyne traveled without some staff. His father was very particular about that, as I recall."

"Mother! You knew Lord Reyne's father?"

"I had my Season, my dear. He was married then, of course, but I remember vividly how proud he was of his rank. If any hostess made an error about who went into dinner first, Lord Reyne would leave at once, never to return."

"So I have heard also, Mrs. East. I'm happy to say Alaric isn't like that in the least. Barton usually accompanies him everywhere, though. Now he is in London, preparing Lord Reyne's new house for next Season. It was not kept in the best repair by the former owners, and there is much work to be done."

Their conversation then passed into a discussion of fabrics, styles, and the necessity for good flues in all the rooms. Though Sarah barely listened, she came to understand that Miss Canfield had recently decorated her father's house with as liberal a licence as his great fortune allowed.

When the gentlemen, fragrant with cigar smoke, emerged from the dining salon, Lord Reyne came directly to the settee. He bowed to Mrs. East and to Sarah, but raised his fiancée's hand to his lips. Sarah, awake to his every action, observed that he made no contact with the fine kid glove. "I have been praising your playing to the skies, my dear. Won't you honor us?"

"And I have been longing to touch the splendid instrument I see in the corner. Lady Phelps," she said, raising her voice a trifle, "may I weary the company with an air or two?"

"By all means," her hostess replied, nodding her turban.

The unevenness of the numbers had forced Lady Phelps to seat her guests promiscuously at table. Lord Reyne had been placed beside Miss Canfield, naturally enough. Sarah, near the twins as always, had been unable to keep her gaze long away from the handsome couple. She had wished fervently that it might be she who kept him so attentive. Now, however, when he took the seat his fiancée had left vacant, she could think of nothing to say.

He looked up and said, "Have I stolen your place, madam?"

"Not at all," said Mrs. East, still standing behind her daughter. "I shall sit closer to the pianoforte so that I lose none of the notes." Yet, she half-twisted in her seat when she reached it, to keep close watch upon Sarah, very much annoying Mrs. Dealford who sat beside her.

"Do you play, Miss East?" Alaric asked.

"No, I have never learned." There was wine on his breath, and smoke, mingling with his own woodsy fragrance that she'd noticed from the first. The combination made her dizzy, yet she inclined closer to him to more fully absorb it. Then she remembered the words she'd overheard and leaned away.

"Now Lillian is a most accomplished musician. She not only plays each note with precision, but there is such a depth of feeling in her playing. It brings out the composer's true meaning. Don't you think so?"

"I know nothing about it." She hated to expose her ignorance to him, but she did not even know enough about music to pretend an interest. She sat there, her shoulders once more slumping, as the music, conjured up by Miss Canfield's delicate fingers, floated like a genie across the room.

Sarah's own thoughts shouted so loudly in condemnation of her foolishness that she did not regard the frantic *pssts* coming from behind her. Only two things could have roused her. One—a cannon fired immediately beside her. The other—a single word from Lord Reyne. "Miss East," he whispered. "I believe Miss Phelps is attempting to capture your attention."

Turning, she saw Harmonia summon her with an imperious wave. "I'm sorry," she said. Standing, she drifted forlornly out of the room, noticing only that Miss Canfield smiled and nodded graciously on catching her eye.

"I wanted you to be the first to know," Harmonia said, encircling her friend's waist with her arm. "After Mother and Father, of course."

"To know what?" She hoped that some new epidemic, preferably fatal, had struck, so that she might be the sole victim. A dreadful certainty had struck her in the drawing room. Not only did Lord Reyne think of her as a foolish child, but she was afraid Miss Canfield knew that Sarah loved him. Something about the other woman had been so sympathetic in a loathsome mature way that Sarah shuddered at the shame of it all.

"Did you hear what I said?" Harmonia repeated. "Harlow and I are to be married."

"Married?"

"Not so loud! Father's going to announce it in a few minutes. He's conferring with Smithers on which champagne to serve out. But I wanted you to know first. Aren't you happy for me?"

Something sharp in Harmonia's voice penetrated Sarah's

gloom. Dredging up a smile, Sarah embraced her friend. "But when did this happen?"

"Yesterday. As soon as he was recovered, he said he knew I was the wife for him by the way I nursed him. Of course, he was a very easy patient, so docile and gentle. I'm . . . I'm so happy!"

"And I'm so happy for you!"

The rest of the company echoed her sentiment when Sir Arthur made his announcement. Harlow Atwood, looking thin and pale beside his future brothers-in-law, wrung his hands and said how much at home he felt in the bosom of his new family, and that he truly regretted leaving the comfort of home life so soon.

"What did he mean, Harmonia?" Sarah asked when the engaged girl came to her for her official congratulations.

"Harlow is to be a secretary to some lord in Scotland. He must take up his position within two weeks. His illness has delayed him already. He'll be there for at least a year before we can be married. I wanted to marry at once, but he thought it wisest to wait so that he will be able to support me in our own home." For a moment, disappointment overlaid her radiance.

"Never mind," Sarah said. "A year is nothing. Think of all we must do. I'll even help you with your sewing, if you like."

Mrs. Dealford, who stood near, said, "I personally think a quick marriage often leads to disastrous results. Mr. Atwood is quite correct. You are indeed wise to wait."

Though Harmonia had overcome her dislike of Emma, upon noticing her decided preference for Harvey, she went wary of Mrs. Dealford, suspecting her of still wanting Harlow for her daughter. She now dragged Sarah out of earshot and said fiercely, "I'm sure she'd marry in haste enough if anybody asked her!"

Someone proposed dancing in honor of the engagement. Servants rolled back the carpet, exposing the gleaming parquet in light and dark wood. Harcourt and Harold were seen to flip a coin. Harvey and Emma stood together. After some cajolery, Lady Phelps agreed to honor Sir Francis and astounded the company by the lightness of her tripping. Mrs. East, seeing Mr. Posthwaite gazing enviously at the others, invited him to squire her.

Sir Arthur, Mr. East, Mr. Randolph and Mrs. Dealford were

all adamant that a round of whist would be preferable to
dancing. Though Harriet looked with longing eyes at her husband, she, in the end, agreed to play so that Miss Canfield
could have the pleasure of dancing with her betrothed.
Harold went to turn pages for his sister. They chose a shortened
cotillion in which, as at dinner, the men and women stood
mixed, side by side.

Sarah's feet were heavy with unhappiness, but Harcourt had
won the toss. Besides, if she refused there would be but five
couples, which made for awkward figures. As Harriet began to
play, peering nearsightedly at the page, Sarah followed Harcourt through the round. She kept her gaze on him or on the
floor, for the sight of her neighbor, Lord Reyne, laughing into
his beloved's eyes was more than she could quite stomach.
Even when she passed down the row, though she knew his
touch at once, she did not glance up at him. Only when she
returned to Harcourt did she raise her eyes and smile.

"I say," he said, "are you all right?"

"Perfectly well." It was Miss Canfield's turn to pass down
the row. She called out something to Sarah as she passed,
waving her free hand for an instant before giving it to Sir
Francis. When Miss Canfield returned to her place opposite
Lord Reyne, the gentlemen stepped in front of their ladies to
bow profoundly.

Harcourt's nose and mouth twisted in the effort to contain a
sneeze. He failed. As he grabbed furiously for his handkerchief, Sarah started back to avoid the spray. Her heel slipped on
the shiny floor and her feet went out from beneath her. Her
arms flailed as she strove to regain her balance. She felt as
though she were once more falling into the lake, but winced in
advance, knowing the floor would hurt her.

Instead of grievously injuring her posterior, Sarah found
herself safely caught in the arms of the one man, above all
others, she'd rather not be saved by. She knew she gaped and
felt his forearms tighten beneath her fingers.

As Alaric set her upright, he said, "Bless you, Harcourt."

"You must be the fastest man on two legs," Sir Francis said
in amazement. "I've never seen anyone move so quickly, and
I've been out with the Revenuers."

"Pray continue, Mrs. Randolph. You play very well indeed,'' Alaric said, ignoring this comment. ''All ready now, Sarah?''

''I'd rather sit down now, Harcourt,'' she said, knowing she was red as a hunter's coat.

''Do you need me, dearest?''

''No, Mother. Go on. You have so little opportunity to dance.'' Leaning on Harcourt's arm in a weak and womanly manner, Sarah left the set, leaving the rest to carry on despite the resulting uneven number of couples.

Mrs. East and Lady Phelps exchanged glances and nods of strange significance. Only after the evening was done, and the Easts ready to depart, did they share a word in private.

''What are we going to do, Marissa? When Miss Canfield arrived, I had hopes of Sarah turning to Harvey, but his attentions to the Dealford girl have been most marked.''

''I think it's best if I send Sarah back to my aunt. I was planning to do it after Christmas, but an earlier trip will help her forget. If she stays at home, she will only pine.''

''Yes, new scenes are what she needs. And when she comes back, there will still be Harcourt and Harold. Perhaps at last . . .'' The two ladies embraced.

Miss Canfield came for her visit, but Sarah had warning of it and was not to be found. Her mother had not heart to scold the girl for her rudeness, especially when she had news for her that she feared Sarah would not eagerly countenance. Lord Reyne and his fiancée were leaving Hollytrees the next day. Mrs. East held extra handkerchiefs ready, but Sarah did not cry. Her face became a trifle paler as she nodded to indicate she'd heard. This seemed as good a time as any to broach the subject of a return to Leamington Spa.

''I know Aunt Whitsun will be so pleased to have you with her again. She complained your last visit was too brief.''

What the old lady had actually said was, ''How can you expect me to teach that child to be a lady in six short weeks? It shouldn't take any time at all. It should already have been taught her, but as it stands I shall require months!''

''And then you can go directly from Leamington to London for your Season. I still hope to come to see you during it.''

''Thank you, Mother. That will be splendid.'' But her eyes still turned toward the window as though her vision were miraculous and she could see clear to Hollytrees to witness the

bustle of packing and the harnessing of the horses to Miss
Canfield's elegant equipage.

"I have spoken to your father, and it seems there will be
more money than we thought. His speculations on the Exchange have been quite successful lately. Aunt Whitsun will be
able to take you to the finest dressmakers and the best dancing
masters."

Sarah sighed. "I look forward to it."

"And Lady Phelps has offered you the loan of her coach, so
your journey will be much more comfortable than last time."

"Lady Phelps is always so kind to me."

Outside of Hollytrees, Alaric gathered his caped cloak more
tightly against the whipping breeze. In his mind, he ticked off
a list. Each servant had received his due vail, more heavy
remuneration lying in the hands of Mr. Smithers and young
Fred. He'd promised to introduce Harvey at his club when Mr.
Phelps returned to London, and tendered an invitation to the
elder Phelpses to visit him in Essex whenever they would. A
note had been dispatched to Mrs. East and Sarah, thanking
them for their tender care. He shook his head. That seemed to
be all, and yet . . .

Lillian appeared on the stairs. Alaric smiled and offered his
hand to assist her in entering the coach. Inwardly, he rejoiced
that the movement caused him no pain. When he stepped up
himself, there was no stabbing agony in the repaired muscles of
his back. This country stay, for all its unconscionable length,
had done him good. He felt as well as ever he had in his life,
save for this single nagging doubt.

The door slammed behind him. The coach creaked and
rocked as the footman pulled himself up. Lillian's two maids
sat on the seat opposite, the younger glancing up under her
lashes at him, the other maintaining a precise distance between
his knees and her own. Alaric heard the coachman's whistle as
the coach started forward. He felt like calling out to the man to
stop, but kept himself tightly under control. This was nonsense,
yet once more he went over his mental list, tapping his hand on
his knee to an unheard rhythm.

"You seem restless," Lillian said. "Didn't you sleep
well?"

"No, that isn't it."

"Isn't what?"

"What's bothering me. I can't think what it is. But there's definitely something I meant to do before leaving here, and I'm certain I haven't done it."

"It will come to you when we are twenty miles down the road. I know that is the way my mind works, when it works at all. Did you leave something behind in your room? You'll be able to write to Sir Arthur and ask him to send it on. They are dear people, don't you think?"

"Perhaps I'm imagining it." In an undertone, he said, shaking his head after each item, "Boots, hair brushes, nail brush, tooth brush . . ." He scratched his cheek. Finally, he spread his hands. "I never heard that chicken pox can affect the mind, yet I fear it must have in my case. I have shaken out my brain like a featherbed, yet I cannot think of what I have forgotten."

"Never mind, I know it will come to you," Lillian said, reassuringly.

8

"Remember to stand up straight."

"Yes, Aunt."

"Try to smile when you speak."

"Yes, Aunt."

"Refer strange gentlemen to me when they ask you to dance."

"Yes, Aunt."

"And try not to look bored. It spoils all your looks."

"No, Aunt." It mayn't have been the expected response, but Sarah knew from experience that Aunt Whitsun did not listen to her anyway. She was far from the first young relation Mrs. Whitsun had fired off into the murky, shifting waters of the *ton*. There were times when Sarah felt she was merely another body in a white gown to be ushered about London until, with any luck at all, someone married her.

For the third time in ten minutes, Aunt Whitsun said, "We've not moved a yard, not a yard, closer to the house. Such a frightful crush there'll be inside." They had moved, of course, only so slowly as to make the motion unnoticeable. She darted a quick glance at Sarah from beneath her rather projecting brow. "Don't, dear thing, or it'll come down."

Sarah's hand froze on its upward path. Her hair had been piled on her head by her aunt's freezingly upright maid. A few of the pins seemed to have been driven straight into her head. A tight fillet of silver satin ran through the curls. Only slightly more uncomfortable was the string of small pearls. The clasp scratched her neck every time she turned her head.

Most of all, however, Sarah hated the long gloves of white kid, an important part of her evening ensemble. They were loose around the tops and crept nastily up and down her arms, creasing about her elbows. She should have been used to them,

92

for they were used even in Leamington, but she still found it difficult not to fuss with them.

"Here we are at last. Now remember, Sarah, your future welfare depends, in large measure, on the effect you have on the others here tonight. No one will wish to be acquainted with you if you misbehave. Don't fidget, don't scratch, stand still unless you're dancing, and speak up. But don't be nervous or you'll perspire. There's nothing worse than a sweaty partner."

Sarah waited for her great-aunt to step out. It had rained earlier, and the chilly spring air was cold on her exposed shoulders. Yet, Aunt Whitsun insisted Sarah leave her warm velvet cloak in the coach. Though Sarah shivered, she obeyed.

"You'll do as you are," Mrs. Whitsun said, casting one last glance over Sarah's satin robe, the exact color of fresh, heavy cream. Unlike most dresses of this style, it fell open over an underdress of the same color, instead of a contrasting shade.

Looking up, Sarah saw that the stairs leading into the house were entirely filled up by elegantly dressed ladies and gentlemen, struggling to keep their places in the queue. Mrs. Whitsun advanced boldly, butting the lowest man on the shoulder with her fan. When he turned, his eyes met Sarah's. She didn't know him. It seemed rude to her that her aunt had poked him, so she smiled an apology. His gasp was audible even through the noise of the pushing crowd, and everyone turned to look. A silence fell. The people been pressing forward. Now they fell back.

"Come along, dear thing," Mrs. Whitsun said, nodding to Sarah.

There was now room enough for them to walk up the stairs into the house. However, the interior was if anything more crowded than the outside. If someone blocked the way, Mrs. Whitsun merely jabbed at them until they turned. On seeing Sarah, they stepped aside, eyes wide with astonishment. Though Mrs. Whitsun simply continued forward, Sarah always said, "Thank you," before following.

Sarah asked, "Do all these people know you?"

"A fair percentage do. Why?"

"They let you by."

"It's not for me they do it," Mrs. Whitsun said, and then, after a sidelong look at her charge, shook her head. "Never mind. Come along, come along." They had gone up and up, through the house, and now they reached the head of a staircase from which they must go down.

"Oh!" Sarah said, wavering a moment on the topmost step. She could see everything. The long drop of the red-carpeted steps led to a glass-like floor of polished wood. The scent of hothouse flowers mingled with the sound of sweet music, making her almost dizzy. Looking out at the people who massed about the huge room, she couldn't help but see that they were all staring back. Some even pointed, nudging those who stood nearby. Then they, too, would turn and stare.

She turned smiling to her aunt. "Leamington Spa wasn't like this! Not even the Assembly Rooms."

Mrs. Whitsun merely shook her head once more, the large fake diamond anchoring her turban flashing in the light of the crystal-daubed lusters hanging from the ceiling. "We cannot linger here; we shall appear reluctant. Go on."

Once more, the guests parted before them like a curtain drawing back for the prima donna. Sarah came off the last step and glanced around. The ladies glittered no less than the suspended chandeliers. The gentlemen were but foils to beauty in their dark coats and silken breeches. She heard their laughter, and wondered at its cause, though she did not now fear it was at her expense. At least, she looked as if she belonged.

Despite the price of the gown on her back, Sarah knew she was but a traveler in this strange country called "the *ton*." This was not her true life. For only two weeks, at Christmas, when she'd gone home, had she felt a part of the real world. Sarah reminded herself that she must live through three months more of it—the Season—before she could return home. Though her aunt and mother had promised that the time would fly by, it had not yet begun to do so.

From somewhere near at hand, a voice called out, "Maudie!" Knowing this to be her aunt's Christian name, Sarah turned obligingly about, trying to recall all her aunt's instructions about meeting new people.

"Amabelle!"

The two women embraced, their lips never touching the other's cheek. Sarah remembered Lord Reyne kissing the air above Miss Canfield's glove and closed her mind against the memory. She'd honed that talent in the last six months, if none other.

"How do you contrive to look so youthful, Amabelle? There must be a scandal behind it somewhere!"

"Young men, my dear Maudie, and lovely long milk baths." The speaker was too thin, which added more wrinkles than her fifty-odd years had naturally received. She apparently scorned both turbans and trained skirts, as she wore a stunning gold tiara in the latest mode and a low-cut gown that proclaimed her readiness to dance. "But who is this?"

"Allow me to introduce my great-niece, Miss Sarah East."

"Not your great-niece! It's unbelievable." Sarah found herself peered at through a thick lorgnette which magnified the snapping blue eyes of her observer to the size of oysters. "La!" the woman said, letting the glasses drop to the end of the ribbon. "Does she talk? And what difference does it make if she can't!"

Amabelle laughed and then said, with a pleasant smile replacing her wide grin, "You must forgive me, my dear Miss East. The shock, you know. If one's old school friends start arriving with great-nieces and granddaughters, one may be suspected of harboring such things themselves. I'm your hostess, by the way."

Belatedly, Sarah sank into a curtsy. "Forgive me, your grace. I didn't realize it."

"No, how should you? She's charming," Amabelle, better known as the Duchess of Parester, said to her friend. "And you've just arrived? You'd best allow me to find you her partners, then. A few matrimonially undesirable men are here—of course, they are the ones who are the most amusing—and she shouldn't meet them. Yet. After she's married is soon enough."

Mrs. Whitsun sat down in "Dowager's Corner." For all Sarah knew, chairs had never been invented. Her escorts returned her to Mrs. Whitsun at the close of each set, yet she never had the remotest chance of sitting. Another man was certain to be waiting his turn. Though she'd been popular at the Leamington Assemblies, there she'd occasionally meet someone who wanted to sit out. In London, it seemed the choice was dancing or going out past the french windows into the garden. And Sarah had been threatened with what happened to young ladies who left the floor with gentlemen for the pleasures of a breath of cool air. "Cool air would be all very well," Mrs. Whitsun had once remarked, "if it were not that cool air is very frequently *dark* air."

Unlatching her arm from one man, Sarah paused by her aunt's chair a moment, ostensibly to have her see to a possibly torn flounce. "But can't I stop just for a few minutes?" she murmured, thinking of her feet which felt on fire.

"Absolutely not. This is the supper dance. You must have a partner. Sir Augustus Boneview is most congenial. He will take you in. He enjoys hunting. Be pleasant. Smile, Sarah!"

Obediently, Sarah's lips turned up. Sir Augustus was indeed congenial, but, alas, was no more than five feet, six inches tall. His head was near her shoulder. Though it was possible that Sir Augustus enjoyed the view of Sarah's chest more than she admired his bald spot, the dinner gong was welcomed by them both.

"How is the hunting in Bedfordshire, Sir Augustus?" Sarah asked. Her aunt was certain to inquire if she'd raised the subject after such a prompting.

"Are you interested in hunting, Miss East?" Sir Augustus began to tell her about it, without waiting for a reply. As he listed the pedigrees of each hound, Sarah fell into the trap of wondering if Lord Reyne kept dogs. She felt certain dogs would like Lord Reyne. Even Petey had taken to him at once. Of course, the bull was notoriously easy in his affections.

Realizing her thoughts had strayed into remembrances of Hollytrees, Sarah shook herself and said, "How fascinating, Sir Augustus. Do you really mean . . . ?"

"Indeed I do! Thirteen at once, on my word."

He went on talking as he and Sarah traveled into the supper room. So sympathetic and interested a listener did he find her, that he almost forgot his duty to fetch her some refreshment.

While he was gone, a lady, a little past her first youth yet splendid in a blue silk gown that echoed her sapphire necklace, excused herself from a laughing group and came toward Sarah. Tentatively, she offered a gloved hand. "Miss East, is it not?"

"Lady Reyne?" She recognized the former Miss Canfield at once, though the face before her was utterly different in its details from the one she'd so often imagined. The cruel mouth, mocking eyes and claw-like fingers had changed to softness, sweetness and gentleness. The wart on the bridge of Miss Canfield's nose had apparently been entirely imaginary.

The other woman chuckled. "Not yet."

"I beg your pardon?"

"I am not 'Lady Reyne.' Not yet. Alaric and I have not yet made arrangements for our wedding."

"Oh, I . . . that is, I didn't . . ."

"How could you know?" Miss Canfield lifted one smooth white shoulder, smiling. "But what of you? Are you in London to stay?"

"I am living with my great-aunt, Mrs. Whitsun."

"Mrs. Maud Whitsun? I know her very well. She is the dearest friend of my dearest friend's mother. I trust your mother is keeping well?"

"I had a letter from her on Tuesday. She and my father are in excellent health."

"I'm so glad. They were very kind to me when I came to visit your enchanting house. And Sir Arthur and Lady Phelps? And Miss Harmonia?"

"Perfectly well." She realized her answers lacked warmth and said hastily, "I expect Harmonia to visit me soon."

"But how marvelous! Of course, she wants to choose her trousseau for her marriage to Mr. Atwood. I hope . . . that is, may I call upon you? I should so much enjoy seeing her again, and I may be able to offer some help. You know, I am on the point of suffering through that experience myself, and it would be so much more enjoyable if we could all go to the shops together."

"I know Harmonia would enjoy it."

"And you also, of course. One can never have too many pretty things, eh? That is an uncommonly lovely gown. Madame Oulange, is it not? She is a terror, don't you think? But I cannot quarrel with the flawless results she achieves." Sarah nodded, recalling the vivid little French-woman who had scurried about her with a tape and squeals of delight.

Was it possible that, in addition to imagining the hideous-ness of Lord Reyne's choice, she had also been deceived in her memories of Miss Canfield's wicked nature? Her reaction to Sarah's slip about her status had been telling. An elderly countess whom Sarah had once called "Mrs." had complained about it for weeks, insisting her companion wheel her Bathchair out of range whenever Sarah came by.

"How . . . how is Lord Reyne?" she asked, though the sudden jump in subject was perhaps rude.

"Alaric? Would you believe that he did not want to come to London for another two months? Fortunately, his sisters have far more influence over him than I. Had he known his charming nurse would be here tonight, I know nothing could have kept him away. As it is, however, he won't return until next week. His house won't be ready until then, anyway."

"That's right," Sarah said, almost to herself. "You said something about a new house, and a valet named . . . Barton."

"My word, what a memory! That's precisely right. If I had not been present for many of the changes, I would think they'd merely switched address plates with the most fashionable house in the square. The entire building has been altered top to bottom and everything in between."

"I'm sure your taste is perfect, Miss Canfield," Sarah said without sarcastic inflection. Alaric would only marry a woman who knew precisely what to do at all times, exactly what was fashionable, and which was the ideal firm to have in to do it, whether the matter at hand was furnishings or haying.

"Would you believe that Alaric has approved every choice himself? He wouldn't listen to me hardly at all, although I did prevent him using a dark red drape in the drawing room. All the ladies would look like ghosts against so strong a color."

It hurt to say it, but Sarah stood fast against the quick, self-inflicted stab of agony. "Did he approve your rooms, too?"

"My rooms? Oh, I shan't trouble about those until our wedding day is fixed." She turned from Sarah, her smile becoming a little broader, and to Sarah's sensitive perception, a trifle less sincere. "Mrs. Whitsun! Sarah and I were having the most diverting conversation."

"You did not tell me you knew Miss Canfield."

"Oh, yes," Sarah said.

"Oh, yes, indeed," Miss Canfield echoed. "We met during the summer. Lord Reyne introduced us."

"Indeed? Lord Reyne?"

Sarah could almost hear Mrs. Whitsun thinking. She said, "Lord Reyne stayed at the home of some neighbors, the Phelpses."

"The Phelpses? Ah, yes. You know, Miss Canfield, Miss Harmonia Phelps is about to make a stay with me. I hope we may have the pleasure of seeing you at a small gathering I intend to have in her honor. The poor thing is to be married, and thus has only a very little time left to enjoy herself."

"Yes, I was there when Miss Phelps' betrothal was announced."

"Betrothal? What betrothal?" A tall man, very darkly tanned, approached. Though faultlessly dressed, he seemed almost to burst out of his clothing, both by the restless energy of his movements and by the undoubted corporation he sported above the band of his Inexpressibles.

"We were discussing the approaching marriage of a friend of ours, Father. You may recall my mentioning Miss Harmonia Phelps, after my trip last summer."

"Phelps? Phelps? Oh, yes, the house where Lord Reyne was taken ill. And this is she?" He turned his dark eyes, bright with curiosity, on Sarah.

"Miss East, may I present my father, Mr. Jacob Canfield." Sarah curtsied. "How do you do, sir?"

"Gads but you're the loveliest girl here, excepting my own."

"Father, you'll make her blush." Miss Canfield turned from her father and took Sarah's arm. "Come and meet my friends, Sarah. May I call you Sarah? And you must call me Lillian. We shall be friends. I declare it."

On the way home, Aunt Whitsun scolded Sarah. "Imagine not telling me you are acquainted with Miss Canfield, and the Earl of Reyne. My dear thing, whatever were you thinking about? Haven't you realized yet that powerful friends are the most useful thing imaginable? All you need do is smile and what invitations you'll receive! Balls, breakfasts, musical evenings . . . the mind cannot encompass it all."

"Yes, Aunt."

"Mr. Canfield, of course, is socially negligible, save for his fortune. He needs a good wife to . . ." For a moment, Sarah sat petrified as Mrs. Whitsun pursued an idea. What if her aunt took the notion to hurl her at Mr. Canfield's head? To be viewed as the possible mother-in-law of Lord Reyne would be a bizarre situation, indeed. Sarah breathed more easily as the older lady went on with the swift recitation of her thoughts.

"Miss Canfield is a different story. Her mother was a Wentlow, you know, not anything great in the world, yet quality tells. His money makes her success possible, but she is no ordinary Cit's daughter. There are hundreds of those girls, without the slightest idea of how to go on. Overdressed, eager, and pushed forward in the most shocking way. But Miss Canfield . . . her taste . . . her charm . . . her fiancé! The catch of the Season!"

"Yes, Aunt."

"And you know him yet never told me! I'm so disappointed in you, Sarah. Before the war, he was the most sought after bachelor in England. Then he comes back, and hardly has he been in the country a month than the announcement of their betrothal appears. Of course, Mr. Canfield is in bliss! He's been angling to marry her to a title since they came on the scene."

"Yes, Aunt."

"But not just any title would do! No, he's particular. It's got to be someone who doesn't need the money. He's refused at least four gentlemen with pockets to let, including the Marquess of Feddenham. Can you imagine!" Mrs. Whitsun obviously had the greatest difficulty imagining anything of the sort. The effort required in marrying off two sisters, herself, and eight cousins to date had taught her not to be so finicky.

"No, Aunt."

Sarah struggled to stifle the singing voice inside her. Sternly, she told herself that the appearance, or nonappearance, of Lord Reyne was of no significance to her. Yet, her heart leapt and bounded against the confines of her body, and her brain whizzed about like a drunken top. He was coming to London. He was coming to London in a week! Try as she might, the tune the orchestra had played as they were leaving rose to her lips.

"Why didn't you tell me you can sing? Honestly, if you're going to be keeping secrets from me, how do you expect me to . . . to present you well. I thought you had no accomplishments."

"I haven't," Sarah said, swallowing her song.

"You mean you aren't trained. I shall set about engaging Senor Beddini tomorrow. Your father said such things are within your allowance for this Season."

"But I don't wish to learn to . . ."

"You'll like it once you begin. Remember how you hated taking up dancing lessons when you first came to my home? Yet when you returned, you were so eager for them to begin again."

That had been when she was still hoping that some day she'd find herself again in Lord Reyne's arms. Staring out as the dark streets of London passed at a slow clop, Sarah fought to keep her thoughts fixed on trivial things. The moment she relaxed her concentration, however, her mind filled with memories of the brief time she'd spent with Lord Reyne. Awake, she could maintain control. Asleep, she danced again, not with any of the young men introduced tonight, but with the one man who always partnered her in her dreams.

"I'll wager your aunt wears a wig," Harmonia murmured. One week later, Mrs. Whitsun kept her promise of a party for Harmonia upon her arrival in London. Unfortunately, popular though Sarah had been at the balls she attended, the event was not a success. There was, after all, quite a difference between dancing with a beautiful girl and giving countenance to her friends.

"I shan't take your wager. How should we ever tell?"

"Wait until midnight—then shout fire?"

Sarah gave her friend a playful push. "Your engagement hasn't changed you at all."

A shade passed over Harmonia's face. "No, it hasn't." Then, her polite smile reinstated, she said, "Are these all the people Mrs. Whitsun invited?"

"You know it's not. But there's a new play opening tonight, and she thinks most of the guests went there. Perhaps they'll come when it's over." Sarah nodded and smiled at the dozen or so individuals who dotted the shining floor like anti-social icebergs in a vast sea. The orchestra at the far end of the hall played spritely music, which sounded abnormally loud in the great empty spaces between people.

Mrs. Whitsun did her best to turn these few into a cohesive group, the first stage of forming a party. But short of beginning an absurdly small set or arranging two tables of whist, there was little to be done. She chattered relentlessly. Passing the two young ladies charmingly dressed in newly purchased finery, she murmured, "Don't stand here, girls. Walk about. Talk to them."

Sarah raised her hands and then let them fall. "But, Aunt, I don't know any of them."

"Nor do I, Mrs. Whitsun."

Just as the older lady was about to make an exasperated reply, the doors opened and a large party walked in, making a good deal of noise which muffled the announcement of their names. She turned to greet them with a brilliant smile, though it faded immediately. "Oh, dear, it's the Morebinder clique. He's a dreadful young man and goes about with the worst sort of people. I'm sure they've come just to spoil everything. Why couldn't my evening have been a crush, where no one would notice them? What ever shall we do?"

"At least they'll fill up the room," Sarah said, hoping to cheer her aunt. But Mrs. Whitsun only groaned.

The young viscount sauntered over, a young woman on his arm who, although of undoubtedly genteel family, ought to have been warned not to let her dresses hang so low, if only for fear of the ague. "Miss East," the gentleman drawled, raising his quizzing glass to his pale eyes. "What beauty you shine in tonight. The moon will be embarrassed to rise above the clouds."

"Lord Morebinder," Sarah replied, curtsying. "You recall my aunt, Mrs. Whitsun?"

"Yaaas, to be sure." But he did not move his eyes from the contemplation of Sarah's face. He flicked his focus to Harmonia for an instant when her name was pronounced, before returning to his scrutiny of Sarah. The female on his arm yawned openly. "I hope to have the pleasure of a dance, Miss East," Lord Morebinder said. "If your aunt will allow me." He disengaged his arm from the bored woman's grasp and offered it to Sarah.

"Forgive me, but I must refuse. We cannot be the only two on the floor."

"Russell!" Lord Morebinder said, raising his voice a modicum. "Dance with Miss . . . er . . . Miss Phelps."

"Oh, damn, must I?" One of his male friends, painted and

powdered like a woman, said. "That orchestra isn't fit for chickens to scratch to. La, what a dull party!"

"And what shall you do about it?" the viscount asked.

The man looked nonplussed. "I—I hadn't thought. . . ."

"Think about it, while you apologize to Miss East."

"Oh, quite, quite. Your pardon, Miss East." He pursed his reddened lips into a pout.

"I should forgive you, sir, but it isn't my party."

"Here, Jasper, look at this!" Another man, whom Mrs. Whitsun recognized as the dissipated Sir Percy Alvendale, wandered over to the fruit baskets standing sentinel at the sideboard.

Taking up an orange, still somewhat green, he tossed it skillfully from hand to hand. Then, without warning, he fired it through the air, directly at the orchestra. It winged the conductor's wig and landed with a thud against the first horn's brass bell. The entire contingent gave Sir Percy a dire glance, which affected the young man not at all. His fellow bucks applauded and laughed.

"I had a deuced straight eye while at Harrow," Sir Percy said proudly. Then he sighed. "I rather miss cricket, you know. Haven't been to Lords since God knows when."

Sarah asked, "Did you ever play cricket, Lord Morebinder?"

"I do. That is, I did."

"You must have been good at it." Sarah smiled at him. The subject interested her, for she'd enjoyed playing the game with her brothers and the Phelpses. "Are you a bowler, or a batter?"

"I swung a pretty fair willow, once upon a time, that is. Come to think on it, this room is awfully like a cricket pitch, isn't it? Long, straight, and narrow. Infernally like the pitch at home," Lord Morebinder said wonderingly.

He was quite a young man, and possibly had been handsome, before his looks were blurred by the excesses of profligate indulgence. Casting a weary glance over his followers, Lord Morebinder shrugged his world-weighted shoulders. "Blast, we've only enough for one side."

Shyly, Sarah said, "I used to bowl for my brothers."

"I won't hear of it," Mrs. Whitsun said firmly.

"And I am accounted a steady wicket-keeper," Harmonia added.

Mrs. Whitsun said, ''I refuse to have anything to do with this nonsensical notion!'' So Lord Morebinder appointed her umpire.

The canes all the fashionable fellows carried were set up as wickets. ''They're too tall, of course, but I don't suppose we've anything else. Now for the bats . . . ah, Sherwood, Gretcham, you've brought your umbrellas, excellent!''

Sarah and Harmonia won the toss. After hearing an explanation of the general rules of the games, the indolent ladies of the clique were prodded into position, several dimly mentioning their brothers' enthusiasm for the game. A stir of excitement went around the assembled players as Sir Percy carefully selected a new orange with which to open the match.

Sarah loosened up her shoulder, an easy motion due to Madame Oulange's abbreviated notions of a ball gown's sleeve. After a moment of mental preparation, she prepared to deliver the first ball in the smooth, peculiarly graceful arc that had been the despair of Harcourt and Harold in the merry old days when they'd all been friends together.

''The Earl of Reyne, Mr. Canfield, and Miss Lillian Canfield.''

Fortunately, Sarah had not yet begun to bowl. She stayed her hopping through the crease and turned to face the entrance. Alaric stood on the bottom step, the Canfields behind him. She could not see their faces; they were only background to him. Across all the long distance of the hall, his eyes, so very blue, sought out hers. Then, one of his eyes closed in a lightning fast wink, and he nodded as though with approval.

Sarah delivered a straight, medium-fast ball that Lord Morebinder could no more hit than he could sing soprano. His friends jeered. The over continued until six balls had flown down the pitch. Then Sarah took herself out of the game, leaving the next over to a girl whose dainty costume did nothing to conceal the muscularity of her right arm.

''Well played, Miss East.'' Lord Reyne advanced to meet her and bowed. ''I wish I had arrived somewhat earlier. It's been a long time since I played.''

''I think we women will win. Lord Morebinder seems to have overestimated the skill of his team. They don't seem to be very good,'' she added as the orange went skimming past the batter.

"Lord Morebinder is frequently over-confident. I've played cards with him." He took his attention from the game and looked at her. "Lillian tells me you met last week at the Duchess of Parester's. I'm pleased to hear all is well at home."

"Yes, it is." She wished he would take his eyes off her, so that she might study him without blushing. As it was, she kept her gaze fixed on the players, though awareness of him pervaded every breath she took. "Harmonia's here. She's wicket-keeper."

"As I see. She looks in glowing health."

"Oh, yes. Harmonia is never ill." Gliding her hand over her cheek, she wondered if she appeared as tired as she felt. Last night had been sleepless, as many nights had been—nights in which she'd lain awake and writhed at the memory of her foolishness. Tonight would be the same. For, fool that she was, the first sound of his voice, the first glance she'd had of him, this moment with him alone beside her, all combined to teach Sarah one depressing fact. She loved Lord Reyne no less for all the six months that lay between them. She loved him more, so much that her heart nearly strangled her with its fierce beating.

"Do you return to the fray?" he asked. Her replacement had held up her hand for a pause and fell to rubbing her arm, a questioning frown on her brow.

"No," Sarah said. "I'm resigned."

Lord Reyne rubbed his hands together. "Do you suppose it would be . . . cricket . . . if I volunteered my services to the female side?" He smiled more broadly when he saw her doubtful expression. "I'm entirely recovered from my wounds, Miss East. You see, I remember that you were ever concerned for my well-being."

"I saw you are no longer troubled by them, sir."

"How can you possibly know that?" Alaric said, raising his brows at her as thought she possessed second sight.

"It's just that you seem . . . happy, that's all." She did not precisely know how to express it. Every motion he made was free, as though he'd shrugged off some galling fetter.

"I am happy, Miss East." It was a statement of determined fact, allowable of no argument or even discussion. "Ah, she'd given up. Pray excuse me." He walked across the room for a consultation with Mrs. Whitsun, who instantly allowed him to play for the ladies. Taking his place in the crease, he looked about the field as though he'd made a recent purchase of it and deciding where it would fit in his house.

His house, Miss Canfield's future home. Sarah saw Miss Canfield watching Alaric with an expression of mingled pride and laughter. How could he help but be happy with such a woman waiting to become his bride? The wonder was that they were not already married. Without knowing why, Sarah began to circle the room to stand beside Miss Canfield, who welcomed her with a smile. Clapping, Lillian called out, ''Oh, well played!'' Sara joined in the applause.

9

"Bravo!"

"Hurrah!"

"Bravo, bravo!"

The three men sitting in a box with Alaric joined in the cheers. Many voices called out to the actor on the stage. He, having finished a long speech of metaphysical language such as to render him unintelligible, bowed deeply to the audience. A rain of flowers flooded the stage from sentimental ladies.

"Frightfully good, don't you think?" asked Alaric's former subaltern, Mr. Chasen.

Mr. Ward agreed. "He certainly beats Kemble all hollow. You weren't in London for the O.P. riots, were you, Reyne?"

"No, I was otherwise engaged." Alaric tipped his chair back, his arms crossed over his chest. He'd decided rather late to accept the invitation of three friends to this new play tonight, having read in the morning editions that it was a rare experience. Indeed it was, a rare chance to experience pure, exquisite boredom. This was boredom lifted beyond mere torture, into an entirely new realm of agony. He couldn't make out what the story was, let alone what point the orator tried to make.

"You may think Jaspers is good, but wait until you see Mrs. Tovey. I was here last night, you know. She's perfection in the part. And all her parts are perfection." Mr. Hibbert sighed and rested his elbow on the rail, blocking Alaric's view of the stage. Alaric felt rather relieved about it. But in a moment, Hibbert apologized and sat up straight.

"Going to make her the object of your affections?" Mr. Ward asked, leaning over Hibbert's chair. Nimbly, he slipped loose the other man's monocular telescope and applied it to his eye, focusing on the curtained wings of the stage.

"It'll take a warmer man than me to woo her from the Marquis d'Augemont."

"Who the devil's he?"

"A Frenchie who saved his money." The three officers, two still in uniform, laughed, and were shushed by other audience members in the boxes that lined the walls of the theater.

Out came the actress to frenzied applause and coarse comments from the pit. Her declaimed conversation with the actor already present might have been a confession of love, a plot to murder her husband, or both. Alaric couldn't be certain she wasn't asking the time of day and commenting on the weather. The papers had claimed this actress to be of surpassing beauty, lovelier than Venus. She seemed drab and colorless to him. He felt like writing a letter to *The Times* about it.

She came to the end of her speech, and the applause erupted once more. "You're quite right, old man. She's marvelous. What eyes! What expression!" Mr. Chasen said, beating his gloved hands together in ecstasy.

"She's made a quite sensation. Devil of a crush in the Green Room, I daresay. Perhaps we'll shove along and join it, just for *s'amusant*. What do you say, Reyne?" Hibbert asked.

"Whatever you chaps want." What he'd seen of the actress did not tempt him to approach her more nearly. Come to think of it, most females in London these days failed to possess even the rudiments of attractiveness. Casting his gaze about the theater, Alaric considered that all women seemed to come in distressing shades of yellow or fish-white. He'd not seen a one worth the following since leaving Hollytrees. Loyally, he excepted Lillian. She always looked well. But the others—dear lord!

Perhaps, he thought, tipping his chair further back, teetering on the danger point, chicken-pox affects the eyesight adversely. Or perhaps it had rendered his vision so sharp that he could see past artifice to the real beauty beneath.

Lillian was supposed to be here, somewhere. He'd not spotted her yet. He brought his chair forward with a thud that brought hisses from the crowd, for the actor and actress had begun ranting again, complete with over-emphatic facial contortions. Alaric ignored both the crowd and the performance. He scanned the house. A glint of something like gold attracted his attention in the box across the way, on the same tier as his own but back two. He dismissed it as the candlelight calling forth reflection from the gilding on a cherub's behind.

But the flickering glow of gold continued to twinkle in the corner of his eye every time he looked in that direction. Finally, he extended his own glass to examine the object more closely. A muffled exclamation escaped him.

The two friends in the rear of the box exchanged looks. Chasen leaned forward. "Are you all right, Reyne?"

"Yes, yes, of course. Sorry to disturb you."

Sarah East leaned her elbow on the rail and gazed at the actors. It was her hair sparkling under the candlelight. Alaric did not know he smiled as he studied the play of expression on the girl's face. Obviously, she'd never seen anything so wonderful as those two clowns, declaiming their hearts out. No doubt some of the flowers littering the stage were from her hand.

"That was uncommonly well put. 'Wearily wandering this orb twinged of torment. . . .' I like that," Ward said. "Comes off the tongue so well."

Alaric raised his small telescope to his eye. Like a diamond slipping loose from its setting, a single tear traced Sarah's flushed cheek. He almost reached out, as though he could wipe it away. For fear someone might have noticed his reaction, he flicked his attention once more to the stage.

The actor and actress embraced. He could see the woman's expression. She looked as if she'd like to hold her nose. Almost without willing it, Alaric once more raised the glass to aid his gaze. Sarah, safely protected by the charm distance lends, pressed her gloved hand to her eyes as though to halt tears that would flow at the tender scene.

Hibbert sniffed and flourished his handkerchief. "Damn that's moving. Pardon me, you fellows."

Coughing, Chasen said, "Quite, quite."

Remembering Lillian had said she'd invited Mrs. Whitsun and her two guests to the play, Alaric dutifully searched the depths of the box. There was a dim shadow in the rear that might have been she, only recognizable because a chilly glitter seemed to encircle the figure's throat. None of the others would have been wearing gems of the quality that throws back candlelight.

Then Sarah sat upright, blocking his view of Lillian. She

turned as though to speak to someone behind her, and all Alaric could see was the graceful line of her back. The sweep of her hair exposed the nape of her neck, and in his glass, it seemed near enough to kiss. Then she turned again, her face aglow with pleasure in the play. She licked her open lips with enthusiasm and leaned forward once more.

Alaric dropped his telescope and had to feel about on the floor for it. He was surprised and ashamed to find that his hands trembled as he searched. Sitting up, he focused with great concentration on the actors as he fought the desire to turn the glass again toward Sarah. Sternly, he took himself to task.

Yes, she was beautiful. Yes, from the first, he'd been charmed by her. She was youthful and completely natural in her reactions and interests. To a man newly returned from war, a young lady was the best antidote to horror and exhaustion. However, she was a hoyden, completely uncontrolled. Climbing trees, losing slippers, yes, playing cricket— all unacceptable behavior. She was still a child, beautiful or not.

Let him keep that firmly in mind, and let him also remember that Lillian was exactly the sort of woman he'd always known he would marry someday. She was beautiful, if not spectacularly so. She was the happy possessor of a calm, well-ordered mind, ideal for a lifetime friend. He could not expect her embrace to stir the wild embers of passion, for they weren't married yet. She wasn't some idle mistress who could be expected to raise his expectations and then fulfill them. No doubt, when the time came, he'd be stirred enough.

The *entr' acte* came, in Alaric's opinion, not a moment too soon. With a click, he closed the tube of his telescope and put the resultant circle in his pocket as he stood up. "I'll see you gentlemen at the next act."

"Ah, off to meet Miss Tovey, then?"

"No, Ward. My fiancée is in the audience and I must offer my respects."

"Quite," Mr. Chasen said. "Very proper. Shall I . . . er . . . come along? Help with conversation?"

"No, thank you. I think I can manage."

"Damn me," said Mr. Ward after the box's door had closed behind Alaric. "*My* fiancée's in the audience and you don't see me slipping out to her between acts. I'll have to see her enough once we're married. I'll wager he's gone to offer La Tovey a slip on the shoulder. I'd do it, if I were as right in the pocket as Reyne.''

"Right as Reyne?'' Hibbert echoed. "I say, that's clever.''

Unaware that he'd just become a *bon mot,* Alaric set off down the corridor. Lillian's party sat on the far side of the theater, and if the house had been thinly attended, he could have walked to it in three or four minutes. As it was, however, it seemed he was forced to stop every yard. Many of his closest friends were still in the field, but there were plenty who knew him to speak to. He concealed his true opinion of the play, not wishing to spend the entire interval arguing, and pushed on.

Outside the door of the correct box, he paused, his fist raised to knock. Though not a man given to examining his motives, he wondered exactly why he'd come. Politeness might dictate that he visit Lillian, yet he could not but be aware of an excitement that had nothing to do with his bride-to-be. But that was ridiculous. His self-respect demanded that he prove to himself that he was not attracted to Sarah East.

Acting the fool over a chit of a girl was an old man's game, and he'd not fall victim to her charms. He'd be polite, show due attentiveness toward Lillian and return, when the half hour was up, to his friends on the other side of the theater. He made a mental note to send flowers to Lillian in the morning.

"Alaric!'' Lillian held out her hand with her welcoming smile. He bowed over it. "I thought you weren't going to come.''

"I couldn't stay away. Good evening, Mrs. Whitsun. Miss Phelps.'' He paused, worried for a moment that his tone might change when he spoke, but then he rushed to continue, thinking his pause might be noticed. "And Miss East. Good evening.''

"Good evening, Lord Reyne.'' She'd turned at his entrance, the candlelight from the theater behind her glinting in her hair, piled and tousled with ringlets hanging. He couldn't help but remember it falling down her back, still wet from the ducking she'd taken in the lake.

Lillian was saying something to him, and he brought himself out of his daydream with a jerk. "I beg your pardon?'' he asked, seating himself.

"I asked if you found the play to your liking.''

"Oh, yes, it seems most interesting. However, I wonder if one of you ladies could perhaps tell me what it is about?"

Mrs. Whitsun gave her whinnying laugh. "Really, Lord Reyne, how droll."

Miss Harmonia, hanging over the edge of the box, said, "Sarah, Sarah, look! Isn't that Sir Percy Alvandale? I wonder where Lord Morebinder is?"

Sarah, Alaric noticed, did not ape her friend's bad behavior, but sat quietly in her seat, looking at her hands linked in her lap. "I don't know," she said softly.

"I much admired your bowling style last evening, Sar— Miss East. Where did you learn it?"

"Oh, don't ask the child to talk about that, Lord Reyne," Mrs. Whitsun said. "Such a scolding I gave her, encouraging those naughty rakes that way."

"I was at school with Morebinder's older brother, Charles. Young Morebinder simply needs steadying. It is not easy to be thrust into a new position by the death of a near relative."

Lillian put her hand on his arm. "I'm sure Mrs. Whitsun did not mean Lord Morebinder is an evil person, Alaric."

He smiled at her. "No, of course not. Perhaps, Miss East, you learned to play cricket from your brothers. Let me think. You said they were in the . . . ah . . ."

"They are both in the navy, Lord Reyne."

"Yes, but she didn't learn to bowl from them," Miss Harmonia said. "Don't you remember, Sarah? Harcourt taught you and the dog retrieved the balls."

"Yes, that's right." Sarah looked up when a knock sounded at the door. Meeting her eyes, Alaric smiled. But instead of her expression transforming by a joyous smile, she only dropped her eyes once again to her lap.

Three footmen entered, carrying filled baskets. "Why, what's this?" Lillian asked. "Alaric, how thoughtful you are."

"I hope you don't mind. I changed your order for biscuits and wine for this light supper." Though he spoke to Lillian, he found his head turning toward Sarah. Would his effort please her? Sternly, he reminded himself that her reactions were no concern of his. But why didn't she seemed pleased?

Apparently, Harmonia's notice of Sir Percy had been reciprocated. In a few moments, the party was increased by Alvandale and Morebinder, this time unaccompanied by their entourage. Lillian was as welcoming as always. They could have been South Sea Islanders, naked save for paint, and she still would have been charming.

The box began to grow crowded. Alaric stepped out of the way, toward the front of the box. Harmonia was absorbed by the new arrivals. He stood alone beside Sarah. The pearls in her hair were dull in comparison with its shine, and the purity of her skin eclipsed their moon-like luster. Alaric clasped his hands to keep from touching her cheek. He wanted her to look up so that he might savor once more the sensations her gaze aroused.

"And is Sarah enjoying the play?" he asked, striving desperately for a tone that would make it clear she was nothing to him. He managed only to sound, he thought, like an elderly uncle left alone with the baby.

"Very much so, sir. I've never been to the theater before."

Well, that was good. She was using more than one sentence at a time. "It's been a long time for me, too. That is, I've not visited the theater since . . . Covent Garden burned." He thought he saw a brief smile though as long as she kept her head bowed he could not be certain. A loud laugh from behind him made him jump and he looked around half-angrily. "You know, if Harmonia were my sister, I think I should object to Morebinder ogling her in that way through his glass."

"I believe his eyesight is very poor," Sarah ventured.

"What is he doing at the theater if he can't see the stage?"

"The same as you, who do not care for this play." Sarah looked up, then. She went on, in a tone too low to carry to the others in the box, who were becoming noisy anyway. "By the way, the play is about Lady Anne Devries who discovers too late that the man she truly loved was her husband's brother. There is also another story about her maid, who is in love with a highwayman."

Alaric bowed. "Thank you, Miss East. You've saved me from the consequences of my ignorance. At least thirty people wanted to ask me what I thought of it, and I was having a deuced hard time as I cannot tell one player from another."

"Some are women, Lord Reyne."

This was said with so sweet a smile and in so soft a voice that, for a moment, he could not be sure she was jesting. Then he laughed, and she looked as if she'd like to join him. "I shall keep it in mind, but God save me if the maid puts on breeches. I'll need to come to you so you may explain it to me again.''

"I'm always happy to help you." But the laughter in her voice faded and she fell to examining her hands once again. Just before she dropped her gaze, Alaric thought those large grey eyes moistened as though with tears. She'd been weeping before, from the sentiments of the play, but this was different. He began to shake again, suddenly afraid as war, battle, and the imminence of death had not frightened him.

"Are you thirsty? Would you care from some champagne?" Corks popped, reminding him of his duties as provider of the feast. Alaric moved off and somehow couldn't find his way back to her before the resumption of the play.

While standing beside Lillian, Alaric became aware that every person who approached them had a question in his or her eyes. He'd noticed this before, but put it down to the novelty of his return. Now, though, he seemed to understand what they were silently asking. Behind every statement, behind every laugh, he heard, "Why are you not married yet?" He wondered if Lillian was also mindful that they were the object of such curiosity. This, however, did not seem to be the moment to turn casually to her and ask.

When soft music began again to fill the theater, Alaric took his leave. "Must you go?" Mrs. Whitsun asked, cutting off Lillian, who had been on the point of inviting him to stay.

"I'm afraid so. I have friends waiting for me. We are engaged to go on to White's after the play. Otherwise, I would certainly take advantage of the chance to remain by four such lovely ladies." This gratified Mrs. Whitsun, as was intended.

As he bowed over Lillian's hand, she said softly, "I'll be home from two until four tomorrow if you'd care to call."

"Thank you. I shall. Good evening, Miss Phelps. Miss East." Sarah's white dress glowed as though light itself was molded to her figure. Alaric left rather abruptly, promising himself that he'd send Lillian some small gift in addition to flowers. A pierced ivory fan, a scent-bottle, or perhaps a new telescope for the theater. He'd heard they had some now with two lenses, like a lorgnette, more powerful for longer distances.

Returning to his own box, Alaric was greeted by Hibbert, Chasen, and Ward. He'd returned not a moment too soon; the curtain was already parting, and the noisiness of his friends' greeting caused a storm of furious hushes to arise from the surrounding audience. Alaric tried hard to concentrate on the action going forth on the stage. Shifting in his seat, he cast a suspicious glance at his companions. One of them had certainly changed chairs with him, for it had not been *this* uncomfortable before the intermission. Move though he would, something jabbed him in the back, or bunched up beneath him or made his legs fall asleep. The only comfortable position he could find was more or less turned away from the stage (all to the good) but facing the direction of Lillian's party.

The circle of his telescope seemed to burn in his pocket. His fingers itched for it. The sliding noise as he opened it was gratifying. Sternly, however, Alaric snapped it closed. He turned his head, and his attention, toward the stage.

The actress clutched at her throat. "Ah, cursed house, and cursed hour! The fickle tide of love hast blinded my soul!" She fell to stormy weeping. A sigh of sympathy seemed to sweep the audience, broken into by a groan as, no doubt, some masculine heart was wrung by agony.

Alaric opened his telescope once more. Anything would be preferable to the torture of watching the stage. For a few minutes, he idly gazed about the house, pausing on a sleeping man, a weeping woman, or a fellow sufferer. Yet, as he amused himself, Alaric knew that sooner or later he would reach the upper tier of boxes and search out Sarah East.

Was she ill? She sat up very straight, her eyes fixed, not on the play, but on some internal view. Her face, from being flushed with enthusiasm, was pale and her lips turned downward. If she were not ill, then she must be unhappy. Alaric did not stop to wonder that the thought pricked him like the point of a knife. Perhaps that aunt of hers had taken her to task for displaying so much interest in the performance; some people might take it to mean she was vulgar. Alaric thought her lively attention charming, and regretted he'd not told Mrs. Whitsun so.

Whatever else Sarah might do, she would never feign disinterest for effect, or drawl out praise in a way that was worse than outright condemnation. She was honest, he'd known that from the first, and her emotions were lived fully. If she sat still and quiet, something must be wrong. He only hoped someone over there would notice and help her. He wished he could do it himself, but that would be unwarrantable interference.

As the curtain closed Alaric said, "I'm sorry, you fellows, but I'm going now."

"Now?" Hibbert echoed. "What about the rest of the play?"

"Yes, and what about the club?" Chasen asked.

"You go. I don't feel up to it, somehow. But you must dine with me one day next week. Thursday? Very good. Excellent, in fact. Unless Miss Canfield has other plans, of course."

"Of course," Ward said, laughing. "You lads will have to get yourselves betrothed to find out what real independence of action means. Eh, Reyne?"

"Quite. Good evening, gentlemen."

Walking home through the puddles left by a spring rain, for his carriage was deep in a crush of others, Alaric turned into the square with a sigh that was not entirely one of relief. His carefully chosen, beautifully appointed home was dark, save for a light in the library. He'd given the servants late leave, but he knew Barton would be there, waiting up.

"How was the play, my lord?"

"Don't ask. A bottle in the library, I think."

"Yes, my lord. I'll bring in another glass."

"Another?"

"Mr. Canfield has been waiting for you the last hour, my lord. With the claret." Barton's face, never exactly writhing with expression, was even more impassive than usual.

"Is he drunk?"

"I would not say so, my lord."

"Yes, well, your standards are higher than most, Barton. Bring in that glass."

"Very good, my lord."

"That you, Reyne?" Mr. Canfield's tall, broad form filled the open doorway. Though a waft of alcohol fumes floated out too, the man did not seem the worse for drink.

"Yes, sir," Alaric said, crossing the hall with his hand out. "I'm sorry I kept you waiting."

His future father-in-law shook hands with a powerful grip. "I called on the chance of finding you in, and your man said you'd not be long."

Alaric shot a glance at the imperturbable butler. Though Barton had not ventured an opinion, he must have known the play would not be to his master's taste. "Another bottle, Barton."

"Yes, my lord."

"Let us sit down, Mr. Canfield."

"All right. May as well be comfortable. It's my girl I'm wanting to talk to about."

Alaric poured his guest another glass. The fresh breeze from the square riffled the long white curtains at the windows behind his desk, making the candle flames dance. "Lillian? What's amiss?"

The former miller's apprentice squared his broad shoulders, deepening the shadow behind him. "Just this: when are you two getting married up? It's been over six months, man. Are you trying to slide out from under your obligation?"

"My dear sir!"

"Don't come your fine manner over me. I know what you are, well enough. A nobleman, and the son, grandson and great-grandson of a long line of noblemen. Your blood's blue enough and I'm what I am. But my Lillian's good enow for any prince. So why don't you marry the gel and get on with the raising of my grandsons? Or doesn't that prospect interest you? By God, if you turn out one of those namby-pamby fellers . . ."

Alaric was torn between laughing and anger. However, to give in to either emotion would be to face, he feared, one of Mr. Canfield's large fists, and he was too tired tonight to give as good as he'd get. "I think I can assure you, sir, that my interest is entirely of the sort that would meet with your approval. But people just don't rush into matrimony these days. I'm endeavoring to give Lillian the time required to prepare herself for marriage."

"Dammit, man. How much preparation does a girl need? She'll marry you and like it. Her mother and I married within six weeks of our meeting. I first saw her on a Wednesday and the banns were first called that Sunday. And her father was not nearly so dead set on the match as I am."

Alaric shook his head, wryly smiling. "I'm afraid I'm not so impetuous, sir. But, if it pleases you, I shall ask Lillian to suggest a date for our wedding. No doubt she'll have some notion in mind. As a matter of fact, I believe she said something about wishing to be married around Christmastime.''

''Are you sure she didn't mean *last* Christmas? After all, it's April. She can't mean to make me wait another . . .'' He counted quickly on his strong fingers. ''No. I won't wait eight more months to see her wed. You talk to her, Reyne. And if you've got any feeling, you'll see to it that the date is sooner than that. June, maybe. Two months is more than enough time to 'prepare.' 'Specially when you've had six months before that!''

Mr. Canfield strode toward the door. ''I'll not stay longer, Reyne. Though you keep a good cellar, I've said all I came to say.'' The man hesitated and turned back. ''You'll forgive me for speaking so plain. It's my girl I'm worried for.''

''There's nothing in the world to forgive, sir. Lillian is worth any effort.'' His father-in-law-to-be nodded his head abruptly and departed, cramming a round hat on his head as he went out, without waiting for Barton to bow him away.

When the butler came in, bearing a bottle on a salver, he found his master looking out into the square, the curtain held back. Slowly, Alaric turned. ''You've been long enough with that. Where'd you go for it? France?''

''I considered, my lord, that Mr. Canfield had taken his limit. Too much wine in a boisterous man may lead on to mayhem.''

''Please, Barton. I've heard enough poetry for one evening.''

''I feared *The Ingrateful Wife* would not be to your liking, my lord.'' Barton bowed from the waist, pouring a stream of red wine into Lord Reyne's glass.

''Then why the devil didn't you say so? Leave the bottle and go to bed.''

''Yes, my lord. If I may say so, sir—you have been kind enough not to reject my opinion when I've ventured . . .''

''Barton, I knew you when we had only a blanket for a roof and a box of charges for a table. You needn't talk as if you're an old family retainer with a mouthful of pebbles.''

''Very good, my lord. She ain't for you, Captain Naughton.''

''I beg your pardon?''

"Miss Canfield. She ain't for you. Not sayin' anythin' against the lady. She's fine. But anyone can see with half an eye she ain't for you."

"If my boots were off, my dear old campaigner, I'd throw them at you."

"Very good, my lord." The door closed with a soft snick.

As tired and stiff as though he'd spent the day in the saddle, Alaric lowered himself into the chair behind the desk, kicking his feet up onto the clean blotter. He lifted his glass and studied the inverted heart shape of the candle flame in its depths.

Slowly, repeating a lesson learnt by heart, he counted again the reasons why Lillian Canfield was his ideal bride. Listening to the silence of the large house, decorated with a view toward bringing her into it, he tried to convince himself that happiness could be derived from contentment. Alaric strove to keep his thoughts on Lillian. But the girl with laughing grey eyes who held up an apple and asked, "Do you want a bite?" slipped past all his barricades.

——— *10* ———

That night, hours after they'd returned from the theater, Sarah woke to the sound of sobbing. She sat up. "Harmonia," she whispered. "Are you awake?"

Her friend did not answer except by a loud gulp as of tears hastily swallowed. A bar of moonlight filtered in through the window beside her bed, shining across the carpet like a path. Sarah put one foot out from beneath the covers. The floor was freezing and her slippers were far underneath the bed.

"What's the matter?" she asked, stealing across to the other bed. Putting her hair back from her face with both hands, she leaned down to whisper, "Why are you crying?"

"I wasn't. Oh, yes. I was."

Sarah sat on the edge of the bed, her cold feet tucked up beneath her. "Why? Is it . . . is it Mr. Atwood?"

All colors were washed away by the moonlight pouring in through the sheer curtains. Her friend's face seemed like something drowned without her own bright eyes and cheeks to lend vivid life. Harmonia nodded miserably, dragging up the sheet to mop her face. "How did you know?"

"You've been here a week and you've hardly mentioned him. . . ."

"What could I say? I don't know anything. He never writes me. I've sent him letter on letter, and I don't receive anything in return. Not ever. I don't think I've gotten a letter from him since . . . oh, since February. And that was only a brief note, hardly worth franking." She sniffled.

"Have you asked him why he doesn't write more often?"

"I don't like to ask. I don't want him to think I'm the kind of girl who criticizes." Drawing a quavering breath, she went on. "I'm so worried. What if something's happened to him?"

"The people who employ him would surely let you know."

Harmonia shook her head. "Maybe not. Harlow didn't let them know about me. He said it might jeopardize his position if they knew he could only stay a year."

"I see," Sarah said, though she did not. "Write him again tomorrow, and ask him why he doesn't write back. Maybe he just never thought of it."

Harmonia grasped her friend's hand. "Do you think . . . ? I will. I'll demand an accounting. Will you help—oh, I forgot. You're going riding with Harvey."

"Yes, he asked me to. But I'd much rather . . ."

"No, no, you go. This is something I have to do alone." She paused as if in thought, and then said, "Besides, you've not had a chance to ride your horse since you bought him. I can hardly believe Mrs. Whitsun let you do that."

"Russet was a bargain for such a love. And my aunt doesn't object. She told me yesterday that she thinks I should go for rides in the Row more often. But that first time out, there were too many other people riding to find out what she can do. Early in the morning, or so Harvey says, there aren't so many riders to get in the way."

"I don't know why you call your horse that. She's not red."

"No, I know. But she's the apple of my eye. Is there anything I can do for you, Harmonia? Would you like me to make you a cup of tea or chocolate? I know the cook won't mind my being in her kitchen." She knew no such thing. Her aunt's cook was a tartar, who defended her stove and hearth like a demon.

"No, I don't care for anything. I just wish he'd write to me! Even a word would be welcome."

"I know. Try to sleep, Harmonia." Feeling helpless, Sarah returned to her own bed. The girls had decided from the first to share a room, both for company and late-night gossips. Now that Sarah was awake, she could not go back to sleep. Not even the rhythmic breathing of her friend, finding slumber quickly through sheer exhaustion, could stop her thoughts from racing, despite how well she knew the track.

When Miss Canfield first suggested visiting the theater in her company, Mrs. Whitsun had taken her up at once. Not even Sarah's pleading the headache had dampened Mrs. Whitsun's enthusiasm for the plan. She had talked for an hour to Sarah about all the important people who would be there, about the eligible men who would fall in love with her, like Romeo and Juliet, admiring her in her balcony setting. But it was not until her aunt sighed, complaining that Lord Reyne would not be joining them, that Sarah's heartache dissipated.

She had even given in to Mrs. Whitsun's insistence that she sit up in front of the box, despite feeling like a bolt of cloth in a draper's window, because she could watch the play so much better from there. Though the high-flown language was a trifle difficult to follow, Sarah had enjoyed herself until the door opened and in walked Lord Reyne.

How splendid he'd appeared in his evening dress, with the brilliant white linen throwing back the candlelight. And then, wonders of wonders, he'd come to her side. They'd talked for a time, and he'd smiled. But those moments had been too brief; he'd returned to Miss Canfield. Sarah had not the faintest notion what happened during the next two acts. She lived only for the moment when the curtain dropped down, and yet, Lord Reyne never came back.

Lying back against her pillows, Sarah decided to forget that he'd gone from her, that he'd not returned. She smiled in the darkness, remembering what it had been like to have his entire attention focused on her alone. She invented a thousand witticisms to keep him laughing, conveniently forgetting she'd never have the boldness in real life to deliver a one of them.

Early in the morning, noticing her niece was heavy-eyed and yawning, Mrs. Whitsun said, "It will be an early night for you, dear thing. We can't have you falling ill."

"I just had a difficult time sleeping, Aunt."

"Over-excitement. My, that habit was an excellent investment. There are not many girls who can carry that shade of pink." Mrs. Whitsun gave the antique-colored lace at Sarah's throat a straightening pat. "Do be careful of that train; I know you are not used to it, and nothing looks worse than a girl tripping over her own clothes."

"Yes, Aunt." Sarah heard a jingle as of harness and went to the morning room window to search the street. "It's Harvey, already. Doesn't he look fine? Those clothes must be new. Yes, they are. Look how proud he is of them."

The lanky young man stopped on the steps of Mrs. Whitsun's townhouse and inhaled a great draft of morning air. Then, suddenly somber, he painstakingly plucked a piece of invisible lint from his sleeve. With a word to the groom who held the two horses, Harvey rapped the knocker. Sarah was there to open the door before the sound had the chance to echo.

"Good," he said, looking her over. "You're all ready then."

"Yes, I am. But I'm surprised you're so early. Harmonia said you'd be late." She waved her riding crop to her aunt, still peering out the wide front window.

"What does she know?" Harvey asked, making a cradle of his hands so Sarah could stand on them to mount. "I hate girls who keep you waiting, on and off for an hour while they fuss. Especially with a restive beast like this under me." The big bay, as rangy as his master, blew out his breath as though in agreement and danced, kicking his black feet. "That's not a bad animal you've got there, by the way." They rode away, leaving the groom sitting on the steps.

Upon reaching the Park, Harvey, only in town a week, was busy greeting friends and nodding to his acquaintances. Sarah found that even at seven the rides were not empty as she'd hoped. A few of her admirers were out and her cheeks ached from smiling so much so early. She could feel beneath her the tense muscles of her mare and, as much as the horse, longed to go bounding over the empty expanses she knew existed beyond the Row. Yet, as Harvey had brought her, she felt compelled to remain beside him.

Harvey half-rose in his saddle, looking off into the distance. "Isn't that . . . I believe it is!"

"Who? What is it?"

"That girl. Emma Dealford. And without her mother for once, by God!" Harvey gazed eagerly at the dim figure of a girl on a white horse. Then he slumped down and cast a sheepish glance at Sarah.

"What eyes you've got, Harvey. I can just see that is a horse. Do you want to greet her?"

"I don't want to leave you."

"Oh, I'll come with—" Sarah recognized the expression in Harvey's eyes. It was the same a dog she'd once owned would wear whenever someone went for a walk without him. At a word, Harvey's ears would no doubt prick up. "Go ahead, Harvey. I'll wait for you down this lane."

Quickly, before anyone noticed she was now alone, Sarah

urged Russet to turn aside from the main thoroughfare. Not knowing the ground, she dared not let her mare entirely off the rein, but she could not resist moving up from the leisurely pace of the Row to a brisk trot. Though a few patches of mist still clung to the low spots on the path, a breeze stirred her hair as her heart beat freely for the first time in days.

Then, a small man appeared almost under Russet's hooves. Sarah pulled sharply at the reins. The horse, surprised, reared back. As Sarah fought to keep her seat, she glimpsed a long object of wood and steel in the man's hands. Shocked, she let go and fell off.

"Are you hurt, Miss?"

"No, I don't believe so." For a moment, she thought she was back in her own woods, staring up into an autumn sky. But this man's eyes were brown. He was small and scrawny, his clothes patched together with dark squares and ragged threads. The object in his hand was definitely a pistol.

Sarah sat up, her hand on her head. The universe still gyrated. She took her hand away and the reeling slowed. "Where's my hat?"

He searched around with his eyes. "'Ere you go," he said, bending to pick up a squashed and dented object. Handing it to her, he stepped back and leveled his pistol once more. "Give me . . . yer money and ah . . . yer jewels."

Rising, Sarah found she rather towered over the man. He wore a tattered cap on his greying brown hair. "I'm afraid I haven't anything. I'm riding this morning, not going to Court."

"Ain't it my luck?" The man lowered his pistol, shaking his head as though he'd never expected any better success.

"I'm sorry to disappoint you," Sarah said. "Aren't you going to shoot me?"

"No, miss. I can't hurt nothing, after being in the wars."

"Oh, were you a soldier?"

"Yes, miss. With the Army of the Peninsula."

"Were you? Maybe you knew a friend of mine—his name's . . ."

Hearing a rumble of hoofbeats, they turned to see a huge black stallion galloping down the lane. The rider shouted, "What the devil . . . ?" as his horse nearly trampled the would-be hedge-robber. The little man threw up his arms and the pistol went off with a shattering bang.

Lord Reyne hurled himself from the saddle, landing on the man. He gathered up the filthy neckcloth in one fist and brought the other around in a swing. "Packer?"

"'Allo, Captain. Don't hit me, if you please, sir."

"Do you know him?" Sarah asked, coming to stand beside Lord Reyne. His stallion moved over to become acquainted with Russet.

"Miss East? It is you! I thought . . . What is going on here?"

"Oh, do let go. He's turning blue." Alaric opened his hand and Packer fell backward, gasping for breath. "It's very interesting," Sarah said, coming around to help him up. "I've never been robbed before."

"He robbed you?"

"Oh, no. I don't have anything worth stealing. It was very gallant of you to rescue me, all the same. Just like the play, except there the highwayman saved Lady Anne from the lecherous Lord Lunge. Of course, you wouldn't remember that." She brushed the hair out of her eyes and dared to glance at Lord Reyne. He'd pushed his own hat back on his head and rubbed his forehead.

"No, I don't recall much about the play."

"I suppose you had rather a lot to drink at your club. Are you feeling better, Mr. Packet?" The robber coughed and rubbed his throat, while nodding his head.

"His name's Packer, Sarah. He was in my regiment, one of those who carried me behind the lines when I was wounded."

"It were no trouble to me, Captain."

"What brought you to this?" Alaric asked, stunned by the difference between a uniformed soldier and a ragged robber.

"These are 'ard times, Captain. Turrible 'ard, and my health h'ain't so good. That there mal-aria. But I know you ain't no choice in the matter but putting me down on the charge sheet, Captain. I'll go 'long quiet-like. Guessed I'd come to this any road."

Alaric's eyes met Sarah's, her hand still on Packer's thin shoulder. "I can't help them all," he murmured, hoping to see understanding. She nodded sadly, and somehow that seemed worse than any indifference would have been. Sarah, he felt, shouldn't know anything about the limitations of one person's charity.

"Look, Packer," he said. "You go to my house. Ragnor Square, number ten. You used to be a fair man with horses; tell Barton . . . do you remember him? Tell him I said to put you onto something. And get a meal. But look here! You're taken on conditionally; this is no sinecure. Cock up and you're out!"

"Yes, sir, Captain," Packer said, sketching a salute. "Number ten, Ragnor. Good old Barton." He picked up his pistol and stood a moment, polishing it up with the corner of his coat.

"You can't walk about London carrying that. Give it to me."

"Yes, sir. It's yours, anyway. I found it on the field, but I couldn't never get up with you after you'd been carted off."

Alaric took the pistol. Though the metal was scarred, his enshielded arms were still incised in the butt. "By heavens, I've the mate of this at home. I'm glad to have them both again; the one looks so lonely in its case. Thank you, Packer."

When the little man had gone, Sarah stepped up shyly to Lord Reyne's elbow and looked at the long pistol that he still held in his hand. He turned it so she could see. But though she seemed to be examining it intently, in reality she was filling her senses with his nearness. The brief struggle caused a line of sweat to trickle from the close-cut hair beside his ear. Her height made them equals, and she could study every feature of his face from beneath her lowered lashes.

"You were kind to offer Packer a job," she said. "And what a coincidence his having kept your gun. He could have sold it."

"It's not important what I did. Listen, Sarah." He took her upper arms and faced her squarely, the pistol firm against her shoulder. "What do you mean wandering off like this? What are you doing riding alone?"

"I'm not alone; Harvey is with me."

"Harvey? You mean Phelps? Where is he?"

"He went to speak to a friend."

"Haven't you got a groom?"

"No, Harvey said we wouldn't need one."

She frowned with confusion when he searched the sky as if pleading for help, but as long as he went on holding her, he could do whatever pleased him. She didn't even mind that the gun was probably staining her habit with its oiled works.

Gently, Alaric shook her. "Hasn't your aunt ever told you not to go anywhere alone in London?"

"She warns me so often; I can't remember everything."

"Well, remember this. London is a dangerous city. It's not like home where you know everyone and everyone . . . loves you." Abruptly, he took his hands away, leaving her bereft. Shoving the pistol in his pocket, he brushed his fingers together as though removing contamination.

Sarah bowed her head, knowing he was remembering all the foolish things she'd done since they'd met. What good did it do her to make any attempt to please him? The moment they met again was sure to be the moment she fell into some bramble or other. She was only fooling herself, believing a dream that one day he'd forget his obligation to Miss Canfield and turn to her.

Sniffing, Sarah refused to cry before him. That would set the seal on his poor opinion of her. Despite her efforts, a tear escaped and rolled down her cheek. She shut her eyes tightly.

A warmth enfolded her. She rested her head on a firm, gently surging surface. She breathed in the fragrance of leather and citrus, mingled with another scent she knew was Alaric's alone. He tilted up her face, his fingers caressing her cheek, and she pressed her face into the palm of his hand.

Almost too softly to hear, he said, "Oh, my dearest."

Sarah slowly, slowly opened her eyes. She'd had dreams like this before and always, when she raised her lids, the blissful images vanished. This time, the vision lingered. She felt his hand tremble and rejoiced. But why, when he spoke again, was his voice so sad?

"Sarah, please don't. Don't make this difficult for me."

Suddenly, Sarah realized she'd betrayed herself. Her hands against his chest, she thrust herself away and stumbled out of his arms. She felt with what reluctance he released her. The knowledge did not make her happy.

"Sarah," he said again, pursuing her. Catching hold of her arm, he tried to draw her near. "Please. Listen to me. I know that at this moment you feel—"

"Oh, let me go!" She tore away violently, though it pained her like pulling away oiled plaster in a sharp jerk. Beside her horse, she hiked up her skirt and placed her foot in the stirrup. Sarah swung up into the saddle, not caring that she'd probably shown him her leg to the knee. She'd just exposed her heart, so what mattered immodesty? Pulling hard, she tried to turn Russet about. But the horse locked its knees and refused to move from beside Reyne's large stallion.

"Damn!" Sarah exclaimed, and dropped her hands. "Take your horse away, sir, so that I may leave." She made an effort to speak freezingly, as Aunt Whitsun had told her the right tone very often discouraged unwanted attentions, though Sarah was not certain how to rid herself of wanted attentions.

"Yes. I'll take you back to Harvey."

"I don't want you to come with me."

"Nevertheless, I have a few words to address to that young bast—gentleman." He mounted his horse. Sarah's mare followed closely. "How long have you had that animal?" he asked.

"Years!"

"It's strange, then, that she's not better trained."

Sarah wished she'd picked up her riding crop so she could hurl it at his head. The desire grew when he told Harvey that she'd fallen off her horse, to account for her air of disarray. "Fallen off?" Harvey echoed. "That's not like you, Sarah. I must tell you. She's invited me to call. Miss Dealford, of course. I beg your pardon, Lord Reyne? You were saying?"

"I was saying, you young fool, that only a cad lets a lady ride alone. What the devil were you thinking of?"

"Miss Dealford, sir."

"Take Sarah home, then meet me at Jackson's. It'll give me great satisfaction to render you *hors de combat*." He turned his horse away and rode off, without a glance at Sarah, and without acknowledging Harvey's ecstatic thanks.

"Did you hear that, Sarah? I've never been to Jackson's Saloon. What a dashed good fellow he is. A bit of a cross crab, but I don't let that put me off. It's amazing how many fellows will do anything for you, as long as you don't thank them."

"Take me home, Harvey, will you? I don't feel very well. I'm probably going to have a large bruise on my . . ."

"You do look rather a mess. 'Course anyone would after Emma—I mean, Miss Dealford. You should see the way she sits her horse, and a quiet, dark habit—nothing flashy for her. I say, Sarah, I mean, is pink quite the thing, do you think?"

"Oh, Harvey, I don't know."

But he wasn't listening. "She's got a splendid seat, but she's not unfeminine. I hate a woman who thinks she can ride better than I. Miss Dealford was quite startled when that shot went off, but I grabbed the reins, and her horse soon knew who was master. Docile little thing, really.''

''Shot?''

''Didn't you hear it? I think . . .'' He urged his bay closer to Sarah and whispered, ''I think someone's fought a duel. I looked up when I heard it, same as everyone, but nobody moved. We'll hear all about it later, when the gossips get hold of the story. I promised to come tell Miss Dealford the entire tale, once I knew it.''

The bonging of a church clock prompted him to ask, ''What time do you suppose Lord Reyne meant to meet me? Although, it's awfully good of him to take me to Jackson's, I hope he won't keep me too long; I mustn't disappoint Miss Dealford.''

''You'll have to visit her after the swelling goes down.''

''Oh, it won't be a real match. Just sparring. Won't Miss Dealford be bucked when she hears where I've been? I tell you, Sarah, I've never met a girl so sweet and sympathetic. When she looked up at me with those big eyes, that first day, when Petey came at her, I, well, I . . .''

Sarah peered at Harvey in amazement. He was actually blushing! It was hard to believe that a few moments alone with some girl could reduce a boy she'd known all her life into a flowery lover. But, turning red herself at the memory of Lord Reyne's arms about her, she found it easier to understand. How unfair that fantasies should become so hideously embarrassing when realized!

''Here we are,'' Harvey said, breaking into her thoughts. He helped her to dismount.

Though she wanted nothing more than to be alone, to sob into her pillow as Harmonia had last night, politeness demanded she show Harvey some consideration. ''Won't you come in? You haven't met my great-aunt yet.''

''Yes, I did, when I brought Harmonia up. I don't mean to criticize, but does she look at everybody that way?''

''What way, Harvey?''

''It's difficult to say. As if she were hungry? Made me nervous as a cat, I can tell you.''

''Aunt Whitsun's not so dreadful as that. She's been kind to me and good to Harmonia. If she hadn't agreed to let Harmonia stay, you wouldn't have come up to London until next month.''

"That's true. But I'll cry off coming in, nevertheless.'' He tugged at the fronts of his coat and fluffed his cravat. "I'd better hurry to Jackson's. I don't want to keep Lord Reyne waiting. And then, Miss Dealford did ask me to call.'' After escorting Sarah to the door, Harvey remounted. "I'll come by in a few days. If you're going to Lady Gordon Lloyd's ball, I'll meet you there.''

Sarah nodded and waved. Then she said, "Harvey? Harvey, *can* you box?''

"'Course I can,'' he said, pausing. "What did you think I learned at Oxford?''

"Good. I hope you black both Lord Reyne's eyes!'' The butler opened the door and she went in, leaving young Mr. Phelps to clatter down the stony street, shaking his head at the strangeness of women. He did not think about this long, as in a few moments he was wondering what his mother thought of Miss Dealford, a speculation which occupied his mind until he reached the stables.

—— 11 ——

"Damn!" For the third time, Alaric caught his leg on a tree root. He felt certain it was the same knobby stem that had tripped him twice before. Glimpsing a tree stump, shining whitely in the gloom beneath the trees, he hopped over to it and sat down.

This natural seat was ridged and beastly uncomfortable. Alaric wished he could leave it to the elves, who were no doubt abroad on this witching eve. Above him, the sky held the lasting purple glow of the spring midnight. A few stars shone like netted fish in the swaying branches above. At his feet, all was impenetrable shadow, full of things that could not be alive and yet moved with malevolent intention.

Finding his thoughts irresistibly running over the foolish stories of his childhood nurse, Alaric crossed his arms and concentrated determinedly on his boots. No doubt they were now buffeted and scarred beyond repair. As soon as he could get back to the house, he would change them. The next order of business would be to find some potion rather more substantial than fairy dew sipped from a wild rose, or whatever the liquid that the Duchess of Parester's butler had been ladling. Despite its medieval associations, a'Maying all night was not for the middle aged.

Alaric looked up once more at the stars and defied them to bewitch him more. Tree branches swayed before his eyes, weaving complex runes across the sky. Floating on the flower-filled breeze came the voices of the other house guests. Lillian was among them. So was her father. And so was Sarah. It had been at the sight of this last that he'd ducked into this grove.

Though it was beyond foolish to be afraid of a mere slip of a girl, he knew it was the better part of wisdom to avoid

Sarah. Sitting with the wind whispering around him, Alaric acknowledged that he was indeed afraid, afraid of the giddy feelings she aroused in his heart. Safer by far to cower in a dark wood than to be tempted anew into folly by Sarah's beauty. He knew he would not find the courage a second time to resist her youthful enthusiasm for him as he had in the Park. And even then, he shamefully confessed to the night, he'd had to beg for her help. Trying to think of brandy and bruises, Alaric was prey to the strange sensation that it was not the stars that had been trapped by the trees but himself.

He did not hear the girl behind him until her hand came down caressingly on his shoulder. "My word!" Lillian said, retreating. "I did not mean to startle you, Alaric."

Having leapt to his feet, Alaric bowed. "I beg your pardon, my dear. I seem to be somewhat . . . edgy?"

"Perhaps spring has got you." Lillian came a hesitating step nearer. "It seems to be in the air. After all, there are young girls down in the meadow performing magic rites. Such things have an effect on everyone. I even saw Father cutting a caper in the moonlight."

"I have not seen a moon."

"Well, starlight then. Magic light, Alaric." Hastily, as though afraid she'd be stopped, Lillian laid her hand on his arm. With a smile, Alaric raised her fingers to his lips and kissed them exactly as he'd done a hundred times before, in greeting or farewell. Exactly as he'd done before.

"Frankly, Lillian, I can't quite see why we shouldn't go back to the house like reasonable mortals. There's such a thing as carrying respect for a hostess' wishes too far."

"The duchess wants to carry on May Day in the traditional style."

"Tradition's well and good for Druids, Vikings and such, but not for sober-minded people like you and I. Come, let's go back. We can play cribbage."

"I don't play, you know that."

"That's right; it's Sarah I'm thinking of. I suppose she's washing her face in the waters of seven flowers or something. At least you needn't bother, my dear. You've no need for the fairies to show you the man you'll marry."

"No, I've no need for the fairies. But still . . ."

"You know," Alaric said, pursuing his own thoughts. "I

don't know what it is about that girl. I don't think she cares much for me."

"Who? Oh, Sarah."

"Have you noticed it, too? She stops smiling and never talks when I come in the room. I wonder if I've frightened her."

"I shouldn't think so."

"Well, I am much older than she is."

"Fifteen years isn't very much. I know many people who are happily married with greater difference in their ages than that. And do you forget that I am only four years older than Sarah?"

"There's no comparison to be made between you, Lillian. You have much the advantage. But still, I don't like frightening young girls. I'm not an ogre, you know. I shall have to show that I approve of her, although that aunt of hers is a dreadful toad-eater."

"Mrs. Whitsun has had a difficult life. And you are rather important, socially. Quite a feather in her cap if you show attentions to her ward."

"Nonsense. I'm no one of any use to anyone with social ambitions. Or do you want to continue the giddy round once we are wed? Not that we won't come up to London fairly often; I'm not going to wall you up in the country. Girls get rather silly if they live completely bucolic lives. That's half Sarah's trouble, I'm sure. She doesn't know how to get on in society. You know, she hardly spoke to me at dinner. Rather rude, really."

"I like the country very much."

"Oh, you'll be an ornament to Reyne, I've no doubt. Did you say your father is dancing on the green?"

"Yes, just over there. Or at least, he was."

"I must see it. I'm afraid I'm rather in awe of your father, you know. Did I tell you he called on me after the theater the other night?"

"No. What did he say?"

"He wanted to be certain of my intentions toward you. I believe I reassured him that my heart had not changed."

"Really, it's too bad of him. I've told him that sort of thing isn't done. He keeps telling me that he married Mother in six weeks."

In imitation of Mr. Canfield's serious tones, Alaric said,

"Aye, met her Wednesday . . . banns up Sunday mornin'."

"Oh, he *didn't* tell you that old story! I'm sorry."

"No, it was charming of him to confide in me. I hated to disappoint him by not running out to post ours on the nearest church door."

"He just doesn't understand. Does he think he can force you to marry me?"

"Lillian, force doesn't come into it."

"But say you decided that I do not suit you. He'd think I should continue with the ceremony willingly, even if you hated the idea. He can't see that anything would be preferable to being married to a man who did not love me."

"Lillian!" Now Alaric took her hand in both of his and rubbed it anxiously. "Lillian, this is nonsense. I'm not about to hate the notion of marrying you. The thought of a life with you makes me quite happy. There's no need to talk of force or unwillingness. We agreed to wait. . . ."

"Yes. Yes, we agreed to wait." She laughed a little. "I think May madness took me away for a moment. Perhaps you are right and this staying up all night and romping in the woods is only for Druids and fairies. Walk with me to the house?"

"Of course, if you're feeling . . . that is, if you can find the way out of this wood. I've ruined my boots already with tripping over roots."

Sarah held her breath. The meadow was hushed as a church, the giggling and foolishness of the girls past for the moment. The carefully chosen flowers lay like many Ophelias on the surface of each ewer, calmed now after the splashing of pretty faces. Long hair flowing over each back had been brushed to the quality of silk. Sarah, like the others, waited trembling for the May miracle. A breeze stirred the water. No face appeared in the mirror beside her own.

Some other girl in the field screamed and the rest streamed over to hear her news, or to comfort her if the face was not that of the man she wished to choose. "I shall have to become reconciled to being an old maid," Sarah said to Harmonia, who was still gazing into her own mirror. "What did you see?"

"I . . . I don't know. I thought I'd see Harlow but it . . . I didn't see anything. Of course not. It's just a superstition, isn't it? It doesn't mean anything."

"No, as the duchess said, it's only a tradition."

"I shouldn't even be here, as I'm engaged, that is. If her grace hadn't insisted, I wouldn't have come." Harmonia yawned the last words. "Excuse me!" she said in some surprise.

"It's all I can do to keep awake myself. I hardly slept last night."

"Was your bed as hard as mine?"

"Like a pavement." It was easier to agree than to confess she'd lain awake because she'd not expected Lord Reyne to be at the duchess's May house party. She'd come around a corner and there he'd been, talking easily to his elderly host. Somehow she'd contrived to nod, to smile and to pass by without a word.

Dinner had been an ordeal. Some evil chance had placed her at his left hand. Her tongue had stuck to the roof of her mouth and neither water nor wine could move it. Mrs. Whitsun had beamed and made motions, suggesting in pantomime that she start a conversation. Every time Sarah thought of something to say, the memory of the moments in his arms choked her. It did not help to see Miss Canfield smiling on his other side.

"Do you want to stay out all night?" Sarah found herself asking Harmonia.

"Do you?" The two girls looked at each other and then smiled. "I would if Harlow were here," Harmonia said wistfully. "But without a sweetheart . . ."

And somewhere in the darkness, no doubt, Lord Reyne strolled arm in arm with Miss Canfield. "No, it's not much without your sweetheart. How cold it's growing. I'd rather go back to the house and have a cup of tea."

"Oh, so would I! Do you think anyone would mind if we did?"

"I don't see why they should." They started back, their long dresses rustling in the tall grass. The other girls had run off, perhaps to the garden to see what the unattached young men were doing.

Harmonia's steps were slow. "I did hope I'd see him in the mirror. I know it's just superstition, but I would have felt better if I'd seen him."

"I'm sure there'll be a reply to your last letter when we return to London."

"Oh, yes, he must have written this time. He must have." When they reached the house, Harmonia had lost interest in refreshment. She wanted only her bed where, Sarah knew, she'd sigh and sob out the night.

Sarah asked a passing servant for tea. Apparently, though, the duchess had given leave to her people for the evening, to go a'Maying in the woods, gathering fronds and flowers, just like their betters. The young footman promised he'd do his best.

While waiting, Sarah wandered out onto a stone-flagged terrace along one side of the long, low house. As in a dream, she heard the soft music of a flute, accented by the giggles of young lovers. She sighed and leaned against one cream-colored pillar, wishing for wonders without names. Hearing a step behind her, Sarah knew, before he spoke, that Lord Reyne had come.

He cleared his throat and then said, "I keep expecting to find I'm living in a vase at the Ashmolean Museum."

Though his words were not what she expected, they made her laugh. Turning, she asked, "Why?"

"I seem to have gotten into some sort of pastoral landscape. I expect a troupe of fauns and nymphs to come trooping over that hill at any moment."

"I see. And the music is the pipe of Pan?"

"Exactly. And you for Aphrodite."

"Not I," she said, matching his merry solemnity. "I'm just a wandering dryad. When tonight is over, back I'll go to be one with my tree."

"An apple tree, no doubt."

"No doubt." Her eyes fell before his searching glance. Sarah turned from him, struggling to remember that she'd vowed to behave with perfect decorum in his presence. Unfortunately, it was difficult to achieve when he looked at her with such liking. A bubble of happiness grew in her breast so strongly it was as if she'd be lifted up by it to float away. He did like her, at the least. As the music grew louder, not just a pipe now but drums, Sarah pointed toward the hill. "Look, you were right."

Over the hill came the young men and girls, dancing in a style never seen at Almack's. They were led by an odd, twirling figure in trailing robes who was only dimly recognizable as their hostess, the Duchess of Parester, Mrs. Whitsun's friend.

"Come on!" she shouted, waving to them. She held in her right hand some figure on a stick, like the doll a jester of old might carry. Shaking it at the two people on the terrace, she called again, "Come dance with us!"

"Let's go!" Lord Reyne said. Her hand seized, Sarah twirled about under his arm, her long hair of beaten gold flying out to brush his face. He grinned at her surprise, as his feet found the rhythm of the drums. His arm around her waist, he spun dizzyingly around the pavement with her. Sarah felt too breathless to laugh, but gasped a protest she did not mean.

"We can't . . . we mustn't . . . Miss Canfield . . ."

Whether it was the loudness of the music or that he wished not to hear, Lord Reyne paid no attention. He let her go and leapt the low balustrade. Holding up his arms to her, he said, "Come on, Sarah. Come and dance with me."

The dancers were passing. "I can't." Manners, propriety, decorum! What use were they at this moment?

"Can't? Is this the Sarah East who climbs trees, and falls out of them? Who swims and runs and all but flies? Who stands off bulls and beasts and highwaymen?" She could see him clearly in the shimmering light, though the colors had run. He gave her a smile so coaxing that all her good intentions were no proof against it. She leapt over the low wall between them, to be caught and instantly drawn into the train of dancers.

She knew from the first step that whatever hurts his body had taken were healed. So lightly did they move together that she could not feel the grass beneath her feet. The strength of his body was very real. They danced as though they were in no way strangers to one another, as if they'd trod this strange measure during each of the thousand nights before.

Then, the pagan music stopped. Slowly, as though afraid, Sarah turned her head to look after the others. The rest of the party, even the ragged duchess, stared back. A long table had been set out under the trees, loaded with a variety of delights. The fauns and nymphs stood about with glasses in their hands, revealed as proper gentlemen and ladies. Sarah wrenched her hands free of Lord Reyne's, noticing briefly that he was as embarrassed as herself, and smiled shyly about. "What is that?" she asked. "Punch?"

"Yes, my dear," said the duchess, taking pity. "Some punch for Miss East and Lord Reyne, Markham."

"Very good, your grace," said the respectable butler, coming forward with two glasses on a tray. Sarah could not meet Lord Reyne's eyes as she drank. The magic had broken like a crystal goblet, one which made no sound as it shattered.

"A most peculiar evening," Mrs. Whitsun said, going home in the carriage the next morning. "It could have made quite a scandal, if the people had not been so excessively well-bred. Going into the woods all night to see the May in! Had I known Amabelle was planning a party like that, I shouldn't have taken you girls."

"No, Aunt." Sarah had been rather hoping, the next morning, that it would turn out to have been a dream. But as Aunt Whitsun's first words had been an admonition not to pay too much attention to other people's fiancés, Sarah had known her brief adventure had made her the object of gossip.

Mrs. Whitsun returned to the subject now, after a glance to reassure herself that Harmonia was occupied by the view out the window. The weather, from the warm softness of yesterday, had turned grey and cold. "Lord Reyne is most charming, dear thing, but perhaps you should exercise more caution where he is concerned. I don't wish to make you conceited, but you are very beautiful and he is a man. You don't want to take a reputation as a flirt, do you?"

"No, Aunt."

"Enough said, then. I know I can count on you not to be alone with him and not to show any preference."

"Yes, Aunt."

"Why shouldn't she show a preference?" Harmonia suddenly asked. "What's the use of hiding your feelings? I'm sure I'd rather have attentions paid me by anyone rather than sit hiding my face in some corner."

"Miss Phelps!"

Sarah caught Harmonia's hands. "It's all right; I'm sure it will be all right."

"And what if it isn't? What if he hasn't written to me? How much longer can I be expected to keep calm about it when it's driving me mad—quite mad?"

As Aunt Whitsun fumbled in her reticule for her *sal volatile*,

Sarah slid over to the opposite seat and put her arm around her friend. "Please don't, darling. Please don't."

"I tell you, I'm about ready to go to Edinburgh myself. I want to demand an accounting from Harlow! How dare he keep me in suspense this way? How dare he?"

Aunt Whitsun handed Sarah the cut glass vial. "Here, apply this to her nose. She's quite hysterical. What is all this?"

Sarah did as she was told. Harmonia coughed, gasping, and pushed her friend's hand away. "That's awful. What is it?" she said, spluttering.

"Never mind, Aunt. Harmonia's a trifle overset. Her fiancé has not written to her recently."

"Recently!" Harmonia protested. "Not at all!"

"But he will," Sarah reassured her. "And if he hasn't, I'll go to Scotland with you. What do you think of that? Now, don't worry about it anymore."

"I had no notion the girl was brooding about this fellow. Does her father know she's been treated in this way?"

"I haven't told anybody but Sarah. I . . . I apologize for my outburst, Mrs. Whitsun. It just . . ." Harmonia put her hand to the bosom of her drab wool pelisse. "Something seemed to explode here."

"Too much lobster last night, no doubt. You'll take a dose when we come home."

The best medicine would have been some message from Mr. Atwood. But there was nothing for Harmonia, except a letter from Lady Phelps. Sarah did not know how to help her friend, except by staying near to her in case she needed a sympathetic listener. After a day of this, however, Harmonia turned to Sarah and said, "Oh, for goodness' sake! I'm not so addled I'll jump out the window if you're not watching me. There's nothing I can do to make him write, and at the moment I'm so furious with him I don't care if he never does. But you don't need to hang on my skirts. Go out. Change that library book, visit the shops, go riding."

"What will you do?"

"I don't know. Write Mother. Or I've been meaning to see about making over that blue dress. But you ought to get out of the house. You've looked peaky ever since we came back from the duchess'."

"If you're certain. . . . Russet does need exercise."

"Then drop a note to the groom. I'll be right as a trivet; never mind about me. I need to occupy my mind. Maybe I'll change that book. What do you wager they still won't have a copy of *The Curse of Kehama* yet?"

Feeling somewhat less guilty at leaving her friend, Sarah scribbled a note to her aunt's groom to bring her mare around, and then went to change into her habit. Running outside half an hour later, Sarah stopped on the step. Instead of the hulking figure of her aunt's groom, Hannay, there was a small, greying man holding her horse's and another's bridle. "Good mornin' to you, Miss."

Sarah peered at the man. "Mr. Packer, isn't it?"

"Yes, miss. At yer service." He grinned, showing a gap on one side. His smile was shyly engaging despite the flaw.

"But you work for Lord Reyne, now. Or have you been discharged?"

"Oh, no, miss. I like it there, I do. Me an' Barton talk over old times in the evenin' when I'm polishin' up a bit of leather. The beer's right regular."

"Then what are you doing here?"

The small man scuffed his boot along the cobbled street and a flush of embarrassment came up on his thin cheeks. "It's loike this, miss. You done me a good turn, an' I try to pay back. That feller yer aunt's got workin' in the stables ain't no good. He drinks, don't he?"

"Does he?"

"Yerss. An' it's a shame. A nice ol' lady like this ought get her meals regular and not be stinted on the oats." He rubbed the mare's velvet nose, and Russet held her head still as if she enjoyed it.

"Thank you. It's very good of you." She walked down to the street and Packer helped her mount, quite as if he'd never pointed a pistol at her in his life.

With an instinct she'd not known she possessed, Sarah did not tell Packer she'd inform her aunt about Hannay's inadequacies. It would make Mr. Packer feel badly if his information lost another man his job, though he must have known that would be the outcome. For the first time, Sarah became consciously aware that sometimes it felt better not to acknowledge what was perfectly plain.

She realized she'd been doing this herself for quite some

time. If she once let herself think about the fact that Lord Reyne obviously felt no love for Miss Canfield, liking being something quite different, it would become impossible to keep from throwing her arms about his neck whenever he came near. She found it difficult enough to constrain her feelings as matters stood.

Mr. Packer behaved in every regard as the perfect groom during Sarah's ride. Though he never permitted her to leave his sight, he kept up so beautifully she hardly knew he was there. It was only on their return to Mrs. Whitsun's house that he once more dropped into his own personality. "There, miss, and 'ow was that?"

"Heavenly, Mr. Packer."

"I know the horse liked it. Didn't you, old lady?" He helped Sarah down. "Now, about this feller . . ."

"Hannay?"

He shook his head. "This other feller. The one what'as been 'anging h'about the square. All white-faced 'e is. Skinned to the nubbins, near enough. 'Orrible-lookin'. I run 'im off myself a couple times, but you just tell yer butler to look out sharpish for 'im. An' if 'e comes h'around, t' call the watch or send for me and my mates."

Sarah would have questioned Packer more about this mysterious person, who sounded rather like a character from one of Harmonia's favorite type of stories, but Mrs. Whitsun opened the drawing room window and said, "Sarah! Come in at once."

"Thank you, Mr. Packer," Sarah said, turning to go.

"A pleasure, miss."

"Really, Sarah!" Mrs. Whitsun said, as soon as her greatniece entered. "Bandying words with a common groom in the street! Will you never grow sense?" She slit open a letter with her long paper-knife. "Another appeal from charity! Do these people think we are made of money?"

Even when Sarah told her aunt about the groom, Mrs. Whitsun pooh-poohed it. "Hannay has been with me for years. I'm not about to take the words of some stranger about him. And as for this loiterer, no doubt he and this groom are in collusion. I shall tell the servants to be on guard against *all* strange persons." She shook open the next letter. "Oh, dear. Mrs. Lampert won't be able to come to supper. The catarrh again. Remind me to send her some jelly. Go and change, dear thing. You reek of horses.''

As Sarah opened the double doors to go out, she heard her aunt give a vexed exclamation. ''What is it? Is something the matter?''

''It's really too bad. You might as well know what consequences your actions have, Sarah. If you hadn't made such a cake of yourself over Lord Reyne at Amabelle's, we'd be able to attend this party at Miss Canfield's. Last year, her soiree was the hit of the Season. And you have that charming Aetherial blue crepe that would have been so suitable.''

''But, surely, if Miss Canfield isn't scandalized by my actions . . . after all, Lord Reyne is her betrothed. . . .''

''Oh, she'd be putting a good face on it. I've known girls who'd throw a man over for that sort of behavior. Dancing with another the moment she'd retired! Men did not do that sort of thing when I was presented. You should have refused him, Sarah.''

Sarah wanted to protest that she'd not known what she was doing that mad May Eve, but it would have been a lie. ''Perhaps . . .'' she said slowly, ''perhaps Miss Canfield is wise to invite us. If we went, that might stop all this gossip, for it would show we are still friends.''

''Well, it's certainly the only *new* invitation we've received today. Have you assurance enough to face all those people?''

Though she pretended not to hear, a little voice whispered that Lord Reyne would certainly be at an evening party given by his betrothed. That, naturally, was no factor in her decision. ''Of course, I do.''

She needed all the confidence she could muster or the gold-trimmed chemise robe could lend. Entering the pink-and-cream ballroom was daunting enough to make her face pale, for every head swiveled to observe her. She'd grown used, during these weeks in London, to being looked at, but always before she could feel the approval in the air. Now, the faces frowned and voices whispered behind raised fans. Sarah knew that every pair of eyes, aided and unaided, watched as she approached Lillian Canfield. Harmonia, guided by Mrs. Whitsun's hand on her arm, fell back to let Sarah go on alone.

Her garlanded head held high, Sarah waited for Miss Canfield to notice her.

"Miss East!" her hostess said, holding out both hands with a warmth more vibrant than that offered to her other guests. "I'm so very happy you could come. What a charming gown! And you must show me that style of hair. So pretty! Come, you must meet all my friends. Alaric isn't come yet. He's bound to be late; he always is."

Sarah blushed then, at the kind greeting. The pressure of all those gazes suddenly seemed an intolerable burden. If Lillian had not been so determined to make Sarah known to her friends, Sarah might have committed the error of apologizing for her mistake in dancing with Miss Canfield's husband-to-be. She realized just in time, however, that by continuing to be stubbornly unaware that any solecism had been committed, Lillian Canfield could avoid the worse burden of the pity of all her large acquaintance.

Lord Reyne arrived before eleven o'clock. Despite the crowd of people, for Miss Canfield's ball was to be given that highest accolade, "a sad crush," Sarah knew the moment he entered. She faced her partner a little more squarely and spoke to him a trifle more gaily than she had a moment before. So emboldened was he by her increased interest that he dared ask her for a third dance. Sarah was on the point of agreeing, though she knew she'd find herself in further trouble with her aunt, when a male cough sounded at her elbow.

"Miss East, I believe this is our dance," Lord Reyne said.

"Is it, sir? I don't believe so." Mrs. Whitsun had warned her that any expression other than polite boredom would be taken to mean she was eating her heart out for him. "If he's fool enough to notice you," her aunt had said, "don't compound his folly by encouraging his attentions. Be cold, be distant, be uninterested."

Lord Reyne did not seem taken aback by her impoliteness. With a second bow, he said, "I am but obeying the orders of our hostess."

"In that case, I cannot refuse you." She curtsied to her former partner. Touching his arm as little as she could, Sarah strolled off with Lord Reyne.

"I don't know, Miss East. This floor appears rather slick. Perhaps I should abrade the soles of your shoes so you do not slip.'' He smiled down on her, and Sarah felt her heart give an impetuous bound. She sternly called it to heel.

''I don't think that will be necessary.'' The music began. A country dance, thank God, she thought. To be held by him after their temporary madness would be more than she could have stood.

As their fingertips touched in passing, he said, ''I'm sorry I have no orange to offer you.''

''Do you want oranges? There are some by the refreshments.''

''Ah, but they are too ripe for cricket.''

''I suppose they must be.'' Sarah chewed the inside of her cheek to keep from smiling back. If only Aunt Whitsun had told her *how* to behave with the necessary aloofness. Try as she might to make her eyes hard and cold, Sarah greatly feared their expression told more of her feelings than her unsmiling lips.

Though the first dance of the set kept them apart, the second made the exchange of confidence easy. Though not a waltz, the dance involved a good deal of touching and standing by with arms entwined while other couples sashayed down the line.

''Miss East . . . Sarah, how have I offended you?'' His voice was intense, sending a shiver of response down the back of her neck.

''You have not.''

''Obviously, there's something I've done to hurt you. Please believe my intentions were never . . .''

''Our turn,'' she said, and smiled brightly while passing beneath the linked arms of the other couples, swinging in and out with Lord Reyne. Though she met the eyes of strangers, she felt nothing save his fingers locked with hers. So soon they'd slip away for ever. She couldn't remember how the dance ended, only that he never again used that particular tone when speaking to her.

Then it was done, and Mrs. Whitsun was nodding approval from across the room. Sarah went to stand beside her aunt, feeling more drained than after an entire day in the summer sun. She sipped from a cold glass as someone called for silence. With the rest, Sarah turned to see what was happening.

''Friends,'' Mr. Canfield said, raising his arms in his tight coat like a successful prize-fighter. ''I'm a lucky man tonight.

I've been told the one thing I've been longing to hear, and that is that my girl will be married before the end of August!''

"How vulgar!" Mrs. Whitsun whispered, though she joined in the gasp of surprise and the polite applause that greeted this unusual announcement. The snap of the breaking stem of Sarah's glass went unheard amidst the noise.

"Now, then, lift up your glasses and drink to the happy couple." Mr. Canfield took his daughter's right hand, joining it forcefully with Lord Reyne's left. There was some laughter at the expressions of surprise on the happy couple's faces. The toast was drunk willingly, the wilder spirits calling out jests.

"I have the headache," Sarah said, bending to whisper beneath the edge of her aunt's silver turban.

"What? Don't be ridiculous."

"I'm going to send for the carriage and go home. I'll give orders the driver is to return at once. Don't disturb yourself, Aunt."

Mrs. Whitsun stood up, gripping Sarah's arm strongly. Though she smiled and kept her voice low, the outrage in her tone came through clearly. "Don't you understand anything, you silly fool? If you go home now, after that announcement, don't you know what people will think? They'll think you're heartbroken, going home to cry because you can't face the fact that he's marrying another. If you go home now, you daren't show your face to the *ton* again. Then what good will your beauty do you?"

Sarah freed her arm, not roughly or with strength, but as easily as if no bond existed. "Let them think what they like," she said, without lowering her voice. "It's true, anyway."

She had to stand for some little time in the marble-lined entrance, as Mrs. Whitsun's carriage was lost behind a myriad of others. If anyone looked upon her, Sarah was not aware of it. At last, the carriage came. After pulling across the curtains, she sat with her head in her hands. Her fingers felt comfortingly cool over her hot eyes. She did not cry, not yet.

A few sentences to the yawning butler explained the ostensible excuse for her early return. Dismissing her aunt's maid, Sarah removed her clothes and clambered into an old nightdress, not fine like her others but darned by her mother's loving hands. Getting into bed, Sarah sat up, looking at the mountains and valleys of the rumpled white blanket.

As squarely as she could, Sarah faced facts. There'd never really been any grounds for hope. Alaric had been betrothed before he'd ever met her. If he did not love Miss Canfield, how much less likely it was that he should ever love her.

Sarah decided she never would marry now. Her great-aunt's lessons, carefully instilled, had as their main point the fact that any girl who transgressed the rules of society would have no chance at marriage. It had been Sarah's responsibility to find herself a suitable husband during this sojourn in London. She'd failed, not through lack of beauty, charm, or dowry, but by daydreaming over someone who could never be hers. Even if she'd not ruined all further opportunities by her bad behavior, Sarah could not stomach the idea of finding another man. The whole process of charming a stranger left her feeling completely exhausted.

A clattering as of rain outside her window reminded her of the lateness of the hour. She slid beneath the covers, leaving only her forehead exposed. Once the rain began in earnest, she promised herself a good cry. The noise of the downpour would hide any sobs she would make, and then she'd not have to explain her mood to Harmonia, who had enough troubles of her own.

The rattle at the windowpane repeated, and Sarah came upright. That did not sound like rain. It sounded like . . . She recalled the frequent summons of gravel against the glass. If she opened the window, would she find herself in a dream of Harold and Harcourt, and the laughing days of long-ago?

Sarah turned the brass handle and leaned out over the sill. In the street below, a man stood, half-illuminated by the flickering lantern light. A long cloak muffled his figure. Seeing her, he raised up on tiptoe and waved something white at her. It did not flutter like a handkerchief. It was square and stiff like a sealed letter. "Harmonia?" he called. "It is I. Harlow."

"Mr. Atwood? What in the . . . ? Stay there; I'll be down directly."

— 12 —

Cautioning him to be silent, Sarah led Mr. Atwood through the hall to Mrs. Whitsun's morning room, their path lit only by the candlestick she'd picked up from the console table. The breeze through a window, opened a scant inch, set the flame to flickering. The huge shadows cast on the grey-blue wall behind them bowed and swayed as if in an evil dance. The color, chosen to flatter an aging complexion, did nothing to improve Mr. Atwood's sallow face. After putting down the candlestick, Sarah shut the heavy door. "We can talk now," she said.

"You're . . . you're looking very well, Miss East."

"Thank you, Mr. Atwood. Aren't you supposed to be in Scotland?"

The man's prominent Adam's apple rose and fell in his skinny neck as he gulped. He cast a glance over his shoulder, as though expecting to see pursuers. "Yes, yes, I am."

"Harmonia's been quite worried about you. You do remember Harmonia? Your affianced wife?"

"Yes, of course, I do. How is she?" He seemed to realize his curiosity was not as lover-like as it should be. "I've been thinking of her rather a lot just lately. I wonder if you would mind giving her this?"

Sarah took a grubby paper from his hand. It looked as if it had been much handled. "What is in this letter, Mr. Atwood?"

"Uh, it's . . . that is . . ." Fixing him with a steady eye, Sarah repeated her question. Harlow Atwood crumpled. "It's an apology."

"For not having written?"

"For marrying someone else."

"What?" His muttered words were so low, Sarah could not be certain of their sense.

Mr. Atwood shushed her, patting the air with his hands.

"I've snuck out," he said. "If Lucy finds I've gone, especially to come here, I'll never hear the end of it."

"Why should she find out?"

"You don't know Lucy. This is the first place she'll look. She's always been jealous of Harmonia, seeing as Lucy's so much older. Er . . . Harmonia's not here, I take it?"

"No, but she'll be back in less than two hours."

"Oh, good. I needn't see her, then. You give her that letter, Miss East. It will explain it all."

"It cannot explain away her humiliation and pain, sir," she said, flicking it indignantly onto a table. Sarah's face was red for her friend's sake. It burned all the more brightly because she suddenly understood what Miss Canfield's position would have been if Lord Reyne had left her for another.

"Well," Mr. Atwood said, after a long pause. "I'd better be going along. Lucy, you know."

"I insist that you stay to see Harmonia." Sarah advanced on him. "To leave now would be an act of cowardice."

The gangling fellow raised his shoulders in a continental shrug. "You don't know Lucy."

"I have no wish to know a woman who would steal another's affianced husband. Didn't you tell her about Harmonia?"

Still backing up, headed by a poltroon's sure instinct for the front door, Mr. Atwood said, "I made every effort, but she never seemed to want to listen. I had no choice but to marry her, Miss East, once that incident in her room came out. She promised me she'd not tell a soul, but the next thing I knew, I was standing up in the kirk . . . er . . . church. You'll tell Harmonia that, won't you?"

"I think you've behaved abominably, Mr. Atwood. If Harmonia's brothers were here, they'd take a horsewhip to you!" Feeling a strange breeze, Sarah looked around to find that she stood in the street. Glancing up at the windows that reflected the street lamp, she realized, after a moment's alarm, that they were still unobserved, save by a distant figure striding towards them at the end of the street. "You are not a gentleman, sir. I'm happy Harmonia isn't at home to learn of your perfidy."

Mr. Atwood also seemed to discover that his escape path lay open. "I'm sorry you feel that way, Miss East. I know Lucy would have liked to meet you. Good-bye.'' Off he darted on his long legs, only to collide with the sole other person in the street.

"Aha!" said a familiar voice as strong hands caught hold of Mr. Atwood by the slack of his coat.

"I say, Reyne, old man, let me go! There's a good fellow.'' Mr. Atwood pleaded, twisting and turning in the peer's grasp.

Sarah was dumbstruck. She felt she'd not only forgotten how to speak but that even the ability for conscious thought had departed. Lord Reyne seemed so much bigger than usual, like an avenging spirit, that she wanted to fall at his feet, but she could not move.

"I suppose you were just arriving?" Alaric demanded. "All the more shameful if you are going. Miss East, have you no moral sense whatever? Receiving gentlemen in the middle of the night and in your nightclothes!"

"He . . . he isn't in my nightclothes. . . ." she said in a tiny, ridiculous voice.

Alaric only turned on her a look of scorn before giving his attention once more to the interloper between his hands. "Be gone, sir, before I call the servants to thrash you. No, by God, who needs them?" Loosening his shoulders in the tight black coat, he hurled Mr. Atwood away as lightly as if he was an old, dried-out branch.

Landing with his arms and legs curled up, like a spider cut loose from a web, Mr. Atwood scrambled to his feet. "Remember to give it to Harmonia!" he said as he turned to run away. He tripped over a loose cobble and sprawled like a beached starfish for a moment before finding his footing again. A brief whizzing noise and the street was empty save for Sarah and a furious Alaric.

"That was Mr. Atwood," Sarah said, still softly.

"So, not content with carrying on illicitly with a man, you betray your dearest friend? Did that add more spice to the proceedings?"

It was absurd to think, at this moment, of his arms about her, foolish to wish that he might embrace her again, only this time without pausing to remember all the reasons he should not. But when Alaric did nothing beyond glaring at her from across the street, a new sensation began to bubble up inside her. It burgeoned and grew: a mood very different from what she was accustomed to feeling in his presence.

"I think . . . I think I ought to be insulted. What are you doing here, Lord Reyne, anyway?"

His angry color had ebbed, only to be replaced by a sudden flood of abashed red. "I happened to be passing by, that's all."

"Passing by? But Miss Canfield said you lived at the other end of town. Besides, I thought you'd still be at the Canfields', making arrangements for your wedding."

"And so I should be, if I had any sense. Miss East, go into the house before you catch your death."

"I will!" In slippered feet, Sarah trotted up the steps, preparing to slam her way into the house and never give Lord Reyne a backward glance. But, putting her hand to the brass knob in the center of the door, she found it would not turn! She tried it again, a frustrated moan escaping her lips.

"Go on," Alaric said from the street.

"Don't you think I want to?" she asked, glaring at him with hot eyes. "It's locked. Someone locked it."

He stepped up to stand beside her, and Sarah pulled her dressing gown more tightly around her. Impatiently, Alaric raised his fist to knock on the door. Sarah put her hand on his arm. "Don't. If the butler tells my aunt about this, she'll think I've lost my mind."

"So, you're not entirely dead to propriety."

"I don't know what you mean. Mr. Atwood simply stopped in to give me a letter for Harmonia."

"Where is it?"

"I beg your pardon?"

"If you expect me to believe that highly unlikely story, I want to see this so-called letter."

Sarah plunged her hand into the patch pocket of her robe. "Here it is and . . . oh. I left it in the house."

"As I thought."

"Besides, it's Harmonia's. You couldn't read it, even if I had it with me. That wouldn't be right."

"Kindly keep off irrelevant side issues, if you can."

"It's not I who can't keep my mind on the business at hand. However am I to get in again?" She looked at the shiny white door with anger sparking in her grey eyes. As if she'd not taken about all the abuse she could for one night!

He searched the front of the house. "Could there be an open window somewhere?"

"There shouldn't be. My aunt is severe on the idea of burglary. All the servants have been warned."

"What about that one?" He pointed to the tiny opening at the base of one of the morning room windows. The marble sill was perhaps eight or nine feet above the street, set in the brick wall. Though the closest window to the door, it was too far away to be reached even from the top step.

Taking Sarah roughly by the arm, he led her to stand beneath it. "If I lift you up, can you open that window and climb in?"

"Of course I could. But there's another . . ."

"Be quiet, Miss East. I'll do you this favor, but then our association is at an end. I have been grossly deceived in your nature and have no wish to continue our acquaintance."

Wishing she could kick him in revenge for his odious tone of superiority, Sarah stamped her foot, a mistake as her slippers were thin. Through a sudden tide of tears, which she put down to the pain in her foot, Sarah glowered at him and replied, "That pleases me above all things, my lord."

Meeting her gaze, Alaric regretted the strange impulse that had sent him walking home from the Canfields' soiree. He seriously resented Mr. Canfield's presumption in announcing an undiscussed wedding date, and had hardly stayed long enough to hear the first congratulations. His thoughts dwelling on the unpleasant situation Mr. Canfield had forced upon Lillian and himself, Alaric did not think of the path his feet were taking until he looked up and saw Sarah East letting a strange man out of her great-aunt's house.

"What does this supposed letter say? Did he tell you that?"

"It explains why he cannot marry Harmonia. Are you going to lift me up, or are we to stand here until the watch comes round?"

In answer, he turned her so her back was to him. His hands squeezed against the quilting over her rib cage, but it was not this pressure that made her breath come short. Sternly, Sarah took herself to task for responding even inwardly to his touch. He'd made his attitude toward her beautifully clear. She was, in his eyes, low and contemptible.

"Go on," she said, bracing her hands on his.

He lifted her as though she were of no weight, without jerks or panting effort. Sarah reached out. Though she struggled, she could not quite manage to lift the window. It slid upwards a scant inch and stuck. Sarah gritted her teeth and tried again, to no avail. She'd slid down between his hands and his strength began to hurt her. "Put me down," she gasped.

Standing, she bent this way and that to try and ease her sides, which felt as if they'd collapsed. "You didn't have to hold me so hard."

His face was heated from his exertions. "You would have rather I dropped you? Move aside; I'll do it." He put her out of the way with one hand.

Sarah watched as he stretched upwards to attempt to reach the window. Even in her exasperation, she could not but recall the glimpses she'd had of his person under other circumstances. She could imagine the flexing of his muscles and the rippling play of his skin as he reached up. Though the lateness of the hour had brought a chill with it, Sarah felt too warm.

With the intention of irritating him, she said, "Shall I fetch you a footstool from across the street? That window's a good two feet higher than you can reach. Do you want to pick me up again?" She hoped he'd refuse, yet her heart sank when he did.

"No, that's worse than useless. I'm afraid you'll just have to face your butler."

"Are you willing to listen to my alternative? After all, it won't look very good for you either, me in my nightclothes, as you pointed out."

"Very well. What brilliant scheme have you?"

Sarah explained.

"That's won't work. He's bound to suspect something. People don't call at half-past eleven."

"Yes, but a mere butler isn't very likely to question the Earl of Reyne, is he? Just be haughty and look down your nose. That's right, like that."

His scowl darkened. "Why can't Atwood marry Harmonia?"

"What? Oh, are you still harping on that! He can't marry her because he married a woman named Lucy while in Scotland! I don't think he wanted to. It sounded as if her father made him do it."

"That's preposterous. What any woman could find attractive about Atwood is beyond me. Yet you seem to expect me to believe that armies of girls are hurling themselves at him every minute of the day and night.''

''I expect you to believe nothing but the truth!''

''Keep your voice down, Miss East, or not all your subterfuge will serve you. Hide in the shadows by the steps, and I thank God this is the last scrape I ever need rescue you from.'' With that, he stomped up the steps, his broad shoulders squared.

His knock at the locked door sounded like the hooves of the Four Horsemen. When the portal did not instantly open, he thundered at it again. At last, Mrs. Whitsun's butler appeared. ''My lord Reyne? What is it?'' he inquired tremulously. ''Has there been an accident?''

''Not yet,'' Alaric replied grimly. ''I'll wait for your mistress in here.'' He pushed by the elderly servant with more discourtesy than Sarah had ever seen him use. The butler looked heavenward as though asking for help to deal with the humors of hasty young bucks and slowly closed the door. Sarah listened anxiously, but did not hear the snap of bolts being thrown. From the morning room, she heard Alaric say, ''Come in here and light more candles. It's dark as a funeral.''

''Very good, my lord.''

Sarah pushed open the door. She took the stairs two at a time and in a moment was safely on the landing. After one moment to kick off her slippers, she was in bed with the covers pulled right up. Then, she had a ghastly thought.

Without pausing to reclaim her footwear, Sarah dashed down the stairs and burst into the morning room in the nick of time! Alaric had already Mr. Atwood's letter in his hand, peering at the red blob of wax with which it was sealed.

''Give me that!'' Sarah demanded, approaching with her hand held out. When he hesitated, she snatched it from him and jammed it into the bodice of her robe. Defiantly, she crossed her arms.

''Sarah,'' he said, a frown drawing his brows down over his eyes. He dared not look down, for the sight of her bare pink toes caused a strange constriction in his heart.

''You should not call me that, not if you think what you have been thinking about me.''

''Let me see that letter.''

''No. It should be seen by Harmonia before anyone else.

It . . . it's going to break her heart, and it's not fair that anyone else should see it first."

"I demand to see it!"

"Sssh!" Sarah waved her hand at him for silence and turned her head to listen. If the butler heard that shout . . . A quick flick against her breastbone and the letter was once more in Alaric's hand. She jumped for it, but he held it over his head. "Return that at once!"

"Don't you see that I have to open it, Sarah? Otherwise, how am I ever—" Alaric damned himself for the faint note of supplication that had entered his tone. Why in the world should it matter to him if the girl before him had a thousand lovers or none? Only, it did matter.

Through the open window came the clatter of hooves and the rumbling of wheels on a cobbled surface. In the face of this new danger, Sarah and Alaric instinctively moved closer together. They heard the coachman say, "Ha!" as the equipage halted outside the townhouse. "Oh, heavens," Sarah whispered. "My aunt!"

A fresh awareness of her costume and the invidiousness of his position came to Alaric. With a half-bow, he returned the letter to Sarah. "I am, of course, compelled to accept your account of what I saw this evening, Miss East. Nevertheless, I am confirmed in my opinion that it is better we do not meet again." He hated sounding like his own grandfather, but he felt safest from her charms in the refuge of pomposity.

Sarah, with a pang, knew that tone meant he had retreated from her and had once more become the correct English gentleman. She feared indeed that she'd never again meet the merry friend she'd sometimes glimpsed behind that facade. Looking at him now, it was hard to believe she'd ever been the cause of even one of his smiles. "As you wish, Lord Reyne. I think you'd better leave by that window, if you can get it open."

Behind her, she could hear the whispers of the butler. "Lord Reyne?" Mrs. Whitsun exclaimed. "At this hour? You must have been asleep and dreaming."

Sliding his fingers under the frame, so slightly ajar, Alaric brought his hands up. The window squeaked, resisting. He glanced over his shoulder at Sarah and exerted one more ounce of effort. The knob of the morning room door was turning.

Sarah turned a white face toward the window. Only the movement of the curtains betrayed his departure.

Instantly, Sarah flung herself into her aunt's own armchair. Snatching up the second volume of a novel, Sarah opened it so fast the spine cracked. She hadn't time to bring the candle closer but was apparently so deeply engrossed that she'd not noticed the lack of light. She started to hear Mrs. Whitsun say, "Still up, dear thing? Good. You should hear how we were forced to come home at this hour. Snubbed by all and sundry. Your flight did not go unnoticed. Oh, no, it did not."

"Where's Harmonia?" Sarah asked.

"I've sent her up to bed. She shouldn't hear the peal I'm going to ring over you. Why are you barefooted? Now, Sarah, I think—"

"Yes, Aunt. In a moment. First, I must talk to Harmonia. You'd better come, too. She may need you."

Harmonia poked her head around the door just in time to hear this last. "Why will I need her?"

"Because . . . because Mr. Atwood was here."

"Harlow?" With a brightened face, Harmonia stepped into the room, looking around for the visitor.

"I'm sorry; he's gone."

"Gone?"

Sarah came over to her friend and put her arm around her. "He left this letter for you. I don't know what he wrote, but he told me why he has not communicated with you before this."

Harmonia took the letter in hands that shook. Casting a look at Sarah's face, she said quaveringly, "Is it ill news?"

"I'm afraid it is. He's . . . he's no longer free."

Mrs. Whitsun strode past them. "I'll make tea."

Shrugging off Sarah's restraining arm, Harmonia walked to the candle. In a single motion, she broke the seal and shook out the page. Sarah could see that there was no more than a single, closely written paragraph. Harmonia read it over twice, and then once more. She sighed. Holding the page to the candle, she waited until one corner was alight. Carefully, she carried it across the room and dropped it onto the cold grate. She stretched out one hand to the cold marble mantel. In a moment, the message was ash.

"What . . . what did it say, Harmonia?"

"Just what you said. I'd wager his wife wrote it for him, as

it did not sound like Harlow at all. There was only one apology
in it." Her voice seemed to hold a laugh. Then, she dropped
her head onto her arm and began to cry.

"Oh, please don't," Sarah said, starting impulsively toward
her. "He's not worth it, you know, not in the least."

Harmonia raised her head to look, with reddened eyes, at her
friend. "Oh, you wouldn't know. You've never been in love."

"No, I haven't," she said forlornly.

"Sarah!" Harmonia forgot her own heartache in the sheer
amazement of the discovery. "Who is it?"

"I don't know what you mean. Do you want to know what
Mr. Atwood said to me?"

"Later. Who is it? Lord Morebinder? Sir What's-his-name
Boneview? That other fellow—the one who's Harvey's
friend . . . ?"

"Harmonia, I think you're overwrought. Where's Aunt
Whitsun with the tea?" Who knew but that Harmonia might
guess that it was Lord Reyne she loved? Despite his coldness
toward her during their dreadful last adventure, Sarah knew she
still loved him. At least, there were a few happy memories to
cling to in the lonesome days ahead. Lost in a reverie of the
past, Sarah did not heed her friend until Harmonia shook her.

"Sarah Marissa Clivenden East, if you don't tell me who it
is you've fallen in love with, our friendship is at an end."

"Oh, please don't say that. If you knew who else said that
tonight . . . and I'm afraid he meant it."

"Who? Who?"

"Oh," Sarah sighed, and said from the depths of her heart,
"I wish Mother were here."

"Then I'm glad I've come," Mrs. East said.

Sarah spun about to see the soft figure of her mother, still
cloaked and bonneted, standing in the doorway with her arms
outstretched. "Mother?" Sarah said, unable to believe the
miracle. She dashed across the room, to bend her head down to
rest on her mother's shoulder and put her arms about Mrs.
East's waist. Only then did she realize her prayer had been
answered. "Oh, Mother, things are in such a muddle! How I
wanted you to talk to!"

"Did you, sweetheart? Sometimes all my children seem so
grown-up that it's lovely to find I'm wanted, still," Mrs. East
said, looking down into her child's face, wrung by the misery

she saw there. She smiled and blinked eyes in which tender tears threatened to spill over her red cheeks. Mother and daughter clung together.

Then Sarah, shaking the long hair out of her eyes, said, "Mother . . . poor Harmonia . . . could you . . . her own mother is so far away."

Mrs. East untied her bonnet and put it in Sarah's hands. "There, there, Harmonia. What's the difficulty?" She reached up to kiss Harmonia's cheek. "Your mother's charged me with so many messages for you, I hardly know where to start! Wait until I tell her how fine you look in your ball gown. That pink is so lovely with your hair and eyes. Have you been crying, child?"

The story of Mr. Atwood's defection came pouring out. Mrs. East held the sobbing girl, her face as hard as Sarah had ever seen it. She said, "I think he must be a very foolish young man to pass you over for anyone. But come, you mustn't cry anymore. I've been telling Mortimer what a beauty you've turned out. He doesn't believe me."

"Me? A beauty? Mortimer?"

"Mother!" Sarah said. "Is Mortimer home?"

"Home? He's here!" Mrs. East noted with satisfaction that Harmonia began at once to hunt for her handkerchief and wished that there were time to send the girl upstairs for a splash of cool water and the touch of a comb. But already the sound of rolling steps was heard in the hall.

"Mortimer!" Sarah shrieked as she was tossed up in the arms of her eldest brother. Young Commander East stood at least six feet tall and, in his blue-and-white uniform, looked six feet wide as well.

"Children, children. My bonnet."

"Here you are, Mother," Mortimer said, taking it from his sister and tossing it lightly on a chair. He dropped Sarah to her feet and kissed her cheek.

"You've been promoted again?" she asked, admiring the shiny new epaulet decorating his left shoulder.

"Last month."

"Good, then Sam is certain to receive a promotion in the next six months."

"Sooner than that, I'd water. I can't tell you where the lucky dog's been sent—I saw him two weeks ago off Brest—but he's bound to come back an admiral at least. Don't worry, though, Mother. There's no danger in it.''

"Of course not," Mrs. East agreed bravely, though she knew that promotions appeared most quickly when battles removed the senior officers. "Mortimer, you remember Miss Phelps, I know."

The family grey eyes looked very bright in the tanned face of the naval gentleman as he directed a single glance toward the wan figure by the cold fireplace. "Miss Phelps," he said, bowing. "I say, Sarah, it's not too late to find something to eat, is it? Mother wouldn't stop on the road, and I'm ravenous. Even a week of home cooking isn't enough when all you've had is hard tack and boiled beef for six months."

"I should say not. I'll show you to the kitchen."

Once there, Mortimer set about charming the sleepy cook, already summoned by Mrs. Whitsun to make tea. After a wink and a further description of naval-style meals, the plump woman stirred and chopped with a good will. Sitting on the table, kicking his long legs, Mortimer said, "Was that Harmonia Phelps in truth, or was Mother making a game of me? I can't believe it."

"Because she's changed so much?"

"Because she hasn't changed at all. She was crying when I left, and she's crying now. Did she weep all of the last four and a half years, or am I always going to make her cry?"

"Did you make her cry when you went away?"

"Yes, I suppose it was my fault, in a way. Of course, I didn't know she felt that way about me. How could I? She ran like a frightened hare every time I looked her way. Besides, she resembled a baby porpoise at fourteen," he said, as his voice dropped away to a wondering murmur.

Two hours later, after the uproar of accommodating two more persons at one o'clock in the morning, Sarah and Harmonia were once more preparing for bed. "Why didn't you tell me you formed an attachment to Mortimer when he was home last?"

"I hadn't. Where did you get that notion?"

"He told me."

Harmonia dropped her hairbrush. "Don't tell me *he* knew? Oh, goodness, I had hoped no one knew."

"Then it's true?"

"Sarah, I do believe that I'm the most fortunate girl alive today."

Thinking that the strain of the evening had been too much for the balance of Harmonia's mind, Sarah said, "I don't understand. Mr. Atwood . . ."

With a new radiance shining in her eyes, Harmonia came to sit beside Sarah on the white counterpane. Half-laughing, she said, "What a narrow escape I've had. Imagine if I were still betrothed to Mr. Atwood, or worse. What if I'd married him already and then Mortimer came home? Oh, when he came into the room, I felt as if my heart would bound right through my side."

"Mortimer?"

"Sarah, you've got to help me. When he went away before, I thought I'd die. I was fourteen; of course it was hopeless. But I'm nearly nineteen now. If he'd only . . . I suppose it's impossible. He's so wonderful. There must be a hundred . . ."

"What's impossible?" Sarah asked, taking both her friend's hands. "You'll be his bride if I have to tie him up. I promised you any man you wanted, remember?" Between giggles and plans, not unmixed with sighs, neither girl slept much before dawn.

13

"Would you care for more haddock, Mortimer?" Harmonia said, bending over him as she filled his cup with tea.

"Yes, thank you." Commander East swallowed what he was chewing. "Are there any more of these little buns?"

"I'll ask for some." Harmonia smiled down on the young officer's sunny hair. "It will only take a moment, I'm sure."

Sarah and her mother exchanged a swift glance, complete with raised eyebrows, over the bowl of flowers that decorated the white-swathed table. Inclining her head a trifle, Sarah saw a happy, if incredulous, smile lift Mrs. East's cheeks. Sarah couldn't help but smile weakly in return, though her head ached and tears would keep forming in her eyes. Every thought had as companion a whispered "Alaric will never . . ." or "I shall never . . ." Though she smiled with her mother, she thought, Mother will never smile like that for me, because she'll never meet Alaric again in my company.

"What are you children going to do today?" Mrs. East asked.

Mortimer looked up from his plate. "I must see about having new uniforms made up. Mine are threadbare after all these months at sea. And the coat I had made in Majorca simply won't do in London, although it's good enough for duty."

"I know Harvey would be delighted to take you to his tailor," Harmonia volunteered.

"Is old Harvey in town? I'll send a note to him at once, if you can furnish his direction."

"I'll get it for you now," Harmonia said, starting up from her chair.

"It can wait until after you've eaten," Mortimer replied, waving his hand in a lordly fashion. Harmonia subsided into her seat, a faint blush rising into her face. She did not continue with her meal, but leaned her head on her hand, elbow on the table, and gazed at the handsome officer.

"I'll give myself today to be with you, Sarah," he said. "Then, I'm afraid I must begin to haunt the Admiralty. I must find another ship as quickly as I can. Half-pay's a misery."

"Oh, but you mustn't spend all day at your tailor," Harmonia said, as though it were a dreadful injustice even to think of such a thing. "Sarah, which of the 'lions' did we enjoy the most? The panorama in Castle Street or the Waxworks? We could go to Saint James Palace, if it hadn't been for the fire. But Kensington Palace is open today. Let's go there! That is, if you'd like it, Mortimer."

"Don't be ridiculous, Miss Phelps," Aunt Whitsun said, speaking for the first time. Except for a disapproving flick of her eyes when Sarah had entered, she'd sat at the head of the table steadily eating her meal. "A man newly home from the sea doesn't want to spend his first day in London walking about some unused palace. Do you, Mortimer?"

The navy had taught young Commander East decision. "Actually, Aunt, I'd like it very much. After months cramped up in a seventy-four, enormous rooms and a bit of gold leaf sound just the ticket. Won't you come with us, Mother?"

"Of course I shall, my darling."

Mrs. Whitsun rapped the table with the handle of her knife. "You'd best not, Marissa. I must speak to you on a very serious matter." Once again her protuberant eyes rolled to Sarah with a hard glance.

"I'm sure it will be no less serious if we put off discussing it for an afternoon. I have never been in Kensington Palace. Let me see, that is the one at the end of Hyde Park, is it not?"

"Yes, Mother, that's right." Mortimer dragged a last piece of bread through the sauce on his plate, ate it, and stood up. Despite his heroics at table, his figure showed trim and neat in his uniform. "If you ladies will gather your fripperies, we'll be off. 'Lose not an hour,' as Admiral Lord Nelson used to say."

"Did he really?" Harmonia asked on a sigh.

"I think it was him. Will we walk, or use the chaise?"

"It isn't very far," Sarah said. "Let's walk." She would have said more, if the image of Alaric walking had not risen before her vision and silenced her.

"That's an excellent idea," Mortimer said. "That way we won't have to wait for it. I know; we'll tell Hannay to send the chaise over to collect us in two or three hours. You ladies will be tired by then, I know. If that meets with your approval, Aunt, of course."

"It does not! Marissa, if you wish to have everyone hear what I have to say about—"

"I'll write to the groom while you girls prepare yourself." The girls gratefully scurried out. Masterfully, Mortimer said, "You, too, Mother. Come along."

"Marissa!"

Mrs. East spread her hands helplessly. "Later, Aunt. The children are so impatient." Mortimer held her chair for her, waiting for her to rise. "I shall only be a moment, darling. I must find my shawl. It may be in the larger trunk."

"Do you need my help, Mother?"

"No, I think I can find it."

"Then I shall write that note. Pray excuse me, Aunt Whitsun." Sarah's tall brother bowed out, leaving Mrs. Whitsun in solitary command of the dining table.

Somehow, upon leaving the house, it seemed natural that Harmonia should take Mortimer's arm. After considerable heartburning, Harmonia had accepted Sarah's advice. A woodland hat, tilted to one side to show glossy brown curls, complete with a rippling ostrich feather for a dashing accent, was far more becoming to her round face than a close-fitting cottage bonnet, demure though it might appear.

Sarah was quite startled by Harmonia's sudden descent into meekness and her stubborn insistence that Mortimer would prefer a docile girl to a lively one. Sarah, however, agreed with Aunt Whitsun so far as to believe that a sailor, newly home, would appreciate something piquantly feminine to offset the sturdy reliability of the able-bodied seamen with whom he spent so much time. Not that all men felt that way. Alaric, for instance, made his preference for elegant and gracious ladies splendidly clear.

"I think I won't go after all, Mother," Sarah said, hanging back for a moment as Harmonia and Mortimer walked on ahead.

"The fresh air will do you good. I believe the sun is going to shine for us."

Perhaps in honor of Mrs. East's visit, the sun emerged from behind the clouds. London looked like a marzipan replica of itself, newly made and faintly sticky with the remnants of last evening's haze. Though many people walked or rode in the Park, the East party had the palace largely to themselves, except for a group of rather noisy Americans who romped like true rebels through the princely chambers.

"Coo-ee, Martha. It ain't a patch on the Presidential Mansion!"

"Say, I like that staircase, huh. Which one of them gals is that painter fella's lady-friend, if you take my meaning?"

The Easts followed along behind the Americans, as they had hired the only guide on duty, an elderly lady in a grey stuff gown. At first, Mrs. East had been hesitant about joining the group, but the older of the American ladies said, "You might as well come along with us. These old ruins don't mean a thing unless you've got someone along who knows which king is which. I can never keep them straight! They all look alike, don't they?"

"H'in 1762," the guide said, pushing back her mobcap to glare at the American lady, "our good King George chose not to live 'ere h'at Kensington, preferring the modern comforts of Buckingham 'Ouse. Step this way, if you please, gentlemen, and don't point at the paintin' with your h'umbreller, there's a good sort, sir. The ceiling in the Presence Chamber is famous for its h'imitation of the H'italian style. That there bright red's never had to be redone, not in ninety years. Move along, please, ladies and gentlemen."

Gazing up at the brilliant, mysterious decorations of caryatids and sphinxes, and the roundel of Apollo driving his chariot against a flaming red background, Sarah did not at first notice that the group had gone on. "Come and sit down, Sarah," her mother said, patting one of the low settees covered in soft red velvet. "I'm tired."

"But don't you want to hear the rest?"

Faintly, she heard the strident voice of the guide saying, "It was 'ere, in the King's Gallery, that good King William the Third collapsed after his riding accident at 'ampton Court. . . ."

"Look," an American man said. "Stop callin' them good

King this and that. We all know what these kings are really like. Scalawags and scoundrels, the whole boiling of 'em.''

"See here," Mortimer said. "I resent that."

"Oh, you do, do you?"

"Mother," Sarah said. "I think Mortimer's about to fight with someone."

"Let Harmonia handle him. She'll have to get used to it. Mortimer has always been ready to defend his honor at the drop of a hat."

Surprised, Sarah sat down beside her mother. "Then you think they'll . . . ?"

"Bound to, dearest. To confide in you—and you mustn't tell Harmonia—Mortimer has hardly been able to talk of anything else but her. Even before they met again yesterday. He didn't realize he was doing it. Every subject whether it be the weather or . . . or vegetables seems to remind him to some story with her as the heroine."

"I can't believe it."

"Oh, they are exactly right for one another. Marriage will steady her, and having a wife to care for may persuade Mortimer not to take so many frightful risks. And if not, at least we may have grandchildren." Mrs. East patted her daughter's knee. "But enough about them. My dear, if I asked you about vegetables or the weather, who would be the hero of your stories?"

"I don't understand," Sarah said, turning her head to look at a portrait of a silk-and-satin lady smirking only a few inches above the narrow wainscoting.

"You have never told an untruth to me before, Sarah." Mrs. East smiled and said, "Well, then, never mind. I'm sure Aunt Maudie will tell me the whole tale. Someone lay on his back for *weeks* to paint that ceiling. His clothing must have been fearfully spotted by the time he was through."

"Mother . . . don't believe all the bad Aunt Whitsun is bound to tell you."

"Then you had best tell me all the good."

Sarah hardly knew where to begin. "Alaric—that is, Lord Reyne and I . . ."

"Lord Reyne? The Earl of Reyne?"

"Yes, Mother. You remember him; he stayed with the Phelpses and took the chicken pox."

"Oh, yes, I remember him perfectly well. Has he been annoying you with unwanted attentions, dearest? I shall have your father call him out. He was accounted a very fair shot, your father."

"There's no reason for Father to do anything of the kind! Mother . . . I love him so dreadfully much. He's going to marry Lillian Canfield, but I know he doesn't love her. Not that there's much hope he'd ever be mine, even if he didn't marry her. They announced the date of their wedding; that's why I left early, as Aunt Whitsun will tell you. And there's more."

"More?" The paintings of gaudy creatures who had lived on the crumbs of politics and gossip seemed to vibrate at this revelation of one more scandal. They almost turned painted ears to catch the whispers of the young girl confused by the flattering notice of a man of the world.

"I . . . I danced with him on the lawn at the Duchess of Parester's May party. I didn't know it was wrong. You see, Miss Canfield had already retired to bed. Aunt seems to think I'm disgraced."

Mrs. East breathed more easily, and the great silent room shrugged and returned to the fifty-year-long dream of glory gone by. A shy tale of unrequited love was not sufficient to stir it into wakefulness. Only the recitation of the steps of a stealthy seduction could have had that power. The silk-and-satin lady seemed to sneer at a mere dance causing this much concern.

"And that is all?" Mrs. East asked.

"Yes, except that I'm so unhappy." Sarah stood up and drifted toward the entrance to the King's Gallery. The group was in the act of turning out of this immensely long chamber. Mortimer and Harmonia stood together in a great square of light, shed through windows behind them, apparently enraptured by a huge wind-dial over the chimney-piece. Sarah supposed a sailor would be interested in such a device. That Harmonia was too seemed clearest possible proof that her feelings for Mortimer were deep and real.

"Don't dawdle! There are more visitors waitin' for me, and at this rate we won't never be through," the guide complained. "The White Court is shut up today. Pass along to the Great Cupola Room. Watch that h'umbreller, sir, reely. You nearly 'ad that bit o'statuary h'over."

At the end, after tipping their lady usher profusely (a thing the Americans took great exception to), Mortimer said, "That was precisely what I needed. Now I can go back to sea and enjoy myself. A cramped cabin will seem positively restful after all that magnificence. Imagine, Harmonia, bulkhead after bulkhead with not a picture in sight!"

"No red flocked wallpaper, either," Harmonia said.

"Now that was one thing I approved of. Red wallpaper with gold furniture. Just the combination to make a cottage cozy. No one would ever look ill with that shade reflected onto their cheeks. I like healthy cheeks, myself." He peered under the tilted brim of Harmonia's hat. "The rosier the better, I always think." If that were true, he must have been pleased by the color that flooded the girl's face at his words.

That day at Kensington began a romance between Mortimer and Harmonia. Between her amazement at the speed with which their love developed, and sightseeing with her mother, Sarah almost failed to notice that she'd been dropped by the *ton* like a too-hot chestnut. Persons who, two weeks before, would greet her with particular notice now passed her by without a nod. Aunt Whitsun made her displeasure known.

"Almost two weeks without an invitation from a single respectable person. Although there have been plenty from the other kind. The only flowers she receives are from notable *roues* to whom I would not trust a potted plant! Marissa, your daughter has ruined every chance she had of finding a worthy husband."

"There are many worthy young men at home, Aunt."

"Cabbage-heads! With her beauty, she could have aspired to the highest in the land. Did not one Gunning sister marry a duke?"

"Two dukes, I think. One after another. And as for invitations," Mrs. East said, lifting her attention from her embroidery a moment and squinting beyond the circle of light shed by the candle at her elbow, "Miss Canfield asked us to dine."

"Which invitation Miss Sarah insisted I refuse."

"Never mind. We were out to dinner three times last week alone."

"Yes, but to whose houses? That Mrs. Armistead—married to a banker! And Mrs. Greendial—her husband is in trade!"

"They are old friends of mine from my own Season, as I explained. The kind of friends who married for love and have stayed true to their husbands and to me. When I was young, I had many acquaintances who married well, even brilliantly. But they did not continue to know me once I married—a nobody.'' With a soft smile that Mrs. Whitsun did not understand, Mrs. East returned to plying a slow needle.

''I only hope your precious daughter is aware of how much she has thrown away by this foolish infatuation with a man who is as good as married.''

''Do not tell her, Aunt. It will do no good for her to know.''

''I like that! What is to prevent her falling in love again if she is not warned?'' The amount of disgust Mrs. Whitsun loaded onto the phrase ''falling in love'' made Mrs. East glance up again.

''I hope nothing prevents her. I would not like her to believe that marriage is only for security or gain.''

''If that is to my address, Marissa, I cannot but think you horridly ungrateful. If I had not warned her, do you think she would be wise enough to refuse the *carte blanche* Lord Reyne might have been on the point of offering. Yes, I don't wonder you're surprised. He'd be a perfect idiot not to realize the girl's in love with him, and you know nothing makes a man a fool faster than having some young girl obviously mad about him!''

''Are you talking about me, dear Aunt Whitsun?'' Mortimer, resplendent in a new uniform, entered the room. ''I knocked, but you didn't hear me. And as for young girls in love and the fools who love them in return . . . Mother!'' He knelt by her chair. ''Mother, did you always know that it would be Harmonia?''

Mrs. East searched her son's face. ''You've asked her?''

''Yes. She was sitting by the window all alone, and the candle shone on her hair, and . . .'' His tanned face darkened by a blush, Mortimer lifted his light eyes. ''She's telling Sarah about it now. She didn't think it was fair to make Sarah wait until you knew.'' From his tone, it was obvious that there was now only one ''she'' in Commander East's life.

Sarah turned from counting pale London stars through a closed window to stare blankly at her friend. For a moment, she had the strangest notion that she stood again outside the drawing room at Hollytrees and would have only to walk a few steps to stand beside Lord Reyne.

"I'm sorry," Sarah said. "Will you repeat that? I thought you said that you and Mortimer . . ." At Harmonia's patient nod, Sarah reached out to embrace her. "I thought perhaps I dreamed it. I dream so much these days. Sometimes they seem so very . . . But tell me. When and how did he ask you?"

"Just now. Downstairs. I wasn't expecting him to. And look at me. This is the oldest dress I brought with me. He couldn't wait until I looked like something besides a fright, could he? He didn't seem to notice, though."

"Mortimer kissed you? Mortimer? He used to say he'd die before he'd kiss a girl—but I suppose I shouldn't repeat tales out of school. I promise myself I shall tease him about it!" They laughed, though with a sob in their throats. Sarah sobered first. "What about his ship? He has to take command soon, doesn't he?"

"I asked him about that. It won't be commissioned for a month, though he'd like to go on, that is, he'd like to go aboard her as soon as he can. He says we can go home to be married and then travel to Plymouth. Then we'll have two weeks together, if he can get permission to sleep out of the ship." Though her blush deepened at this mention of matters she should know nothing about, the sparkle in her dark eyes told of her anticipation.

Sarah hesitated a moment before embarking upon a delicate subject. "Harmonia, you're certain about this? I mean to say, it has only been two weeks since you were engaged to Harlow Atwood. I know Mortimer will wait. . . ."

"Oh, no. Not that mistake a second time! Delay is too dangerous for a man. If they have the chance to look about them and think it over, good-bye to the first girl. I'm going to marry him as soon as I can; it may be the only way to keep him!"

"Then you think he's like Mr. Atwood?"

"Nothing like him. I thought I wanted a man I could influence. What am I saying? I wanted a man I could rule. I can never rule Mortimer, though I think I can influence him. He's going to be captain in the house, as well as aboard his ship. I've quite made up my mind about that!"

Seeing Sarah was about to say something further, Harmonia held up her hand. "Please, Sarah, as you love me, never mention Mr. Harlow Atwood again. That episode is over, most happily over.'' Hearing a footstep on the landing, Harmonia stood up, her face alight with the joy of knowing she'd see her beloved in a finger's snap. More than that, for when Mortimer walked into the bedchamber, he stretched out his arms to take her in.

''We're all going home for the wedding,'' Mortimer said. ''My mother's writing yours at this very moment, no doubt making the paper very soggy. But the letter will hardly arrive before we do. I want to leave day after tomorrow. What do you think of all this, Sarah? Were you surprised?'' Mortimer asked, gazing down into Harmonia's face.

''Yes,'' she lied. ''I hadn't the least notion how matters stood until Harmonia told me just now.'' She saw Harmonia wink approvingly over Mortimer's broad shoulder. Sarah turned her gaze out toward the blackness beyond the window, doing her best to ignore the tiny sounds from behind her. She sighed. At least Harmonia was happy, secure in the embrace of the man she loved. As happy, no doubt, as Miss Canfield. As happy as Sarah knew she'd never be. Idly, she wrote ''Alaric'' in the fog left by her breath on the glass, and then rubbed it out.

''You don't mind spending the day shopping, do you?''

From beneath the tilted brim of his tall hat, Alaric smiled at his fiancée as her chaise started forward. ''For the third time, Lillian, I don't mind in the least. I may purchase something myself. Seals, or fobs, or a shiny new snuffbox.''

''You don't take snuff, and should you begin, you shall have to find a new fiancée. What a ghastly habit. Almost as bad as the betel nuts the natives chew in the East. I'm not sure I don't prefer that. It makes their teeth such a lovely shade of red.'' She grimaced at him comically, showing all her straight, white teeth.

Alaric laughed. ''Charming. I shall recommend it to all the ladies I meet. Tell me honestly. Wouldn't most of your friends look far lovelier with bright red teeth sharpened into points? Shall we begin the fashion?''

''I'd prefer a new dress—of bright red silk with pointed trimmings. Where do you suggest we go for such things, Kendall?''

The fortyish maid, sitting with her back to the horse,

brightened at hearing something she could understand. "Grafton House, miss. They have everything."

"Excellent. Tell Briggs to take us there."

As they tooled along in the bright morning sunlight, Alaric allowed his gaze to travel where it would. An organ-grinder, two bucks shaking hands on horseback, an increasing lady and her worried husband circling her like a frantic lapdog, and a friend were all pointed out to Miss Canfield. Then a frown rumpled his forehead and he turned, sitting up from his lazy posture to look over the back of the open chaise.

"What is it, Alaric?"

"I thought . . . I thought for a moment I recognized someone, but it couldn't be he." He shook his head and, feeling he'd been remiss, asked about his future father-in-law.

"He's well."

Alaric noticed Lillian's infinitesimal hesitation. "What has he done now?"

"It's only that you'd think, after the fearful trimming I gave him over his behavior three weeks ago, that he'd have sense enough to stay away from the topic of our marriage."

"But he hasn't."

"No. He was complaining this morning that . . . oh, it's too ridiculous to mention!"

"Mention it, then, so I may laugh."

Lillian let out half an exasperated sigh. "Just so long as you don't imagine this complaint is from me."

"I shan't. What is it?"

"Father, with his usual elephantine tact, wanted to know why you had not, as yet, equipped me with some token of our betrothal." Her face impassive, Lillian's distaste flavored every syllable.

"Shall I buy you a ring today?"

"I don't want a ring. Father thinks I should have something imperial—hen's egg size at the least—to decorate my finger, but I like to lift my hand without using a derrick. Father's behavior has been disgraceful throughout. I could have sunk through the floor at dinner last night when he was going on and on about the arrangements for our wedding. You were so very polite, yet I knew you must have been angry."

Alaric did not answer. Partly because they'd now arrived at Grafton House, an enormous columned emporium, and partly

he kept silent because he was afraid that to speak would reveal
much that he wished to hide from Lillian. At dinner, with his
host demanding an open discussion of private matters, he'd felt
as trapped as a criminal on his way to Tyburn. Already he
could feel the coarse fibers of the noose. He'd known a
strangling fear and had hoped that a glance across the table at
Lillian, so calm and lovely, would ease it. She'd smiled and
nodded understandingly, but the fear remained. Perhaps, he
thought, handing Lillian down out of the chaise, his had only
been the natural reaction of a bachelor facing the dread specter
of Matrimony.

Undoubtedly that was all this feeling was. Turning to follow
his fiancée into the dusky interior, he paused to tug gently at
the fine cravat about his throat. He couldn't be more delighted,
Alaric told himself firmly. Lillian would make a perfect
countess. Together, they'd put down deep roots as they
followed his plans for the future. With her beside him, the
course ahead would be as untroubled as the straightest road,
without bend or hill to spoil their easy progress.

Two passersby stared open-mouthed at the elegantly dressed
gentleman clutching at his cravat in Bond Street. Prying loose
his fingers, Alaric bowed coolly. During a supercilious glance
around to see if anyone else had noticed his bizarre actions, he
paused. Coming toward him was the lady in delicate condition
that he'd noticed before. Though he'd dismissed the idea
before, he now saw clearly that her escort was none other than
that notorious lover, Mr. Harlow Atwood.

"Harlow," the lady said, tossing up her red head with a
boldness that must have been very charming five months ago.
"Does that gentleman know you, or is he crazed?" She
narrowed bright hazel eyes at Alaric.

"It's the Earl of Reyne, Lucy. Should we not hurry . . . ?"

"You never told me you were on speaking terms with earls
and other quality. Go and speak to him. Go on, I say."

Shaking off his amazement, Alaric advanced with his hand
held out. Atwood shied backward, clapping his hat over his
face. He'd obviously not forgotten that the last time they'd met,
Lord Reyne tried to darken his daylights. "How delightful to
see you, Atwood," Alaric said. The hat dropped to reveal a
single eye. "This must be your lady wife?"

"I am, sir. The former Miss Lucy MacKenzie." Though

Alaric hoped they'd been married at least a month longer than the evidence suggested, he noted she still held her left hand so that the shiny golden band caught the light.

"Charming to meet you, Mrs. Atwood. I've heard so much about you . . . from your husband." The eye of her husband gleamed with gratitude as he replaced his hat on his head.

Though Mrs. Atwood was loath to let a bona fide earl go, pressing upon him many offers to visit them in their lodgings, Alaric finally tore himself away. Finding Lillian once more in the depths of the shop, he duly admired the bolt of cloth on display for her and then said, "I hope you'll forgive me, Lillian. I have to leave you. An important matter has come to my attention."

The shop assistant withdrew to a respectful distance out of earshot. Lillian said, "I understand. Shopping is dull. Shall I see you later? This evening, perhaps? I promise you Father will behave."

Guilt heated Alaric's face. Grateful for the murky light, he hastened into extra explanation. "I've misjudged someone, Lillian. Grievously. I must apologize at once. To let it go on any longer would be adding injury to insult. I can't in good conscience do that."

"You misjudged someone? I can't believe that. You are always so confident and clear-sighted."

"Thank you for your kind words, Lillian. But I've been a fool, and I've hurt Sarah more than I can ever tell you."

"Hurt Sarah? Sarah East? How could anyone misjudge someone so open and honest about herself?"

"I did, at any rate."

"I do see that, yes, you must apologize to her immediately. I like her tremendously, and it won't do to have her feelings wounded by you. Hurry along. Kendall and I shall carry on without you. But promise to tell me all about it later."

"I promise." Alaric kissed her hands and left.

Ordinarily, he would have walked, though Mrs. Whitsun's house was far from Bond Street. But a sense of urgency, welling up from somewhere inside, propelled him into waving down an unoccupied hackney. Restless on the seat, he leaned forward as though willing the horse to greater speed. Hopping down in the street, he had already fished up a sovereign. The driver eyed it suspiciously. A quick bite later, he drove off, grinning. Alaric crossed the street to stand outside the narrow house.

Shutters linked hands across the windows, a sure sign that the house was now unoccupied. He stood beside the very one he'd leapt lightly from on a night three weeks ago. It was as if he could still feel the jar that had met his feet when he'd struck pavement, no less startling than the jolt his heart had received when he'd believed Sarah East to be false.

Alaric rapped on the door. The echo, searching empty rooms, seemed to resonate in his chest. He knocked once more, solely because a ragged, shivering hope still lived in his heart. But when the second echo faded, his hope died. "They've gorn, sir," said a sweet voice.

Looking from side to side, Alaric finally espied a small maid in a mobcap and apron, wielding a broom on the steps next door. She bobbed a curtsy, finding she had his attention. "They've gorn. Yesterday morning as ever was. Gave the staff a holiday 'cause of the young lady's wedding."

"Wedding? What young lady?" Good God, how had Sarah found herself a bridegroom so quickly? Not that there weren't plenty of men who'd snatch up such a beauty before a star could twinkle.

"I dunno, sir," the maid said.

"Was she a blonde?"

"I dunno, sir, but he was ever so handsome in his uniform."

"Uniform? Of which service?"

"Navy, of course." She looked at him as if he were quite mad to think of any other. Her expression grew even more ludicrous when he handed her a half-crown for her information. She reached out for it twice before mustering her nerve to take it, then she disappeared inside with her broom before the madman had a chance to change an already unbalanced mind.

Alaric did not trouble to search for a second hackney. He walked slowly up the street, his hands clasped behind his back. Remembering all the cads and fribbles that had clustered about her until that unfortunate business at the Duchess of Parester's party, he felt distinctly grateful that Sarah had found herself a respectable naval officer to marry.

His frown deepening, he chastised himself for never having apologized to Sarah for having involved her in such a brangle. Nor had he taken the time to clear her reputation, though he knew Lillian had made an attempt to invite the Whitsun party to dine. He'd thought the entire silly business would blow over, and perhaps it would have, with Lillian's support, but it didn't matter now. Alaric walked along, wondering why nothing seemed to matter anymore. A sudden fog seemed to have moved in on London, and he wandered in it, darkly.

Sighing, he looked up. There was no fog. If anything, the day was as clear and sunny as any he'd known. The street looked familiar. Studying the houses, he realized this was the street where the Canfields made their London home. His sense of direction, invaluable in the smoke and battle of war, had brought him here without conscious thought, even as he'd once walked in similar turmoil of mind to Sarah. He shied away from the thought of her, as he'd winced from the surgeon's touch.

Feeling for his watch, he discovered that it was half-past four. Lillian would certainly have returned from her shopping expedition by now. She might even be pouring out tea. Good old Lillian, Alaric thought. At least I still have her. With this lover-like thought, he mounted the steps and tugged on the bellpull.

Ascertaining that Lillian was alone, Alaric entered the blue and white drawing room without waiting to be announced. With a pleased smile, Lillian rose from her chair to greet him. Silently and swiftly, Alaric crossed the room, put his arms about her, and kissed her smiling lips. He felt her hesitate and then try to draw away. Assuming she was only surprised by the suddenness of his kiss, Alaric pursued her, but she put the heels of her hands against his shoulders and pushed. "Stop, please."

"Why? Mayn't a man kiss his fiancée? And I've decided your father is entirely in the right. We shouldn't wait any longer to be married. June is the perfect month." He smiled down on her, hoping she'd reassure him.

Lillian pushed him again with a new strength. He opened his arms to let her go. "Alaric, I . . ." She grasped a chair back for support and then, shaking her head a trifle, stood on her own. "Very well. Come here and kiss me, then."

Confused, Alaric did as he was bid. He'd kissed many girls before, at his expense usually. He was used to the yielding sigh that went through them all, sooner or later. He put his arms around Lillian and touched her lips lightly with his own. There was a moment of cold hesitation. Perhaps she simply needed to get used to the idea. After all, he'd never made the slightest attempt to kiss her before.

But when the moment lengthened, Alaric began to feel ridiculous, and moreover, bored. It was exactly as though he were kissing a girl during amateur theatricals—less interesting, if anything. Lillian did not giggle or blush. She simply stood there, enduring his embrace in patience. Alaric lifted his head. "This isn't going to work, is it?"

Now she smiled as she slowly shook her head. "I knew, somehow, that it would not. I respect you, Alaric, and love you, but exactly as if you were my brother. I realized it, I think, three weeks ago, when Father made such a fool of himself, and of me and you. Standing in front of all those people, I did not feel pleased or excited, only tremendously embarrassed."

"Then you are much cleverer than I. I came here with every intention of encouraging you to marry me immediately."

"I thought you might. I meant to free you as soon as you suggested it, but you didn't grant me the opportunity. I'm happy you kissed me, as it makes explanations so much easier." Alaric sat down, rather heavily, as Lillian returned to the desk in the corner of the room. She picked up a piece of paper and stood turning it in her fingers. "Alaric," she said, as if bringing up a delicate subject, "I also know why you wanted to marry me at once all of a sudden."

"You know? Pray explain that to me, for I am not certain why myself."

"It wouldn't have anything to do with a young lady's departure for her home, would it?" She came and put the paper in his hand. Squeezing his shoulder, Lillian said, "I found this waiting in the post when I returned this afternoon. When you came in just now, I put one and one together, as you should do." Leaving the note for him to read, Lillian crossed the room to ring for their tea.

Alaric frowned at the neat writing that covered the page. Though at times verging on incoherence, Sarah's regret for any pain she might have caused Miss Canfield came through clearly enough. The letter closed on a note of thanks for all Lillian had done for her. "This bracelet," Lillian said, holding up the glittering strand, "was enclosed. I gave it to her at Hollytrees for nursing you so well. Please take it back to her."

"Take it back? I'm not going anywhere."

"Now you're being very stubborn. Listen to me a moment. When you offered your kind proposal to me, I knew you did not love me, although I was prepared to love you. I didn't understand then that love cannot be prepared for and cannot be arranged. It enters your heart like a king to command or it doesn't come in at all."

"Are you in love with someone else?"

"No. I don't believe I ever shall be in love. I am not one who accepts commands of any sort." Lillian appeared to be gazing inward, and she smiled sadly. Then she looked at him, and he saw laughter sparkling in the depths of her brown eyes. "To tell the truth, Alaric, I'd not marry you if the Archbishop of Canterbury were to perform the ceremony and the Prince Regent were to give you away. When you think about my father, you'll see how positive I am that I could never be brought to marry you."

"What about your father? He'll kick up a deuce of a fuss. I'll see him before I go."

"Never mind. He's not your difficulty now. I give you your congé. Please take it. There's a young lady waiting for you that you've made rather unhappy by being engaged to me. The sooner you clear that up, the sooner you'll be happy."

"Happy? Do you think I'll enjoy delivering Sarah from one scrape only to see her fall into another?"

"Enormously. Are you going?"

"May I have tea first?"

"No, you may not."

They laughed together, companionable as old friends. Lillian made him promise that he'd bring Sarah to dinner as soon as their honeymoon at his house in Essex was over. Alaric left, whistling. Lillian drank her tea, fortifying herself with several cups, then knocked on her father's door. No doubt he'd be noisy, yet she felt certain she'd bring him around in time. Despite his ambitions, she felt he'd never force her into a marriage that would make her unhappy, even if that meant no marriage at all.

14

"Yellow iris and jasmine to match Harmonia's ribbons!" Lady Phelps said, with the air of a conjurer bringing a three-foot sword out of a six-inch handkerchief.

"Dorothea, how perfect!" Mrs. East said. She wrote a note on the sheet of foolscap by her elbow. "I shall tell Marsh to search by the stream. There should be plenty there. And, if not, I noticed this morning that my yellow rose bushes are in bud. By next Wednesday, they'll bloom; no doubt about that!"

The two ladies smiled contentedly at one another. The happy tears of the return from London with the betrothed couple were past. Harmonia and Mortimer meandered about Hollytrees, holding hands, far removed in thought if not in distance from the hubbub of the library, where mothers made plans. After two days of brain-squeezing, they'd completed the list of food to be served out at the wedding breakfast and had turned to the question of decorations for the church and hall.

Lady Phelps said, "Dear me, there's still so much to be done. Sarah, how are you proceeding with those letters?"

Hearing her name called, Sarah began to drive her pen across the page with more industry. "Very well, ma'am. This one's to your cousin Cecilia."

"Oh, yes. She'll never come, but she always likes to hear about the children. Although, to think on it, she did come to Harriet's wedding and while suffering from a sprained foot. Perhaps she will make it."

"It's very short notice," Mrs. East said reassuringly.

"Nevertheless, you'd better put her at the table with Mrs. Harleigh. They'll be able to compare doctors and have a lovely time." Mrs. East nodded and scrabbled among the many pages of notes for the arrangement of the wedding breakfast.

Sarah bowed her head once more over the list of addresses.

Her task was to copy the meticulous announcement Sir Arthur had drafted. The twins were supposed to be helping her, but they'd ridden off with Mr. Randolph to oversee the delivery wagon which was to bring the two kilderkins of rum ordered in for the wedding breakfast. There'd also be brandy, but that would be brought in at night, due to a small question of Revenue.

As the two mothers continued, discussing now how much white bunting they'd require versus how much the draper was likely to have, the rhythmic scratching of Sarah's pen slowed again. If they'd been planning a funeral, Sarah could have been miserable and caused no comment. But to be sad when everyone else is ecstatic smacks of rudeness, if not perversity. So Sarah struggled to seem as delighted with her brother and friend as custom demanded. Indeed, she was happy for them, but as though they lived in another country, separated from her by heavy seas and roiling mists. She sighed, and the salutation to a distant cousin blurred.

Lady Phelps stopped in the middle of a sentence. "Listen! Is that Mr. Gerard with the post? Yes, yes, it is. Hurry, Sarah. Take the ones you've finished in to Sir Arthur for his frank and we'll get them off." Sarah gathered a rustling armload to her chest. "And be sure to tell me if the bishop has sent the license. I'm so glad you arranged that before you left London, Marissa. What a clear mind you have!"

Sir Arthur happily complied with his wife's request, laughing that, "Those two years in Parliament are going to save me a fortune. Must all these people know about Harmonia's wedding?"

"Lady Phelps and Mother says they do."

"Then they do." He signed his name to the last one. "There you are, my dear."

Outside in the sunshine, the postman whistled and scratched his head, shoving aside his three-cornered hat. "If I'd known about this, I'd of brung a bigger bag, Miss Sarah."

"It's very good of you to make the extra trip to pick it all up. I hope we'll see you and Mrs. Gerard at the breakfast."

"Oh, she's looking forward to it mightily, Miss Sarah." He opened his satchel, and Sarah helped him fit all the letters in. "They'll be twice as many for yours, won't there? I'll have to bring a wagon for all them invites." He chuckled and remounted his nag, not noticing that the young girl had gone white.

Feeling as if her velvet slippers were anchors, she dragged herself back to the morning room. Flustered by Lady Phelps' commands and with her hands full, Sarah had neglected to fasten the door securely. As she approached, she heard Lady Phelps say, "I just can't help wishing that there was to be another wedding after Harmonia's. Or even at the same time. I do love a double wedding. Sir Arthur and I were married at the altar with his older sister and her husband."

"Yes, I know. But, as I told you, things became very complicated for Sarah in London."

"It's a great shame the advantage those dreadful men take of young girls. One of my boys would never do such a thing. Was he really pledged to another?"

"I'm afraid he was. I can only hope that, in time, she'll see that other men have merit and not waste her youth dreaming of something that can never come true." Her mother sighed, and Sarah forgave her for telling Lady Phelps about her disappointment. She could only hope that the name of the gentleman had been kept from her mother's friend. Sarah knew she'd hate to be the cause of Alaric's losing even a jot of his reputation.

Though the ladies were unaware that she'd overheard their conversation, Sarah did not feel that she could face them so soon after being intimately discussed. It would be impossible to meet their eyes. Remembering her other commission, she went in search of Smithers. Finding him in the kitchen, the air steaming and fragrant with smells of baking, for Mrs. Smithers was hard at work creating the wedding breakfast, she asked if anything had come in the post from the Bishop of London. The butler regretfully said, "Nothing as yet, Miss East."

"But that's dreadful. He promised . . . I shall have to tell Lady Phelps."

She went, leaving the butler to shake his head and say to his wife, "Miss East lost all her bloom in London."

"Late hours," the sweating lady cook said with a censorious sneer.

"Lost love," her husband replied. "I heard Mrs. East telling her la'ship the entire tale. They never said the name of the fellow it was, but I can guess."

"Who?" Mrs. Smithers leaned nearer to him across the work-scarred table, holding up a dripping spoon.

"Never you mind. And watch it! You've got batter all down your arm."

Upon hearing the news, Lady Phelps beat her hand on the leather blotter. "They must have a license. If only Mortimer had applied for one while he was here."

"Considering he did not know he was going to marry Harmonia before he went to London . . ."

"But it's the sort of thing a man may find himself needing at any moment."

Sarah said, "I'll send for Father."

"Why do you need me?" Mr. East entered and stooped to kiss his wife.

"Oh, Edgar, you always know when to arrive. The license hasn't come *yet*. The bishop promised it would be here by today. Whatever shall we do if it doesn't arrive in time?"

Mr. East said, "I don't know. But Sarah has an idea. What is it?" He turned his bright blue eyes on his daughter and a smile of pure pride lit his face.

Sarah responded to it with something like her old spirit. "I'll tell you in two words: Baggers Ashton! I've heard you mention him often."

"Old Baggers?" her father asked, a frown rumpling his shaggy blond eyebrows. Then his expression cleared. "You're right, of course. How clever of you! My dear, don't you recall my telling you that old Baggers had made bishop at last? It took him years, as he knows rather less about Scripture than my boot. Where was he promoted to?"

"Blanstonbury, wasn't it?" Mrs. East said.

"That's right, that's right. I remember him telling me in his last letter how splendid the hunting was. Very good, Sarah. All our problems are solved! I shall ride over at once."

"But," Lady Phelps said, rather hesitatingly as though bringing up a subject of doubtful respectability, "isn't Blanstonbury thirty miles from here?"

"Something like that," Mr. East agreed. "Don't worry about me. Fathers aren't much use at weddings. I shall enjoy seeing old Baggers again. I last saw him . . . let me see . . . at about the same time as I saw my last nappy."

Mrs. East said, "It's four days to the wedding, Edgar. You

don't have to leave at once. Why not wait until tomorrow to see if the Bishop of London has sent his license? Then you'll have enough time to ride over to Blanstonbury, collect a license, and still be back a day early. No, I forgot. The first license might come before you came back, and then you'd have had your trip for nothing.''

"Not for nothing. I'd see my dear old schoolmate, which is worth something any day. And, at the worst, Harmonia and Mortimer will have two licenses which, as we all know, is better than none.''

Their minds relieved, the ladies went on with their plans. Mr. East came to Sarah's side and peered over her shoulder as she worked. "How many of those have you done today?''

She checked the addresses. "Twenty-four.''

"Twenty-four! Your poor hand must be aching. Let me take over for a little while. I'm used to writing long screeds; these will take me no time at all. You go out and get fresh air into your lungs. We can't have you falling ill.''

"There's no danger of that.''

"Go along, go along,'' he said, scooping the air with both hands. With a slight smile at this pleasantry, Sarah stood up. Her father sat down at once, reaching out to dip the pen in the chased silver inkwell.

"Run about and shake away the fidgets. Don't come back for hours. You can work on these tonight, if I leave you any to do,'' he said, falling to work, apparently taking no notice of the feather-light kiss Sarah dropped on his permanently wrinkled brow. Under his breath, as he finished the first line, he said, "Pish-tosh, what a driveling way to put it . . . 'honor is mine to tell you' . . . how like an M.P. . . . no wonder they sent him down. . . .''

Finding her hat, she left the house by the front door to walk to her home. Molly wanted to refit the dress Sarah was to wear to the wedding, as it hung loosely on the girl's figure. Though making every effort to think only of the upcoming festivities, Sarah found her thoughts dropping into a well-worn groove. What if, she thought, watching her feet kick out the front of her dress, what if things were different?

What if it were Alaric on the horse I can hear approaching? What if the animal came to a sliding stop only feet away from me and I could look up and there he'd be smiling down at me?

What if he vaulted down from the saddle and grasped me in his arms, begging me in broken tones to marry him?

"Yes, yes, I will," Sarah murmured.

Harcourt kissed her cheek. "I knew if I made it back here before Harold you'd accept me," he said, exulting.

"What? I . . . what?"

"I gave him the slip at the wine merchants. He thinks I've gone to buy Harmonia's wedding present." Harcourt chuckled at his cleverness and the lunk-headedness of his twin. "It's the first chance I've had to be alone with you, and by the Great Harry, I'm glad I took it. Harold will be blue-green with envy. He'll bite his pen when I tell him."

Sarah blinked and refocused her eyes. Thick dark hair, a strong smell of horses, stronger arms, and a long, narrow face wearing a grin that seemed to split it in half. Yes, it was Harcourt holding her at the side of this dusty road, his horse breathing heavily just behind them. This is what came of dreaming incautiously. "Harcourt, I don't know what to say."

"Why say anything?" He kissed her again, noisily, still on the cheek. "You've just left the house? Come, ride with me, and we'll go tell them the news. They'll all be so happy, especially Mother. She's been hinting around for days, now Harmonia's marrying your brother, that one of us ought to get cracking to marry you. We tried to tell her that this was no new thought, but you know what Mother's like."

"Yes." She contrived to put a little distance between them, if for no other reason than fear he'd might break one of her ribs in his enthusiasm.

"Now, I've always thought your mother likes Harold better."

"That's not true."

"Good! Then you don't think there'll be any objections to me as son-in-law? 'Course, I don't understand your father, but I'm willing to love him for your sake." He had taken one of her hands and led her toward his horse. Unthinkingly, Sarah followed along. "I don't care for double weddings, though Mother's a fiend for 'em. On the other hand, I hate to wait too long."

"No," Sarah said, catching up to his side. "Let's not wait too long."

All Harcourt's talk about their families decided Sarah. Even if she'd not overheard the regrets of her mother and Lady Phelps, she still would have been aware of their strong desire to see their families inextricably linked, by more than one couple. She'd marry Harcourt, making everyone happy.

"I don't know if we should tell them now," she said. "I'd hate to take any of the attention away from Harmonia."

"Why not? You always do."

"That's why not. Let Harmonia have her day."

"All right, but dash it—can I tell Harold at least? I want to see his face when he hears the news."

"Yes, you may tell him, but warn him to keep it all a secret, for Harmonia's sake."

Harcourt turned and put his hands on Sarah's waist. "I'll lift you up."

Had he been Alaric, Sarah would have yielded to his touch. This thought made her step back out of Harcourt's reach. "No, I'm going home. Molly's waiting."

"You can ride with me and be there in half the time."

"I prefer to walk, Harcourt. I've been shut up in the morning room all day. You run home and decide how you're going to tell Harold."

"Yes!" The boy grinned. "He'll gnash his teeth down to nubbins! We'll have to feed him gruel." With athletic grace, Harcourt bounded into the saddle. "Shall you come to dinner?"

"I don't know. We'll see what Mother has to say."

"I hope you can. It'll be such a pleasure to see Harold glowering at you. Stand back now." Sarah stood away and he clapped his heels against the horse's sides. With a snort, the animal took off. Harcourt stood up in the saddle and waved his hand above his head, whooping like a Red Indian.

Sarah walked on. Except for the dust still hanging in the air, the entire episode might have been a dream. Inhaling deeply, Sarah revised that opinion. Such sore ribs never resulted solely from imagination. She'd accepted his proposal and was now the future Mrs. Harcourt Phelps. Someday there'd be a procession of little Phelpses. Harcourt, while not witty, not blue-eyed, and the possessor of footsteps that resounded rather than whispered, could be called handsome in a boyish, outdoors fashion. She'd get over Alaric Naughton, Earl of Reyne. One day, no doubt, she'd be unable to remember even his voice. It would be drowned out by the clamor of young Harcourts.

The quiet woods along the road beckoned. She'd be alone and peaceful there, with no great horses and loud boys to disturb her daydreams. Sarah turned and entered the green coolness. This had always been her shelter.

The six months between October and March had not served to rid her of his image, and their meeting during the Season had reinforced her love. Perhaps it would take six years before her heart healed, though it was not fair to ask Harcourt to wait so long. There must be a way, she thought, to pretend to be in love with her childhood friend. She tried to invent a daydream of happiness with Harcourt at the center. But her thoughts danced away, like so many butterflies, to hover about Alaric. Chasing after them only exhausted her. In the end, she let them drift where they would.

When she came home, she fell asleep. Her mother and her maid found her there when the supper bell had rung twice. Drawing up the blanket over Sarah's motionless body, Mrs. East said, "Let her sleep as long as she likes tomorrow. She's been working too hard."

"Lovin' too hard's more like it," Molly said.

"You know about that?"

"Find me a single soul in the county as doesn't. If I had him here, he'd soon regret playing fast and loose with my girl."

"You'd have to stand in line behind me," Mrs. East said with a fierce look. "What can the man be thinking of? Why doesn't he do something about it?" she asked, closing the door.

It was late in the morning of the next day, when Sarah woke up. Wandering downstairs, she begged Molly for a cup of tea. "You'll be having something more than that, it's to be hoped," Molly said, her hands on her hips.

"No, thank you," Sarah answered with a slow smile.

"That wasn't a question. Sit down and I'll make you some nice toast, with my special damson plum preserve."

"You only give me that when I'm ill." Obediently, Sarah sat down at the kitchen table.

"It's the end of the pot, and you may as well have it as the next person. When you're through, put on that dress and I'll start fitting it to you. I'm ashamed to see you in my kitchen in your dressing gown. Is this the fine way you learned in

London?'' The maid's heart dropped another notch when Sarah did not answer back in her familiar hasty way. Stabbing the bread with a toasting fork, she held it to the flame as if it were the body of a certain earl.

Two hours later, Molly stepped back a last time, squinting above a mouthful of pins. ''That's as straight as mortal hands can make it,'' she said indistinctly.

''I beg your pardon?'' Sarah said from the dizzying height of a straight-backed chair.

After spitting out the pins, Molly said, ''That's as good as I can do. But don't you dare lose another pound before that wedding, or this dress will fall off halfway through the vows. Let me help you down.'' Reaching up a worn hand, she grasped Sarah's smooth fingers and steadied the girl. ''Now slip out of that and put on your pretty blue silk, so I can see if it still fits you.''

''What for?''

''Dinner at the Phelpses. Never say you've forgotten tonight is their pledging dinner.''

''I thought that was the night we came home.''

''No, that was the-night-you-came-home dinner. Tonight is when Master Mortimer lifts his glass to his lady. You must be there. It's oh so romantical.'' Her white-swathed bosom rose and fell while she gave a misty-eyed sigh.

''I don't know, Molly. I'm tired. Maybe I'll take a quiet supper here, by myself.''

''By yourself? It's bad luck to eat alone, as you well know.''

''Then set a place for yourself.''

Folding the girl's dress over her arm, Molly wheedled, ''Put on your blue silk, Miss Sarah. You'll feel ever so much more like yourself in a pretty gown. And if you're ready early, you can spend some time with the twins. Master Harcourt stopped by while you were still sleeping.''

''He did?'' Sarah blushed guiltily.

Molly misinterpreted the rise of color. ''Put on your blue silk, and I'll bind your hair up with that shaded ribbon you brought home.''

''I will, to please you, Molly. But I don't think I'll go up to Hollytrees for dinner. They won't miss me. I'll send a note so they'll know not to expect me.''

As the maid opened her mouth to further discuss the matter,

a jangling bell sent her to one of the windows to look out. "It's Mr. Smithers! And at the front door! My, if some people don't think they come down from Heaven in a golden chair. . . . Never catch him at the servants' door, you won't. I wonder what he wants.

"Go and ask him. When he leaves, he can carry a message back."

"If he don't think himself too good to take it. *He'll* turn up his nose and send a footman down here to take it, just you wait and see!" She bustled from the room.

Sarah opened the clothespress and shook out her simple silk gown. As if it had occurred in another lifetime, she recalled with what excitement the material had been purchased, and the endless dithering, fascinating in itself, over the cut and make. Aunt Whitsun and she had tromped through a dozen stores, searching for the exactly right braided ribbon to outline the corsage and sleeves. Now, instead of the trophy of a successful adventure, it was merely a more or less adequate covering.

Sarah, dressed, wandered downstairs a second time. A vague surprise stirred when she realized she could still hear Mr. Smithers' voice. She entered the kitchen. Molly turned to her at once. "He's come to raid us," she said, her fingers shaking as she passed Sarah a list.

"Lady Phelps regrets the necessity, Miss Sarah, but these are items of great importance, which Shepherd's does not carry, nor is it likely they will obtain them prior to the great day."

"Let him take what he wants, Molly. Mother sent you, Mr. Smithers?"

"As I attempted to explain." That the butler was offended by Molly's ungraciousness could be told at once from the stiffness of his bow. The doorbell jangled again as Mr. Smithers straightened. "If your maid will begin to assemble these items, I shall be happy to answer for you, Miss Sarah."

"Thank you, Smithers. I don't care to see anyone, but I leave it to your judgment. Molly, I'll be in the garden."

"Humph! Coriander, elderflower vinegar, best preserved peaches . . . goodness, have they nothing of their own?"

A sad smile came to Sarah's face. "We ate all the peaches when everyone had the chicken pox."

The sun warmed the mellow vine-covered stone walls as Sarah followed the brick path around a corner, out of sight of the house. Blue hyacinths bloomed in low masses beneath the tall elms shading the path. A chaffinch sang above her. As she strayed, sun and shadow now brightened, now darkened her splendid hair. She remembered seeing her mother working in this very spot and pointing her out to Lord Reyne, newly met, who stood beside her on the hill, looking down.

She felt hands on her shoulders, gently turning her about. Alaric was there, gazing down on her with a strangely tender smile. He did not speak but with his eyes. When he took his hands away, Sarah protested, leaning nearer to him, determined that this vision would not vanish into nothingness like all the others.

Alaric, his smile growing more loving still, wrapped his arm about her waist and brought her close, off balance. Then his lips touched hers gently, with a pledge Sarah acknowledged at once. Her hands clutched his lapels as she sought to deepen their embrace. Her dreams had never before taken her beyond the point of meeting Alaric once again. Had she but known how satisfying it was to be kissed this way, she would have imagined it much sooner!

"My darling," he murmured.

That was right; he always said that. But he did not usually press his face against her hair as though he would breathe in all the scent of her. And she did not usually feel so light that a single breeze would waft her away. Sarah held on to him for safety. His kiss became stronger, more impatient, and she clung the tighter.

Alaric drew away, just to arm's length, yet even that was too far to please her. He said, "If I'd known what a homecoming this would be, I'd have left London an hour sooner. As it was, I came down as quickly as I could, once I'd known you'd gone. Do you forgive me for the delay?"

Sarah nodded. If this was illusion, why did he talk so much? He must know that to waste a moment now, when they could be kissing again, was to tempt whatever power had control over such things. Molly might call to her and break her concentration. Sarah stepped forward, lifting her face for another taste of Eden. Alaric stroked her face and complied.

"I say, Sarah! What's that fellow doing?"

Shuddering, Sarah opened her eyes and came abruptly down to earth. Approaching from the house, crushing fragrant herbs beneath his shiny boots, Harcourt came, dressed in his best blue coat and carrying a silver-handled riding crop.

"Hello, Harcourt," she said. Only then did she realize that she looked at her fiancé across the shoulder of another man. "Oh, dear," she said, stepping back out of Alaric's arms. Her fingers flew to her lips, which still tingled from the zeal of her lover's kiss.

"You remember Lord Reyne, don't you, Harcourt?" she said, hoping they'd shake hands and that would be the end of it.

Harcourt, however, simply stood in the path, his legs far apart as he swished his crop through the air. "My lord earl, I resent the liberties taken with my bride-to-be!"

"Your what?" Alaric looked at Sarah, who could only lift her hands in a semi-shrug, while a smile she knew to be fatuous crawled onto her lips.

"My fiancée, my lord, whom you were man-handling just now in a fashion unsuited to a gentleman!"

"Harcourt," Sarah began, addressing a young man she hardly recognized in this attitude. "It was . . ."

"I resent that, you puppy!"

"You may call me what you like, but you are a cad and rounder and . . . and . . . a stinker! I demand satisfaction for the insult you've offered Miss East." Harcourt went quite white, but his eyes blazed with outrage. He suddenly looked older and terrifyingly determined.

"Harcourt," Sarah said again. "Don't be silly! It was . . ."

"I don't fight boys," Alaric said, his head thrown back.

"Then you're a Jerry Sneaksby to boot! And so I shall tell everyone I meet in my life." For a moment, Sarah thought he put his tongue out at Lord Reyne, but he seemed to recall that he was a grownup.

"You've a hole in your wig," Alaric said, and turning his back on the furious young man, he said to Sarah, "Are you in truth . . . ?"

About to nod sorrowfully, Sarah's eyes widened as she saw Harcourt raise his crop above his head. Perhaps nothing else could have driven him to attack Lord Reyne save for the maddeningly casual dismissal of his turned back. As the lash came down, Alaric arched his back, a look of pure astonishment crossing his features.

He spun about and snatched the crop from Harcourt's hand even as it swished down a second time. Alaric sent the whip whirling off into the rhododendron bushes. "I accept your challenge," he said coldly. "Will tomorrow morning suit you?"

"Yes!" Harcourt flashed back, then hesitated. "No, actually, I'm supposed to hunt tomorrow morning. Can't disappoint them, you know. May have to spend the night. How about Wednesday?"

"Excellent. I assume there is somewhere we will not be disturbed."

"Certainly, my lord. The meadow behind the duck pond is never used this time of year."

"I shall find it."

"I shall send my brother to escort you on the morning."

"Thank you." The two gentlemen bowed, Lord Reyne more stiffly than the younger man. Then Alaric stalked off, without a backward glance.

Sarah rushed up to her defender and clutched his arm. "Harcourt, how could you? It was all my fault."

"I don't blame you, Sarah. How could you resist the blandishments of such a smooth rascal? Coming down here, flashing his blunt, and then believes his title gives him the right to assault our girls. The immortal rind of the fellow!"

"It wasn't like that. He's not like that at all!" Tears swelled in her eyes, but the earnestness of her pleading went unregarded.

"My goodness," Harcourt said, a flash of boyish pleasure lighting in his eyes. "Harold's already sick as a dog that I'm marrying you. He'll bite his cravat when I tell him I'm challenger in a duel with a peer!"

"But . . . Harcourt, you can't mean to go through with this!"

" 'Course I do. I have to, don't I? If it's all right with you, Sarah, I won't stay. Harold's got to hear this, before someone else tells him about it. You'll keep it a secret till it's done, won't you? I don't want anybody stepping in and spoiling it." He bent, kissed her burning cheek, and was gone.

Sarah, her head positively swiveling at the events of the past few minutes, stood in aghast amazement in the garden. The chaffinch still sang its merry song. Almost did she convince herself it was all a particularly vivid delusion when a bearded old man walked out of the bushes. "Ah, then, Miss Sarah," Marsh the gardener said, nodding his deaf old head. "Look here at this," he said tonelessly. "I found it over there. How long do you reckon it's been lying out on the ground? Looks clean, don't it?'' He showed her the unspotted leather and shining silver handle of the riding crop. ''I say one of them boys from over to Hollytrees lost it.''

''Yes, I imagine so,'' Sarah answered, though he could not hear her.

''Your mother wants me to cut them yellow roses. I told her it's too early to cut them, wedding or no wedding.''

''It's too late.''

''That's what I said.'' He watched her gather up her skirts and run to the rear door of the house. ''You tell her, Miss Sarah,'' he bellowed.

''Molly! Molly, is Father still here?''

''Heavens! Don't you know not to shout at me that way? What if I'd been cutting something? I'd have sliced my arm off.''

''Yes, yes, but where's Father?''

''He rode off this morning before you were awake.''

''That's right—the license. Mother's up at Hollytrees, isn't she?''

''Of course.''

''Then I'm going. Have John saddle my horse.''

''Not in that dress. You'll go in the chaise.''

''What does that matter? All right, I'll change. Just ask John to saddle . . .''

Molly shook her head. ''You can't go to dinner at Hollytrees in riding clothes.''

''If I don't go to Hollytrees at once, I may have to wear them to a funeral.''

''What do you mean?''

''I don't have time to explain. Hurry, Molly.''

''I'll send John to harness the horse.''

When the chaise arrived at Hollytrees, Sarah did not wait for the groom to let her out. Glimpsing one of the twins crossing the grass, she ran to him. ''Harcourt? Oh, Harold.''

He took her gloved hand and kissed it. ''My dear future sister-in-law. Let me felicitate you. I cannot blame you for instigating a duel over your charms. Being my brother's widow is preferable to being his wife.''

''Please, Harold, don't be sarcastic now, of all times. You've obviously seen Harcourt.''

"Yes. He's puffed up with pride over the fighting of his first duel. I've told him, of course, that breakfast on the grass is passé. I'm surprised his opponent agreed to it."

"You've talked him out of it? Thank you, thank you."

"You misunderstand, Sarah," Harold said, patting her hand. "Harcourt is determined to continue. I cannot interfere, not because my duties as his second forbid it, but because one gentleman cannot attempt to persuade another to turn tail. This is a matter of honor, after all." He struck a noble attitude, feet turned out and hand to his heart.

"Don't be a fool. Harcourt might be killed. Then what good will his honor do him?"

"You're a girl," Harold said sadly. "What do you know about it? This is a matter for men."

"Men? You're a couple of babies playing a game. Didn't you hear me? Harcourt could be killed. Dead!"

Harold patted her hand again. "Calm down, Sarah. No need to ruffle yourself."

Sarah pulled her hand free. "I'll tell your mother. *She'll* put a stop to it." She walked away, heading toward the house.

"No, you mustn't do that!" Harold danced around her, stopping her progress. "Besides, Father knows all about it."

"Sir Arthur? He approves?"

"No, not exactly. But he won't interfere, either. The code, you know. He exchanged shots twice, when he was young. And he won't let Mother stop Harcourt, either. Besides, if you tell her, she'll just cry."

"Better she should cry now than later." Sarah placed both hands on his waistcoat and shoved, sending Harold's weedy figure over backwards.

The butler opened the door for her. "Smithers," she said. "Did you let Lord Reyne into my house without announcing him?"

"No, Miss Sarah. I refused the gentleman admittance, knowing you were not feeling yourself." He coughed discreetly. "I may, however, have let fall that you'd gone for a stroll about the garden. Am I to wish you happy, Countess?"

"It may interest you to know, my dear old friend, that I am already betrothed to Master Harcourt and by your—"

"What?" Either Smithers' voice had suddenly gone up an octave or Sarah's announcement did not go unheard. Slowly, she turned to find her mother and Lady Phelps looking at her open-mouthed. "What did you say?" her mother asked, coming forward with outstretched hands.

"Oh, Mother, the most dreadful thing . . . But she could
not be heard above the clamor the two women were making.

"My dearest!" Lady Phelps said, kissing Sarah on both
cheeks. "All my happiest dreams are coming true. First,
Harmonia and Mortimer. Now, you and . . . and . . . which
one did you say?"

"Harcourt," Sarah answered. "But you must listen—"

"Harcourt!" Mrs. East signed. "Remind me that I owe
Harmonia twenty shillings. I thought for certain Harold's
poetry would woo you."

"Harold's a beast. He won't even—"

"But we must tell Harmonia. She'll be so thrilled for you!
What a pity there isn't time to arrange for a double ceremony.
I don't suppose . . . can you scratch out the names on a
marriage license and write in different ones?"

"I don't see why not," Mrs. East said. "Sarah, do you want
to share a ceremony with Harmonia and Mortimer?"

"I may not get married at all! If you'd only listen—"

"Of course, most brides prefer to marry alone. Still, it would
have been lovely." Lady Phelps wiped a tear from her eye.
"My goodness," she said as the clock bonged on the landing.
"Is that the time? Come, Marissa, you may borrow one of my
gowns for this evening. There's that purple satin that's gotten
much too tight for me. It will look . . ."

"Please," Sarah said as they walked toward the stairs. They
turned back and looked at her, kindly, lovingly, and with
indulgent smiles of women looking at a child. "You don't
know. . . . Harcourt's going to fight Lord Reyne over me.
They've arranged a duel on Wednesday, at the duck pond."

The two women exchanged a look in which concern and
affection mingled. "There, there, my dear," Lady Phelps said.
"You're overwrought. I know how exciting this time is for a
girl. Exciting and frightening, too. We shall arrange to end the
evening early tonight. See to it, Smithers."

"Very good, my lady."

"Oh, please," Sarah said. "You must believe me. It just
happened. Right after breakfast. No, wait. After Molly fixed
my dress. I went into the garden. Everything was so beautiful.
Lord Reyne came in and . . . and kissed me. Then Harcourt
challenged him to a duel. . . ." Even the butler was shaking
his head at her now.

"You'd just woken up when all this occurred?" Mrs. East asked.

"Yes. No, that was hours before."

"Obviously it was all a bad dream. You're sure Harcourt proposed marriage?"

"Of course, I'm sure. That was yesterday."

"Ah!" The two ladies exchanged a wink. "It's perfectly natural to have strange dreams after so unsettling an experience," Mrs. East said reassuringly. "I shall give you a nice dose of laudanum tonight, and there'll be no more bad dreams. You'll be right as nine-pence in the morning."

The two ladies linked arms and walked up the steps. Her mother's final words floated back down to Sarah. "Purple satin, you say? How intriguing."

Sarah stamped her foot on the shining parquet. As a last resort, she turned to Smithers. "I want to send a message to Lord Reyne at the Saddle. Give me five minutes, then send Fred to me."

"Very good, Miss Sarah. Are you sure?"

"If one more person asks me if I am sure about something that's as plain as sunrise, I'll do violence!"

The message was sent. During dinner, which gave Sarah galloping indigestion, the missive came back, the seal unbroken, the letter unread. Sarah threw her napkin down on the table and hastened from the room. Mrs. East put her hand over Harcourt's and said, "Never mind. All girls are emotional when they first become engaged."

"I wasn't," Harmonia said, then blushed as Mortimer whispered something in her ear.

Later that night, Fred sat in the kitchen, massaging his aching feet. "You coulda let me take a horse, Mr. Smithers."

"Sorry about that, me lad. I didn't know she'd send you five times to the village. And he never opened a one?" He pushed his own ale mug down the table toward the boy.

After Fred wiped his dripping mouth, he said, "Never a one, Mr. Smithers. He just looked at 'em like this. . . ." He twisted his open face into a proud scowl. "Then he shoved 'em back at me. Each time, exactly the same. Never said a word to me; though he gave me a shilling each time. That's not a happy earl, Mr. Smithers."

── 15 ──

The hour had gone midnight before Sarah decided she could bear Alaric's silence no longer. She'd tried hard to see this disastrous situation from a male perspective, but images of Harcourt and Alaric dead on the stained grass in the bright morning dawn kept coming between her and rationality. That two men should face slaughter for her sake seemed horrible. She didn't know how medieval maidens withstood the strain.

Waiting for dawn seemed beyond her powers. Sarah rose from her rock-like bed and hurried on some clothing. As Harcourt refused to hear reason, turning her aside with a laugh, and Harold only quoted from *chansons de geste,* Sarah knew it was time to see Lord Reyne in person. She'd gone to the inn earlier today and he'd not been there. Though she'd waited for two hours, he'd not come back, and she had to hurry off to help Harmonia deal with last-moment wedding worries.

Carefully, Sarah avoided the squeaky riser at the bottom of the stairs. She lifted down her dark green cloak from a hook by the kitchen door and swung it around her shoulders, concealing her white dress. The latch moved easily. Sarah filled her lungs with the cool night air. An owl hooted like a conspirator concealed in the top of a tree. Sarah listened for any further sound, from outdoors or from within. Hearing nothing, not even the rush of the owl's wings coasting through the air, she slipped around the corner of the house.

There was no moon to dim the swirling stars, thick like daisies in the meadow, each alive and individual, though all the same if seen from far enough away. Sarah thought of those flowers, smashed and bloodied, and walked on faster.

On the main street, the white plaster of the Saddle-Bow Inn gleamed like milk behind the shadowy crisscrossing of the Tudor timbers. A single candle showed against the wave-like glass in the common room. The rooms for the guests were toward the rear, to keep all street noise from disturbing any sleepers. Sarah had come to the Saddle all her life, for teas and hunt breakfasts, as well as to find her father or the twins. Yet, she'd never entered it at night, never alone, certainly never to see a man at midnight. Her hand trembled as she reached out to the brass-bound door.

A noise from up the street, perhaps no more than a cat noising through an ash-pile, sent Sarah scurrying inside. To be discovered in a building was one thing; discovered in the dark on a street corner was quite another. Holding the hood of her cloak up close to her face, she peered around the corner into the taproom. The tapster lay asleep on the long bar, stretched out at his ease. His snores made her fear for the antique plaster-work.

Sarah began to cross the open archway on tiptoe. Then she stopped dead. Something—or someone—held her fast by the slack of her cloak!

Not breathing at all, Sarah turned, her eyes screwed up against what she feared to see. "Oh, for—" She clapped her hand over her mouth. Then she gave a sharp tug and tore her cloak free of the loose nail in the wall. The cloth gave with a rip that sounded like the crashing of waves on the shore. Sarah dashed into the darkness on the other side of the taproom entrance. There was no change in the cadence of the tapster's rumbling snores.

Unlike home, Sarah did not know which step at the inn creaked. So, she crept up them at a maddeningly slow pace, testing each one before putting her full weight on it. At last, she made her way to the rear of the inn. A window at the end of the hall illuminated the three doors cut into the wall beside her, allowing access to the rooms created when the newest addition had been grafted onto the inn in 1678. In the days of five to a bed, three chambers had seemed plenty. To Sarah, they seemed far too many. Which was Alaric's?

Perhaps she could knock on each one, pretending to be a maid. No, for what cause would a maid have to come knocking at one o'clock in the morning? Of course, she could pretend to be Lady Melanie, who hung herself after her husband stabbed her lover in one of these rooms a little over a hundred years ago. Lady Melanie was rumored to walk the inn, calling her lover's name through the keyholes. Sarah wished she'd not remembered that old story; not that she believed in it.

Afraid now to turn around—for what if some ghostly lady stood behind her—Sarah stared hard ahead. Then something impressed itself upon her vision. At the first door, a small pair of lady's slippers stood, heels together as though waiting for a dainty dancer to step right in and began a pavane. At the last two, pairs of boots stood stalwart guard, placed there by the boot boy. Sarah walked forward.

It might have been a reverberation in the floorboard, but as she came closer, one of the boots beside the middle door toppled over, exactly as if a soldier had fallen down drunk in the middle of parade. Suddenly no longer afraid, Sarah wondered if perhaps Lady Melanie, not willing another love affair should end unhappily, had given that little sign to show her the way. Whispering, "Thank you," Sarah pushed open the door.

Throwing queer shadows, a candle flame swayed and nodded, drowning in its own grease. A pair of breeches hung over the back of a chair, and a tall hat gaped up from beside it. On the table, among a confusion of fobs, pens, paper and coins, stood a brandy bottle, unstoppered and empty.

Sarah almost laughed to see it. If Alaric had been drinking, he'd not be fit to fight in but five or six hours. She thought again and shook her head. If Alaric had been drinking, he'd probably go to the meadow and be shot dead on the spot, unable even to defend himself.

Turning toward the shapeless form under the covers of the big testered bed, Sarah started forward impulsively. However, the question she'd thus far avoided asking herself came powerfully into her mind. Which one?

To lose Lord Reyne meant her life would become empty, worthless, useful only for suicide. But to lose Harcourt meant heartbreak for everyone she'd known all her life, and Alaric would be forced to flee the country, and once again she'd lose him. This dilemma had kept her up for two nights already. She'd doze and then start up, sweating and terrified, her sheets curled about her like the entanglements of a snake.

The only thing to do, Sarah decided by the light of a faint candle, was to wake Alaric and attempt to sober him up. Which man would live was not in her power. Yet she could not send

Alaric out into the cold dawn at anything less than his full strength. Her steps now firm, Sarah approached the bed.

He lay on his side, facing into the shadows, his arm flung over his head. "My lord?" Sarah called softly. She could not reach his shoulder to shake it. "My lord?

"Please, my lord. You must wake up." Raising her voice seemed to have some effect. He groaned, muttered some words in a thick, indistinct voice, and rolled farther over on his face. Sarah called him again and poked his back with her forefinger. He wriggled down deeper into the feather bed.

Sarah looked about her for a jug of water. She could dip her handkerchief in and wring it over his face. A basin stood beside his toiletries on the dresser. Unfortunately, the jug was missing. Sarah stood there for a moment, her hand upon the silverback of his hairbrush. Funny, she would have said Alaric's hair was darker than this rather reddish shade of blond.

When he groaned again, Sarah flew to the bedside, her eyes open in anticipation. What she found there made her reel back in horror!

"Pretty girl!" Lord Dudley said, making an ineffectual grab for her. He misjudged the distance and fell out of bed. Sarah closed her eyes and jerked away. Lord Dudley had retired in nothing but his shirt, too minimal to cover all that was necessary.

Hearing no further sounds, she ventured, "Are you unhurt, sir?"

"Fine, fine, fine!" A jovial little giggle persuaded her to open one eye and glance, ever so briefly, at the fallen peer's son. Dudley sat on the floor, his shirt caught beneath his thighs. He met her eyes. His own were rather pink.

"Help us up," he said, holding up his hands like a baby. Sarah almost felt like saying, "Who's a big boy, then?" as she caught his hands and hauled.

He came off the floor about as quickly as he'd gone down. Sarah, caught off balance, was not prepared for his onrush. He caught her about the waist. "Such a very pretty girl," he said. His body felt flabby and hot, and the reek of alcohol puffed in her face completed the unpleasant portrait.

"Lord Dudley!" she protested, pushing him away with an effort. "If you please. . . ." Sarah leapt back out of his grasp, knocking into the table. It rocked, sending the bottle to the floor. She tried to catch it, fearing the crash, but missed. The bottle did not break, but it rang like a muffled bell.

Lord Dudley too made a grab, but not for the bottle. Sarah let out half a scream but managed to swallow the rest. She knocked his hand away, and the table went over with a shuddering crash. Coins danced and tingled away over the floorboards.

"Here now!" Lord Dudley said loudly. "My money! Help me pick them up." He went down on his hands and knees, forcing Sarah to shut her eyes once more.

Someone pounded on the wall. A muffled roar, with opprobrious phrases, sounded from the room next door. Sarah, as eager as that occupant to have silence, backed toward the door. With closed eyes, however, she mistook her direction and walked into the dresser. The mirror propped up on the top thumped against the wall.

"Oh!" As she whirled to catch the mirror, Sarah's cloak swept the basin and sent it to the floor. Made of less stern stuff than the bottle, it crashed like a cathedral falling off a cliff. The mirror didn't fall, which was some comfort. However, the banging on the wall continued.

Sarah knew she had to get out before someone came. Half the inn must be roused by now. As she hurried past Lord Dudley, though, he caught and held her by the ankle. "Ha-ha," he said. "You're the blind man now. Wait till I get my handker . . . handker . . . my wipe."

"Let me go!" Sarah tried to shake him off as he attempted to reach his breeches, hanging on the chair, without releasing his prize. His hold seemed permanent, a fetter hammered closed by a smith.

Suddenly, the door banged against the wall. "What in the bloody . . . ?" Alaric stood in the opening, his hand out to stop the door from swinging shut and his face flushed with anger. He wore only breeches with an unfastened shirt tucked in.

"Help," Sarah said in a small voice, as she balanced on one foot, her cloak falling around her like folded wings.

He observed everything in a finger-snap: the mess, the man on the floor, the fingers around Sarah's ankle. His sky-shaded gazed lingered longest on Sarah herself, though without expression. She opened her mouth to appeal to him again, but he no longer stood in the doorway. Before her heart could make the difficult climb up from her feet, he'd returned.

"Here you are, old man," he said, swinging an uncorked bottle by the neck between two fingers. "You'd better use both hands. You'd hate to drop it."

Slowly, Dudley opened his fingers. With a thud, Sarah put her foot down even as Dudley grasped the new bottle to his chest. "Won't you stay and . . . and . . ." His eyes rolled in his head and he flopped down, the wine spilling on his neck.

"Poor sot," Alaric said. He righted the bottle, crossed the room, and tugged the blanket off the bed. Covering the inert mass he said, "He'll do till morning." Only then did he look again on Sarah. He seemed about to speak when a sound outside the room caught his ear. "Come on; it won't do if you're found."

Absently, he took her hand and towed her along. Safe in his room, he stood for a moment with his ear to the panels. "The landlord and his lady are putting him to bed. Tarle's saying something about her looks, not complimentary, but what woman compares to you?"

Sarah stood in the middle of the room, her hands clasped before her. Lifting her chin, she met his steady regard. Judging by his expression, he wondered what she did here so late at night. Sarah felt keenly the unfairness of blushing under these circumstances. It gave the wrong impression for one thing, and made her feel two feet tall to boot. "Please don't stare, Lord Reyne."

"I can't help myself." He took her hand again in both of his, bringing it up to his lips. That touch confused her brain, sending it babbling.

"My lord," she began, "I have come to ask . . ." His lips touched her cheek. She closed her eyes, or they closed themselves, as she struggled to go on. "Tomorrow you will . . ." Somewhere a clock bonged once. Alaric's breath mingled with her own on her lips. Sarah gave a little gasp, which turned into a sigh as Alaric kissed her, softly but like a man who'd given the matter a good deal of thought.

"This isn't a dream?" she asked in sudden doubt when he lifted his head a moment, merely to bring her more closely against him. He chuckled and kissed her again. No, she was not dreaming, for dreams never clasped her with strength nor looked down with lazy laughter.

Looking up at him, trusting him, she could say what she'd come to say without a hesitation or stammer. "You mustn't fight Harcourt, you know."

"Are you asking me to turn tail?"

"Yes!"

"Impossible." Yet, he still held her, gently refusing her efforts to stand away.

"But you can't kill Harcourt just because he's jealous."

"Sarah, he is far more likely to kill me. I'm not the world's keenest shot."

"Oh, no!" Her arms tightened.

"Then you must save me. After all, it was your kiss that landed me in this position."

"But why . . . ? Why did you . . . ?"

"Kiss you? Because, Sarah, you are irresistible." And he kissed her again.

This time, the shock was less and the pleasure greater, swelling up from her extremities as though a warm spring had suddenly burst up through dead ground. She felt giddy, as though the spring were not water but pure champagne. If it were not for Harcourt, how easy she should find it to float away. Flinging herself out of his arms, she said, "Oh, how can you? Alaric, how dare you!"

"Don't you know why yet? What in God's name possessed you to pledge yourself to that caper-witted farmer?"

"Harcourt at least loves me. He's been in love with me for months and months."

"Ah, well, if time is of importance to you, I have loved you since time began. In the first hour of Adam's awakening, I loved you. You are Eve, you know, fallen from an apple tree."

"Please, Alaric, be serious," Sarah entreated, horrified to feel herself blushing to hear him saying such things to her. She had dreamed of this, but was not fool enough, she hoped, to take him at his word. "We must talk about Harcourt. You must not fight him."

"Devil fly away with Harcourt, Harvey, Harriet, and all the rest of them. I love you."

"Oh!"

"I love you as I never believe I should love anyone."

"Oh!"

"You'd better write Master Phelps a note telling him you've made a mistake."

"It will hurt him."

"Would you rather hurt me? Please don't say 'Oh!'" Lord Reyne had taken her hands in his, pressing them against his heart. His lips smiled still, but his eyes fixed on hers quite as if her answer were all in all to him.

"I believe you do love me."

"I love you," he said, "because when I am with you, I feel so much a part of life. If not for you, I should have been well entered upon the Middle Ages, instead of feeling as young inside as I did at twenty, before responsibility and war got a hold of me." He drew her near once more.

Sarah hid her eyes against his shoulder, strangely humbled she could touch him so deeply that he could speak to her without the least trace of embarrassment. "I don't know why I love you," she said in answer. "I only know that I do. From the moment I saw you . . ."

"As quickly as that? Maybe it was the same for me . . . if so, I wasn't aware of it until Lillian told me."

"Miss Canfield?" For a moment, Sarah's jealousy flared.

"Yes, if she hadn't opened my eyes to the truth of this situation, I might still plan to marry her, instead of you."

In listening to the thudding of his heart, Sarah heard only a word or two of this statement. "I forgot about Miss Canfield. When you marry her, shall I be your light-of-love?" She felt a chuckle run through him. "Why do you laugh?"

"You know, I think you shall be. But first, I suggest we marry. Lillian has given me the go-by. She says love commands the heart. You have certainly commandeered mine."

"I'm sorry you're not going to marry her," Sarah murmured. "I think she'd have made you a very good wife."

Alaric held Sarah out at arms' length. "Sarah East, you're going to marry me."

"Yes."

"That wasn't a question."

"No." How easy it was to be complacent, when acquiescence brought such quick rewards! Kissing someone was easy, Sarah thought, when that someone was Alaric.

He lifted his head to listen. Distantly, Sarah heard raised voices but she paid no attention. She made a sound, somewhere between a cough and a murmur, to remind him he held her still in his arms. "Alaric?"

He couldn't resist the invitation of her softly curving lips, not when he knew already the delights they promised him. But when she opened them to him, and pressed her young yet lush body against his, he was forced to raise his head. "My dearest, it's a scandal your being here, and if you do not leave, there'll be a greater scandal yet."

"But I don't want to leave you." Protected by the circle of his arms, she dared to press closer to his body. A new excitement surged through her as Alaric groaned and brought his lips down to taste her throat. Her breath grew short and fast as though she'd been running. She dared to cling to him as she felt herself becoming part of her beloved.

With a self-control she did not appreciate, Alaric managed to push her away. He was not angry, however, though his smile was tense even as it was tender. "My darling, you must leave."

"Why?"

"Because there is a bed in this room, and if you do not go, we shall undoubtedly use it."

"But I'm not tired."

He laughed and smoothed her hair with his fingers. "Once we are wed, I promise to do my best to tire you. Sarah." He stepped back when she would rush forward. "Go home. I will call on you tomorrow. Keep your father at home, for I will find it necessary to talk to him."

"But there are people in the hall, Alaric. If they see me, how will we avert scandal? I think I should stay until morning, when it would be safe for me to leave." She flickered her eyelashes as Mrs. Whitsun had so often despaired of teaching her.

He laughed again, but continued to hold himself in check. Sarah thought marriage would cure him of that and smiled in a new way. "Minx! You'll be safer if you go. There's a huge tree outside the window. Do you think you could . . . what am I saying?"

"Of course I can. I used to love to climb that one. The boys couldn't manage it. You won't go tomorrow, will you?"

"Only to deliver an apology. Although Harcourt may challenge me again when he learns I've stolen you away."

"I'll tell him it was all my fault." Sarah climbed over the sill and backed out, her toes feeling for each forking branch. Then her head popped up once more. "Say it again."

"I love you, Sarah. Go home. I'll see you in the morning." He watched her go down, sometimes extending a hand involuntarily when it seemed certain she'd fall. But her swift surefootedness brought her safely down. She caught at her hat and waved farewell. He stood by his window until she was out of sight, then, flinging on his coat, Alaric ran down to the taproom. The sleeping tapster awoke with a start as a seeming madman shook his shoulder, demanding pen and ink. Alaric was sorry to wake him, but he had an apology to write.

In the morning, he dressed with extreme care and walked quickly toward the water-meadow, not waiting for Harold to come and show him the way. Halfway there, a figure slipped out from among the trees and took his hand. "Sarah, what are you doing here?"

She shook her head and stopped, still holding his hand. Alaric halted to turn back. It was morning. He kept his eyes open as they kissed, for Sarah in the early light was a glory made of God. Old prayers came back to him, and it seemed he heard the distant music of bells.

A couple of young men on horses cantered by, and then pulled up to stop. "What am I to do now?" Harcourt asked the air.

His twin answered. "You can't fight now. It's ridiculous."

"I knew, somehow, she'd never have me."

"Just as well, really. She doesn't understand what it is to have a poetic soul."

"Hell, neither do I."

"Nor does she really comprehend hunting, shooting, or fishing."

"That's true." Harcourt stared a moment longer at the man and woman embracing in the open. Then he looked at his twin brother. "I hear bells," he said, considerably puzzled. Then two identical pairs of eyes opened wide. "Harmonia's wedding! Sarah! Sarah, the wedding!" Spurring their steeds, they dashed up to the others.

Alaric looked up first and put her behind him for safekeeping. But the twins regarded him without animosity, and soon he understood what they'd shouted. Sarah clutched his arm and said, "I've got to be there. Harold, Harcourt, could you take us up behind you?"

"Certainly," Harcourt said. "Er, take my horse, my lord. I'll ride double with my brother."

"Thank you, Mr. Phelps." When the younger man dismounted, Alaric offered his hand and his letter. Harcourt turned red and scuffed his boots in the dirt.

"Don't do that!" Harold said sternly. "Come on, if we don't hurry, we'll be late!"

Unclouded now by any fears, Sarah realized the extent of her happiness, jouncing along pillion-style, her arms right around Alaric's waist. She laughed aloud for joy and heard his laughter answering. The twins won the race, but both horses reached the church before the last peal had been rung. Standing at the rear of the church, watching her brother and friend become united, Sarah leaned against Alaric. His arm came about her and he whispered, "Soon."